MW01480890

Afterburn

Kathleen Lawless

Published by Kathleen Lawless, 2019.

AFTERBURN

First edition. January 16, 2019.

Copyright © 2019 Kathleen Lawless.

ISBN: 978-1989873335

Written by Kathleen Lawless.

AFTER BURN
by
Kathleen Lawless

Prologue

The little girl's long, white cotton nightie, the one with tiny embroidered pink rosebuds around the neck, rode up around her knees as urgent arms carried her out the front door, down the steps and across the lawn to safety near the street.

She squeezed her eyes shut to block out the surroundings but she could still smell the heavy smoke, still hear the hungry flames crackle as they devoured the wood frame house. The rapid beating of her mother's heart strummed against her tummy.

She was plunked down, the grass cold and damp against her bare feet. She opened her eyes to the darkness of the night, a strange, eerie dark that seemed alive as flames smashed through an upstairs window. Now that she felt safe it was kind of exciting. Then sudden panic clutched her six year old chest and she blurted out a name.

"Stay put! Be a good girl and don't move. You hear me? I'll be right back."

She shifted from foot to foot, shivering in the damp breeze. Why was Mommy taking so long?

The smoke grew thicker, making her eyes tear. In the distance she heard the scream of sirens approaching. She clung to her shabby teddy with the torn ear and, like a good girl, didn't move.

Chapter One

The smell was unforgettable, acrid and dense.

Even before the car sputtered and backfired as she slowed to park, the heavy odor poured through the MG's open window. Smoldering timbers and ash. Charred, water-soaked wood. And something undefinable that made the hairs on the back of her neck prickle.

Erica managed to steer the MG halfway off the street as the motor died, coasting to a stop near half a dozen police and fire department vehicles. A yellow plastic fire line ringed the charred, blackened mass of what had been, until this morning's pre-dawn hours, one of the oldest theaters in San Francisco. Several uniformed and plain clothes officers prowled the site.

Hard hat in hand, she slammed the car door and thrust a thick pair of canvas gloves into her overall pockets. Her old friend, Charlie, was gone; someone new was heading up the Special Investigation Squad. Squaring her shoulders, she approached the nearest uniformed officer. "Erica Johnson, Insurance Crime Prevention Bureau. Who's in charge?"

"Lieutenant Nicols." He pointed. "Over there."

She stopped a few feet away from him. The lieutenant had his back toward her, probing a floor joist with a penknife, testing for depth of char. She wasn't aware of having made a sound but Nicols spun around so fast his movements seemed to blur.

"Who the hell let you in here? This is a secured area."

2

Nicols sported shoulders that would be right at home on a football field. Stepping closer and tilting her head, Erica shifted her gaze to meet his. His eyes were neither green nor brown but an intriguing combination of both.

"Erica Johnson, ICPB, Lieutenant. I just received word about the fire."

He didn't offer his hand, choosing instead to remove his hard hat and rake his fingers through his disordered dark brown hair. All he succeeded in doing was to make most of it stick straight up. Like herself, he appeared to have scrambled into the nearest clothes at hand when the call came through. Rumpled jeans hung over the edges of his rubber boots and the shapeless green sweatshirt was so faded she couldn't read the letters on it.

"I understand the building's been standing empty for some time."

"A couple of years," Nicols said. "Probably well insured. But that's why you're here, isn't it?"

There was no mistaking the patronizing tone, the faint shadow in those hazel eyes. Hostility? Erica shoved her hands into her coverall pockets and squeezed her gloves with tense fingers. Or was she being too sensitive? Expecting, as always, to be challenged? To have to prove herself and her abilities to the new head of the San Francisco Police Special Investigation Squad the same way she'd had to prove it to his predecessor?

She reacted with anger, but deflected it from this doubting man in front of her to wanton, destructive arsonists. Sick, murderous people who laid match to tinder, burning down property and homes along with people's dreams. A picture leapt to mind and she resolutely buried it, along with the memories it raised of a fire scene from twenty-odd years ago. Her job was to concentrate on this particular fire. And soften up her new police liaison.

"Any luck with reconstructing the scene?"

"Minimal." Nicols scowled. "Hell of a mess."

"Any sign of forced entry?"

He shook his head.

Erica glanced up. "I take it the building was originally two stories?"

"Balcony and projection room up top."

"But you believe the fire started on the main floor?"

"Flames have a habit of traveling upward, Ms. Johnson."

Erica ignored the sarcasm. Maybe the lieutenant just wasn't a morning person. It was barely five a.m. "I introduced myself as a professional courtesy, Lieutenant. We do happen to be on the same side here." She was proud of the way she managed to infuse a modicum of warmth into her tone. "If you have no objections I'll just poke around on my own for a bit."

Without waiting for his answer, Erica paced the front of the building, then the alley beside it. Part of the front wall was still standing but the first thirty feet of roof and wall on the alley side was gone. The seating and backstage areas, though black and sodden, were otherwise intact. A strong wind had been blowing last night, too, she recalled, a cold blast blowing in off the Pacific Ocean. No doubt the tall buildings that ringed the site had prevented the wind from carrying the fire from the box office and projection room into the seating area.

She wasn't on her own long before Nicols joined her. He seemed to have thawed a little. At least this time he spoke without her having to ask direct questions. "This was the box office. We found a few remnants of cloth. It's my guess old theater curtains were stored there. We've sent a sample to the lab to see if any hydrocarbons show up."

Erica craned her neck. Where the roof had been, only a few twisted spans of the building's trusses remained, jagged black limbs contrasting with the fog-choked sky, like the skeleton of a corpse picked clean by vultures. Pulling on her gloves, she moved forward and picked up the stump of a blackened beam. She held it toward the light, noting the alligator pattern of charring that traveled deep into the heart of the wood. "It's certain he used an accelerant." She sniffed the beam. "Gasoline."

Nicols nodded. "Not the most original method, but it still works. Too damn well."

"Who turned in the alarm?"

"Anonymous passerby."

"What did he have to say?"

"Not much. Probably long gone by the time the fire trucks arrived."

"Too bad," Erica murmured.

Nicols crossed powerful looking arms against his chest and propped his right foot on a blackened block of concrete. "Maybe he'll have a sudden attack of conscience."

"How often does that happen? Once in a million times?" A muggy breeze stirred a few tendrils of hair clinging damply to Erica's forehead. It was warm inside her coveralls. "Perfect night for a fire," she continued. "That southwester blowing through would be like lighting candles on an explosive birthday cake."

"There's no such thing as a perfect night for a fire." He looked past her, his lips drawn into a tight, disapproving line that emphasized the stubborn angle of his head. A well-shaped head, she noticed. Perhaps more of a work horse than the thoroughbreds she loved, but the lines spoke of classic lineage and a good gene pool. He patted his jeans pockets. "Got a cigarette?"

She shook her head. "Got any coffee?"

Their eyes met and she thought she saw a flash of what could be mutual understanding.

"I'll send one of the boys for some."

Coffee or cigarettes? Erica wondered as he strode around the wreckage of the fire debris and approached one of the uniformed officers. When she caught herself staring at the way the faded denim stretched taut across his well-muscled buttocks she pivoted to look at the burned-out building instead. Lieutenant Nicols was a far cry from his predecessor, old Charlie in his shiny checked polyester slacks and scuffed brogues. The lieutenant also filled out a pair of jeans in a way that surpassed anything Mr. Strauss had originally intended.

"Ms. Johnson!" Hearing her name, she felt hot color scald her cheeks, as if he had climbed into her mind and read her thoughts. She turned in his direction.

"Cream and sugar?"

"Black," she replied. This was not the time to let herself be distracted by the lieutenant's looks. Or his early morning grouchiness. She turned her attention to the rear of the building, which had received the least amount of burn. From there she began the methodical work of tracing a pathway to the area that had suffered the most damage so as to establish the point of origin.

Ten minutes later she straightened up and dropped a chunk of concrete into a plastic bag and tagged it. A second bag held a dirt sample from beneath the floor. Both samples, along with corresponding control samples taken from a different location on site, would go to the lab for analysis and comparison.

A breeze had come up, stirring wet ashes and the smell of burnt wood until it seemed as if her lungs were saturated with it, as if she'd never been away from the job, never filled her lungs with pure Rocky Mountain air for three whole weeks.

She locked the samples in the trunk of her car. As she returned to the theater, Lieutenant Nicols and a second man walked toward her. Pulling off her gloves, she accepted the steaming Styrofoam cup. For once she couldn't dredge up any concern about how bad Styrofoam was for the environment. It was the best thing she'd seen all morning. Second best, she amended, her fingers brushing Nicols' as the cup changed hands.

"Glenn, this is Ms. Johnson, from the Insurance Crime Prevention Bureau." Was it her imagination, or did the men exchange a significant glance that excluded her? "Ms. Johnson, my partner, Sergeant Davenport."

"Sergeant." Erica shook hands with the fair-haired man. Behind rimless glasses his gray eyes were discerning, yet surprisingly soft. She'd bet the two officers made a great team. The sergeant's forgettable looks would allow him to blend unnoticed into a crowd and his casual slouch was the perfect contrast to the lieutenant's flint-eyed, unyielding stance.

"Glenn was checking out the surrounding area. Asking residents if they saw or heard anything out of the ordinary last night."

"And did they?"

The sergeant shook his head. "Not a thing."

"What time was the alarm turned in?" she asked.

"Shortly after three. The fire department arrived at three twelve."

Erica nodded and sipped at her coffee. Almost at once she felt more alert. More conscious than ever of hazel eyes watching her every move. "How long have you been heading up the Special Investigation Squad?"

"Couple of months. One month, officially." Nicols' scowl suggested that he hated to admit he and Davenport were the rookies here.

"You like it?"

The sergeant answered when it became obvious that Nicols had no intention of responding. "It's a change from Homicide."

Erica's smile included both men. "I have to confess, I kind of miss old Charlie. He had a colorful way of expressing himself." Which included peppering his speech with four letter words that started with 'f'. Davenport smiled back.

Not Nicols. The lieutenant observed her from beneath lowered lids while he lit a cigarette. She noticed the way he drew the smoke into his lungs, almost a loving caress, then exhaled slowly, as if with great pleasure. The sensual image gave her a quick insight into the type of lover he would be. She was relieved when Davenport saved her from her thoughts.

"Charlie's quite a guy," he said. "You work with him a long time?"

Erica nodded.

"Once we're finished here, follow us back to the station and we can fill you in on what you've missed. You want a doughnut?"

"No thanks," she said.

Davenport glanced at Nicols. "Matt?"

"Sure."

"Be right back." The younger man headed toward a squad car, leaving Erica alone with the lieutenant.

"Have you two been partners long?"

"A while," Matt replied.

"I understand it's almost like a marriage," Erica said, wondering why the lieutenant couldn't offer a casual comment or two rather than having information pried from him.

"I wouldn't know."

Erica winced at his tone. Did he think she'd been probing? Trying to find out his marital status? It was the furthest thing from her mind.

His eyes narrowed as he inspected her, inch by inch, from her gumboots to the top of her head. "I'm straight, in case that's worrying you, too. And I still have my own teeth and hair."

It was great hair, too, even though it was rumpled because he was forever running his fingers through it. But there was no excuse for his rudeness. "I find your manner demeaning and condescending, Lieutenant Nicols. Homicide was obviously the right department for you. A place where the victims couldn't talk back."

She turned on her heel and, recognizing a familiar figure on the other side of the barricade, made her way to the older man whose uniform identified him as the fire chief.

"Hi there, Erica. Hell of a homecoming."

"What have you got for me, Chief?"

"The fire was a hot one, burned fast. Unusually heavy black smoke."

"Any idea why?"

"I'd guess the projection room up top was full of old celluloid film. Can't think what else would cause it to burn so hot and dirty. Looks to me like the projection room collapsed onto the main floor, which is why there's damn little left of it."

"Could the projection room have been the point of origin?"

"That wouldn't be my first guess."

Erica looked up from her notebook. "Thanks, Chief."

"Lieutenant!" She looked around, hearing the cry from one of the uniformed officers in the restricted area. "Something here you better take a look at."

Erica hurried forward. The lieutenant stepped in front of her, blocking her way. "Stay here." Then he strode toward the officer who'd shouted, apparently never doubting for a minute that she'd obey.

Hands on hips, Erica blew out an impatient breath. Who did he think he was? Charlie had never denied her access to anything. And she had a right to look at whatever evidence they found.

The uniformed officer had been joined by several others together with Glenn Davenport, the chief and the lieutenant. Something about their stance, the way their eyes were riveted to the ground, spurred her into a half-run.

Nicols blocked her approach again. "You don't want to see."

"What is it?" Erica rose on tiptoe but he stood like a tank in front of her. It was impossible to see around him.

"It looks like a body."

"A body?" she echoed.

"Yeah. Charred beyond recognition."

Her stomach lurched at his words. Suddenly the coffee wasn't sitting too well.

With relentless precision, her mind peeled away the years to a different fire and a different body. A body not burned beyond recognition but dead nonetheless. She'd been six years old at the time. The fire's victim had been her mother.

Chapter Two

Matt watched the color drain from Erica's face and hoped she wasn't about to keel over on him. He looked around for Glenn. His partner handled this type of thing better than he did. Inspector Johnson passing out in his arms was just the kind of event the press would have a field day with. Hardly Johnson's usual society page photo, with some over-dressed fop on her arm and enough jewelry hanging around her neck to light up San Francisco in a blackout. Not that he often read the society pages, but he'd stumbled across a few shots of her. Johnson was kind of a puzzle. None of the officers could figure out why she worked so hard when it was obvious she was loaded.

As far as the press went, he was already on their hate list because he'd refused to 'make nice' since being promoted to head of the Special Investigation Squad. He was proud of heading the department's flagship SIS and he was a good investigator. He just wasn't any good at living in a fish bowl. And his screw-up on the Gilbey case would follow him for a long time. If Johnson bested him on this series of fires that had been plaguing the city for the last three weeks, he could kiss his career goodbye.

The bet pool back at the station hadn't done a thing to ease the blow to his pride over muffing the Gilbey case. Not with Johnson the favorite and him the long shot to solve what was now the fifth in a string of arson fires that seemed to have no motive. Five fires and no hard evidence, adding up to a situation that required total concentration and kept him awake nights. He didn't need a distraction named Erica Johnson from the Insurance Crime Prevention Bureau making him look bad.

Matt studied her chalk-white face, noticing the way her pale skin contrasted with soft, curved red lips and dark, deep-set eyes. The newspaper shots hadn't done her justice. She had thick, wavy black hair and her delicate features promised fine bones and enticing rounded flesh. He pulled his mind away from imagining what the reality might be like under those sexless, enveloping coveralls. "You all right? Maybe you need to take a break. Seeing that would be a shock for anybody."

Her chin came up in an obstinate gesture that he had to admire. Color slowly seeped back into her cheeks. "I'm perfectly all right."

"Long as you're sure." Matt turned to the constable who hovered at his shoulder. "Call the Medical Examiner, will you?"

Watching his underling hurry away, Matt felt a renewed energy and commitment. He might be new to arson, but after fifteen years in Homicide, he had no doubt about his ability to deal with bodies. Johnson was clearly not accustomed to seeing them.

He tried to figure her motivation for working at a job that could be damned grim at times. Fires started by arsonists destroyed buildings and sometimes human beings. Weren't women supposed to be more nurturing, more connected to life and growth?

His cell phone rang and he dug it out of his jeans pocket, hoping like hell it wasn't the office notifying him of another fire. The Special Investigation Squad was already swamped with work. Not to mention the dozens of crank phone calls which ate steadily into everyone's time and temper. But it turned out to be an SIS detective who wanted him.

"I got a rundown on the theater, Lieutenant. Belongs to Phoenix Properties, a local investment company. Taxes are paid up and the title's clear."

"You get a name? Somebody we can talk to?"

"Yeah, Ron Grant, the manager." Matt noted the name and address. As he put his cell away, the Medical Examiner pulled up.

"Morning, Harry. Got a messy one for you."

Hodgekiss, a heavy man with a jovial smile, said, "Aren't they all? Especially this time of the morning. I'm too old to be getting up at five, Matt."

Matt wasn't fooled by Hodgekiss's words. The Medical Examiner was on the ball, no matter what hour he was called. "Me, too."

"Come off it. Next to me, you're still in knee pants. Any ID on the body?"

"Too badly burned."

Hodgekiss looked at the rubble and heaved a sigh. "God, Matt, I remember this place when it was used for live concerts a thousand years ago. It was one of the beautiful old classics. A lot more interesting to look at than modern chrome and glass."

"I thought it was a movie theater."

"For the last twenty years, yeah. No, make that thirty. It was converted to a movie house when people were still going to see movies. After the big screen got left behind with the

VCR craze, it was shut down altogether. Now, with DVDs so popular, there's not a chance it would ever have opened again."

"Don't think I was ever inside it," Matt said. "Hell, I never get time to go to a movie."

Hodgekiss chuckled. "If you didn't spend your off hours playing the ponies or hanging around the stable mooning over that mare of yours you'd have time for culture."

"Movies are culture?" Matt snorted.

Hodgekiss grinned, then moved toward the police photographer, who was beckoning him over.

Matt walked over to join Glenn. He gestured toward Erica, who was on the far side of the building. "What do you think?"

As usual, Glenn pondered the question before he answered. "Word is she knows what she's doing. She's got a good reputation."

"Yeah, so I hear." Matt shoved his hands in his pockets and scowled.

"You have to admit she kind of brightens up the place. Uh oh. She step on your toes already?"

"Nope. I'm staying out of her way and she better stay out of mine."

Glenn laid a hand on Matt's arm. "Listen buddy, stop beating yourself up over the Gilbey case. None of us figured that crazy priest would be the one torching all the churches."

"Guess I spent too many years being an altar boy." He shifted his weight from one foot to the other, his mind seeking answers he hadn't found down any of the dead-ends he'd followed. "Anyway, what with the mayor and the Chief breathing down my neck, I've got to produce some answers and damn quick."

Hodgekiss beckoned. The body was being loaded onto a stretcher. Hodgekiss held up two evidence envelopes. "This stuff was with the body."

Matt squinted through the clear plastic. One envelope held a large, blackened, old-fashioned key. The second item was a modern key, lightweight and misshapen. "Don't think these will help much, Harry. We're not going to get any prints off them now."

"The lab might find something," Hodgekiss said. "I'll get the autopsy report to you yesterday, which is when you always seem to want it."

Matt tensed as Johnson's clear, soft tones sounded near his shoulder. "What did the ME find?"

"Just two keys." Matt stared into black-fringed brown eyes and felt a lump settle low in his gut. Lynne's eyes had been that exact same color. "Are you up to date on the other fires?"

Her eyes widened. "Other fires? What other fires? I came home from three weeks vacation late last night. I haven't even had a chance to call my office."

She sounded as if she almost felt guilty about being away and he felt pleased at her discomfiture, yet annoyed with himself for trying to needle her. "This is fire number five. One every five days, almost to the hour."

***

Erica struggled to maintain her composure. Four other fires and a new man heading up the SIS? "Sounds as if we've got our work cut out for us, Lieutenant."

"So it would appear."

Something in his gaze made her uncomfortable. He was looking at her, yet he wasn't. If she didn't know better, she'd say he was a million miles away. Erica repressed a shudder. It was spooky.

Erica marched over to her car, peeled off her coveralls and swiped at her brow with a forearm. She'd almost lost it back there, twice. First, she let the discovery of a body distract her from her job. The second distraction was the lieutenant himself. She had a hunch he was just waiting for her to slip up. He's running scared, she thought. But he was the newbie here. She was the one who knew her way around.

She chucked the coveralls in the back of the car. Who did Nicols think he was, anyway? He had a lot of nerve treating her like a second-rate subordinate. She wondered which of her ICPB coworkers had had the pleasure of working with the lieutenant in her absence. She'd better read the reports so she knew what was going on.

After stopping by her office to pick up the files on the previous fires and inspecting the individual sites, scattered city-wide, she was tired, hungry and smelled like the inside of an incinerator. Her three weeks of vacation in the pristine air of the Rocky Mountains seemed like a dream now. She still needed to stop by the police station to look at the police reports and photographs. After which she'd grab a bite to eat.

At the police station she greeted several officers by name on her way to the back office occupied by the SIS. The SIS was supposed to be the mayor's pet project, but the drab, windowless room was too small for the half dozen littered desks and filing cabinets crammed into it, the men working almost elbow to elbow. File folders were stacked everywhere.

"It's a wonder you guys ever find anything," she told one officer who looked familiar, but whose name she couldn't recall. "Nicols inherit Charlie's desk?"

"Along with Charlie's ulcer," cracked the cop.

"It couldn't happen to a more deserving guy."

"Ho, ho." He arched one brow. "I take it you two have met."

"I've had the dubious pleasure." The wall behind Nicols' desk was covered by a faded city map, punctured with pinholes. Five shiny red pushpins were an obviously recent addition. And they were up-to-date, she thought, noting the site of the old theater was already marked, along with the warehouse, the gas station, the boutique, and the marine-front boat repair. At least the map was organized, which was more than she could say for Nicols' desk.

"This guy certainly didn't confine himself to any one area." Erica studied the map, wondering which spot was earmarked number six, even as she strengthened her resolve that there would be no number six. There had to be a way to stop this senseless destruction before another person fell victim to the flames. The five new pushpins stared back as though reproaching her.

She eyed the jumble of files surrounding the computer monitor on the lieutenant's desk. It had taken her a while to catch on to Charlie's filing system but it didn't look like Nicols had one. Eventually she located the files she was looking for and sat down, shifting her bottom against the hard wooden chair. After three weeks of having a saddle underneath her all day, the transition wasn't an easy one.

Erica frowned as she scanned the files. Hard to say which was worse, the lieutenant's handwriting or his typing. And if there was any evidence that would even find the arsonist, let alone convict him, the pages in front of her didn't reveal it.

"Got the case solved yet?"

She glanced up, noting that the thread of exhaustion in Nicols' voice was matched by his expression of tired frustration as he sank into the creaking chair across the desk from her.

"Did you talk to the theater's owners?"

"Yup. Their front man told us they're trying to dump the place. Which might lead one to believe..." He paused and Erica realized that was her cue.

"That they had the place torched to collect the insurance money?"

"Nice theory. Except he pulls out the insurance policy and we could see for ourselves that the building was under insured."

Erica digested that information, wondering just when the lieutenant had become an expert on insurance appraisals. "Any leads on the victim?"

She watched him rub his eyes with the heel of one hand. "Place had a caretaker. Name of Gus Hilliard. I've got men out trying to locate him now."

Erica longed to lean across the desk toward him and say, 'I have to tell you, Lieutenant. After three weeks and five fires, what you've collected in the way of leads doesn't amount to squat.'

Instead she gritted her teeth and forced herself to be polite and professional. "Is there any other information I should be made aware of?"

Nicols jerked upright, tipped his chair back and crossed his arms over his chest. "Phoenix's insurance premiums were fairly high because there was no alarm system in the building. No sprinklers. No smoke detector. Every arsonist's dream."

"That's it?"

The scowl returned to Nicols' face. "If you mean am I holding anything back from you, the answer is no. Everything we've got so far is right in front of you."

Erica tapped the files with the end of her pen. "Not a whole lot to go on, is it?"

"You think you can do better, Princess, you've got my blessing."

With slow, deliberate movements, Erica got to her feet. That was better. She could look down at him for a change. "Lieutenant. Why don't you like me?"

Matt rose also, and something in his stance made Erica glad the desk stood between them. Palms flat on the desktop, he leaned forward until his face was on a level with hers. "Sweetheart, this is not a popularity contest. This is a police station. We try and catch the bad guys and lock them up so they can't break the law again."

"Well somebody better catch this bad guy. Because the indicators clearly show he'll torch again. In five days, if not sooner."

"It's always been five days."

"Have you run a psychological profile?"

Matt frowned. "We don't even know for sure this is the work of a single perpetrator."

Erica continued as if he hadn't spoken. "In my estimation, it's a serious oversight on your part."

A door opened behind her and the buzz of conversation from the other desks ceased.

"I see you two have met."

"Captain Bailey." Pivoting, Erica extended her right hand, which was swallowed in the beefy grasp of the ruddy-faced police captain. "I hear I missed a fair bit of excitement while I was away."

A sober look replaced the captain's welcoming smile. "Depends what you call excitement. Charlie figures he's well out of it." The smile returned. "By the way, Charlie's retirement party is next week. And we won't hear of you missing it. You too, Nicols."

"I wouldn't dream of it."

The captain didn't seem to notice the faint sarcasm in Matt's voice. He released Erica's hand to clap a fatherly arm across her shoulders. "Erica here is special people, Matt. I expect your full cooperation with her. More than one time she's made us look pretty darn good."

"Yes, sir," Matt said, his voice wooden.

Bailey glanced up at the wall clock and adjusted his tie. "Gotta go. Mayor's trying to light his own goddamn fire. Doesn't understand why we haven't caught this guy yet." He turned to look at Matt. "Anything new I can appease him with?"

"Why don't you tell him Ms. Johnson is back from her vacation?"

The captain was already halfway to the door. "Old news, Matt. I told him that at eight this morning."

Erica flinched at the look in Matt's eyes as they rested on her. It was a look she wouldn't soon forget.

Chapter Three

Matt molded his stiff jaw muscles into a polite expression. So Inspector Johnson was the fair-haired darling of the Mayor as well as the Chief, was she? That figured.

Well, he'd cooperate all right. On his terms. If she wanted a psychological profile, fine. Hell, she could profile him if it would get her off his case. Maybe not, he amended. He didn't want anyone poking into his psyche, theorizing about his toilet training or why losing Lynne had soured him on society-darling rich bitches.

Willing his knotted stomach muscles to relax, he said, "I assume you'll be inspecting the sites of the previous four fires, Ms. Johnson."

"I've already done that, thank you. My colleagues left me very complete file reports."

"Dandy," Matt said, trying to keep the sarcasm out of his voice and noticing she hadn't said a word about his investigation reports. She probably couldn't even read his handwriting.

"I was looking for the police photographs of the fires," she said, her expression bland. "They don't appear to be with the reports."

"They're in separate files. And on the computer.

His words were all but lost as her stomach gave a most unladylike grumble. Her cheeks went pink and she fumbled with the file in her hand.

"Want to look at the photos together over lunch?" he asked.

Her surprise was evident. He shrugged it off. "I haven't eaten yet either. Might as well grab a bite. Talk about the case." There. No one could accuse him of being uncooperative.

"If you're sure you can spare the time," she said.

"I'll make time."

"That's very kind of you. Why don't we take my car?"

He almost said 'no'. Chances were she drove a Jag or a Mercedes. But hell, he'd never sat in a car that cost more than a year's salary.

"Sure." Why not? He shouldn't drive right now, anyway. He was liable to fall asleep.

Matt followed her along the corridor and down the stairs, conscious of the way her snug denim jeans molded the soft, rounded curves of her hips. Her pant legs were tucked into the tops of multicolored, hand-tooled leather boots. A thick leather belt cinched her impossibly small waist, while a satchel-like leather bag, custom-designed no doubt, dangled from one shoulder. Lynne had liked leather, too. Funny, he'd never realized until just this minute how he'd associated the opulent smell of leather with his old girlfriend.

She stopped next to a bright red '52 MG.

Surprise made him abrupt. "This is yours?"

"What's wrong? Don't you like old cars?"

"Yeah, I do, as a matter of fact." His acquiescence sounded grudging, which he hadn't intended. "I just happen to favor reliability over looks any day."

Erica smiled that slow, sweet smile. "She doesn't let me down too often."

He accordioned himself into the confined space of the passenger seat with a grunt. "This thing must've been built by midgets. Or for them." While hardly the latest model, his own car had loads of room. As she leaned forward to shift gears her dark hair swung over her shoulders and he caught a faint, tantalizing scent of lilac.

The engine of the MG coughed and sputtered to life. "Sounds like you could use a tune-up."

"I know. But I never seem to find the time and it's getting really hard to find parts for something this old. Is Matt short for Matthew?"

"Yeah." Short for Saint Matthew, actually. His parents had taken Bible names for all their eight kids. Strange, he hadn't thought of that, or of his old neighborhood in the Bronx, for eons. Why did Erica's presence kindle these half-buried memories of times and places most people would call the good old days? They weren't, not by a long shot. Was it just that she reminded him so much of Lynne?

"Where to?"

Erica's words brought him back to the present. "Go up a couple of blocks and turn left."

She followed his instructions, slowed to a stop, and turned to face him. "McDonald's?"

He noted the faint disdain on her face as she surveyed the famous golden arches. What was she expecting? Top of the Mark or one of her other usual haunts?

"Do I hear an objection?"

She shook her head and pulled into the parking lot. "Next stop cholesterol heaven. Are we driving through or dining inside in style?"

Matt ignored her attempt at humor. If he had to sit squished into this tiny space much longer, smelling her perfume and watching the way her thick, dark hair framed her pale, oval face, it was just possible he might lose control of something other than his temper. The car had barely stopped before he opened his door and jack-knifed himself out. "I've got too much work to take time out for a fancy restaurant," he said, his tone brusque.

"And I have no doubt you know them all, Lieutenant."

As a matter of fact, he did. But that wasn't something she'd expect, or needed to know.

She lagged behind as they entered the restaurant and Matt suppressed a smile. Maybe he'd found the way to freeze her out—give her a taste of how ordinary people lived. Ordinary people who weren't born with upper-crust WASP silver spoons in their mouths.

"You grab a table while I order. What do you want?"

"I won't know till I look at the menu, will I?" She joined him in the line-up, chin tilted at a stubborn angle. The scent of lilac wafted up to tease his nostrils again.

He pointed. "The menu's up there. Oh, would you believe it, they have salad!"

"Are you always this charming?"

"Nah. Today I'm on my best behavior. I'll even treat."

He sat as far away from Erica as the bright yellow and orange booth allowed and wolfed down his first hamburger without bothering about conversation. Between dainty nibbles Erica was doing a lot of looking around. He squirted ketchup on his fries. "Never eaten at McDonald's before, have you?"

"Once. What gave me away?"

Once! So he'd been right in his original assessment of her. Like Lynne, Erica Johnson was not from his world. "What happened? Tried it once and didn't like it?"

She leaned forward and looked him in the eye. "No. I found Burger King."

Matt winced. He was acting like a jerk. It wasn't Erica's fault she'd been assigned to the same fire investigation that he was killing himself to solve. Any more than it was her fault she reminded him so damn much of Lynne that it rekindled all sorts of memories he thought he'd succeeded in forgetting. He fanned the photos on the table between them.

"Any questions about the fire sites?"

Erica dabbed her mouth with a napkin and Matt was amused to note that she'd missed a smear of ketchup at the corner of her lips. "There doesn't seem to be anything in the way of a common denominator." She tilted her head. "Do you see any pattern?"

He didn't need to look at the reports or the photos. The details were etched into his mind, mocking him with the randomness of the sites and the apparent lack of motive.

"Some. None of the five buildings had an alarm system. In the first four, doors were jimmied, but no tools or fingerprints were found and, in all cases, the fire was set with materials existing on site."

"That's really strange. When someone sets fires for fun, they usually use the latest in equipment, not just settle for what's hanging around the site."

"Nothing about these fires makes any sense." As soon as the words were out of his mouth, he regretted them. Sounded like he was making excuses for his lack of leads.

"There was no sign of forced entry at the theater, though, which means it was unlocked or somebody had a key."

"I couldn't see any pattern in the insurance." Erica folded her burger paper. "Each building was insured by a different company. The boat repair shop and the clothing store were underinsured; the warehouse and service station were on the mark. And," she added, "no recent additions to any of the policies."

"That's right; it doesn't look like insurance fraud. We haven't been able to find a connection between any of the building owners either. The thing is ..." Matt paused for effect ... "the thing is, these fires have been exactly five days apart, almost to the hour. It's like the arsonist is thumbing his nose at us, saying, 'Look what I can do. I can even tell you when I'll hit next and there's no way you can stop me.'"

"Do you think it's a pyromaniac?"

He shook his head. "These weren't impulse fires. They had to be premeditated. Otherwise, how do you account for the timing? I get the feeling he scouted for specific targets. None of them had alarm systems and none of them would normally have people inside at night."

"The theater did."

"Yeah." Matt scowled at his coffee. It would taste better with a cigarette and he wanted one so much his mouth watered, but he was trying to cut down. He'd likely need it more later. He reached into his pocket for a sugar lump, blew the lint off, and popped it into his mouth, biting down for a satisfying crunch of sweetness. "I'd like to know if the death was an accident or part of the plan."

"Do you think somebody would set five fires in order to commit one murder?"

"A nut case, maybe. I just hope it isn't. They're a lot harder to catch." As he knew only too well.

Erica looked thoughtful. "And it appears no one benefits from the fires?"

"Nope. Nobody."

"But there must be," she insisted. "If it wasn't a pyromaniac, somebody has to gain something."

"Not necessarily. Could be a clever psycho who's picked arson as a way of proving that he can beat the system. Or maybe he's a fire fan."

"If that's true, then the body in the theater was a mistake, which makes it manslaughter, not murder."

"Whatever. The legal technicalities don't interest me right now. I just want to get my hands on the guy. Three weeks, and I'm still beating my head against a rock wall."

Erica slid to the end of the booth and stood up. "Easy to see why there's a shortage of leads."

"Gee, thanks," he said, unable to keep traces of both weariness and sarcasm out of his voice.

When they folded themselves back into the MG and Erica turned the key, the motor coughed, moaned and died. She tried again, twice, but the engine refused to respond. Matt sighed, levered himself out, and went around to the hood.

She got out and watched as he poked and tested the cables and connectors. "Times like this I wish I wasn't so attached to this car."

Matt merely grunted as he straightened up. "I think you have a starter problem. Where's your tool box?"

"I don't have one."

He stared at her, disbelieving. "You drive a hunk of junk like this and you don't carry tools?"

She looked defensive. "Most of the time my car is very reliable."

"You're damn lucky," he growled. His hands were covered in grease. So was his shirt. He recognized that he was more irritated now than earlier. If he had to put up with having her on this case, the least she could do was drive something that didn't die on her every five minutes.

"Look," he said. "My place is only a couple of blocks away. We'll go over and grab my tools. I think I can fix it so you can at least get it to a garage."

"You don't have to..." She hesitated, turning on him the kind of appraising look she'd been giving to photos of ruined buildings. "All right. Thank you."

As they climbed the steps of his dilapidated three-storey Victorian house, he wondered how she was reacting to it. Probably with disdain. She wouldn't have a clue about renovating a house. He hadn't had time to do much yet, but when he was through it would be a showplace and there was no doubt he'd double his money.

It had been clever of Francie to find the kind of house he'd wanted, in the right area, too. Not that Francie was ever averse to making a few bucks commission. Unlocking the door to his apartment on the third floor, Matt waved Erica in ahead of him.

***

Curious, Erica stepped inside. Matt brushed past her, leaving the door ajar, and somehow the fact that he didn't close it behind them made her feel better. Confident enough to move into the middle of the living room.

Not that it appeared as though anyone actually lived there. The closed curtains gave the room a gloomy, neglected air and her first glance gave her only a vague impression of lumpy, mismatched furniture, bare wood floors and a thick layer of dust.

"I'll just be a minute." Matt's voice echoed from the next room. She glanced at the doorway. This glimpse of his kitchen matched what she'd seen in the living room. Dirty dishes stacked on the counter and a jumble of copper pans and utensils on a ceiling rack.

Wait a minute, copper pans? No, couldn't be him. He must have a girlfriend who cooked.

"Fine." She inhaled and exhaled, each to the count of ten, relaxing her shoulders. It had been a stressful day, negotiating traffic, picking through burn sites and sparring with Matt, knowing he was just waiting for her to slip up.

An old steamer trunk in front of the couch was littered with empty mugs, glasses, piles of newspapers and what, on closer inspection, turned out to be racing forms. So the lieutenant liked to bet on the horses, did he? That didn't surprise her. The man was as predictable as they came. She resisted the urge to straighten the mud-colored blanket that doubled as a couch throw, empty the overflowing ashtrays and organize the jumbled stacks of files and magazines that occupied every chair. She stepped over what looked to be a handful of neglected mail and paused mid-stride, surprised by the large, bright acrylic painting on the opposite wall.

She moved forward for a closer look. It was either an original Hearne or a darn good copy. Familiar with the artist's unique style, she examined the painting with care. Unbelievable as it was, she was looking at an original Hollis Hearne.

"Moon Dance." She spoke the title aloud with admiration, recognizing the picture from catalogs although she'd not seen it displayed at any of Hearne's shows in San Francisco or in New York. The background was dark, misty and mysterious, a cold moon hanging above the tree shapes seen through the columns of a portico. In the foreground the human figures, reminiscent of Picasso, were bright and full of action. One man played a violin, another a piano. A woman handed a bouquet of flowers to a man, while other couples danced.

Erica blinked, half expecting the painting to disappear while her eyes were closed. But it didn't. And it wasn't the kind of wall art a cop could afford.

"Did you hear what I said?"

"What?" Erica spun about. "Sorry. I was admiring your painting." In fact, she could have looked at it for hours, trying to penetrate the mystery and decipher the artist's intent.

Giving it an indifferent glance, Matt shrugged. "Hearne's a little wild for some people."

"He's brilliant. Progressive. The critics predict he'll start a whole new trend in wall art."

Matt hitched the metal tool box higher under his arm. "What do the critics know?"

"I can't believe you're so nonchalant about owning a work like this."

"I know what I like. I don't pay any attention to what a bunch of frustrated, dissecting critics happen to think."

The words were familiar. Her aunt, an artist, expressed the same opinion, even though she was dependent on the approval and good will of the critics. Judging from what she'd seen of Matt, he didn't need anyone's good will.

She smiled. Approval was another matter. He had superiors to answer to, a difficult arson case to crack, plus herself to contend with. She'd bet it was that third factor that was responsible for the frown puckering at his eyebrows and pulling his lips into a thin line.

He didn't seem to approve of her smile. His eyes rested on her lips in a way that she found disquieting. Not really aware she was doing it, her glance shifted from Matt to the half-open front door as, with quick sure movements, he set down his tool box and took a step toward her.

Erica took a step back.

Matt followed.

Erica swallowed, feeling her heart rate accelerate. "What... What are you doing?"

"Hold still." Grasping her chin in one hand he pulled out a hankie and scrubbed at a spot near her lips. "You have ketchup on your face."

His breath was warm, feathering her bangs. Standing so close to him reminded her just how large he was, his height and powerful build making her feel small and vulnerable. As always, she fought against that vulnerability with the best weapon she had.

"Ketchup? You let me walk around all day with ketchup on my face?"

He grinned. He'd stopped wiping but didn't seem inclined to release her. Slowly he balled up the hankie and dropped it on the chair next to them. Erica tried to pull away but his grip tightened a little.

"Why don't you like me, Inspector Johnson?"

His words parroted hers of a few hours ago. Her pulse was pounding and she could feel it throbbing in the vein that ran from her throat up to her ear. Could he see it? Preying on someone's vulnerability was what a tough-guy cop like Matt Nicols would do.

"I like you fine, Lieutenant." Deliberately she made her voice breathy, provocative. As she spoke she placed one hand on his forearm, inching her palm up to his hand, which still imprisoned her chin, tilting her face up.

"That's good," Matt said, his fingers gliding from her jaw up over her cheekbone and past her ear, to sink into her hair and grasp a handful. "Think how much more pleasant it will be working together, now that we like each other."

Erica swallowed. He was bluffing, using the oldest tactic in the book. Physical intimidation. He expected her to cry 'uncle', tuck her tail between her legs and leave him alone with his investigation.

She scanned his face. Whiskers that had been a faint shadow this morning were now more pronounced, as was the tired strain in his hazel eyes, and she felt an unexpected twinge of sympathy. He'd been hard on this case for three weeks without anything resembling a lead. No wonder he was reluctant to have her saunter onto the scene. If she cracked the case she would succeed in humiliating him. In his position, she wouldn't want her around either.

She lowered her arm between them. "Listen, this isn't getting us anywhere. I know exactly what you're up to and it isn't going to work, so why don't we..."

Abruptly her words were silenced by the hard, hot pressure of his lips against hers.

Chapter Four

Erica pulled into the narrow, tree-shaded driveway beside her carriage house and sat for a moment, trying to settle her emotions. She'd been rescued from the lieutenant's cave man maneuver and her own unexpected and embarrassingly eager response by the arrival of his downstairs tenants. As they discussed their malfunctioning shower with Matt, she regained her poise and decided to behave as if the kiss had never happened. Back at McDonald's, Matt had fixed the MG and she'd accelerated away with a breezy wave. Let him find his own way back to the police station.

"He could just grab the nearest vine," she muttered, as she got out of the car and followed the overgrown garden path to where her aunt, wearing her usual long cotton skirt and shawl, was picking flowers.

"You left early this morning," Ronya said, as she snipped a bouquet of the long-stemmed roses that were her pride and joy.

"Big fire," Erica said. "The fifth since I was away."

Ronya's glance was keen. "And no one except you is capable of carrying out the investigation, I suppose?"

Erica evaded her aunt's gaze. "Some new hotshot lieutenant from Homicide is trying to fill Charlie's shoes."

"Do give the poor man a chance." Ronya bent to pet the calico cat rubbing against her calves.

A chance? Is that what it's called? Erica flushed, recalling the firm pressure of Matt's lips, the coarse texture of his unshaven face, the hot invasion of his tongue. For some reason, he was trying to scare her, warn her off. The fact that he'd go to such extremes piqued her curiosity. And the fact that his kiss had sparked instant fire in her blood was unsettling, to say the least.

"What's he like?"

"Sorry?" She felt a rush of warmth to her face, realizing she'd lost the thread of the conversation.

"I asked what he's like. Charlie's successor."

"Big. Prickly."

Ronya nodded as if she'd heard all she needed to. "You look tuckered. Can I fix you some nice herb tea? And maybe a tuna sandwich?"

Erica pulled a face. She liked coffee, strong and black, and Ronya knew it.

"I haven't heard about your trip yet," Ronya coaxed.

Erica glanced at her carriage house, longing to fill her old, claw-foot bathtub with steaming, fragrant water. She'd climb into it and maybe never come out. Ronya would understand if she begged off. Though their homes occupied the same piece of property, Ronya never infringed on Erica's privacy.

On the other hand, she hadn't seen her aunt for three weeks. While Ronya would never admit it, Erica knew she was sometimes lonely.

"I'll pass on the sandwich," she said, smiling. Knowing Ronya, it could be inedible. "But herb tea sounds good. Orange pekoe?"

"Orange pekoe isn't herbal," Ronya chided.

Erica followed her into the Victorian manor house, built in Sausalito's early days. Though the pale green paint was faded and the timbers sagged, the hillside mansion had a fine view of the Bay and still retained an air of elegance and dignity.

Her aunt and the house were much alike, Erica thought, gazing with affection at the woman who had been both friend and surrogate mother for as long as she could remember. Ronya's uncombed long, dark hair was streaked with gray and her figure looked soft and shapeless in the drab, full skirt. The inevitable beads hung over her sagging bosom.

As they entered the sunroom, greeted by a raucous cry from Benny, Ronya's Blue Fronted Amazon parrot, Erica wrinkled her nose at the odor. "Smells as if Benny needs his paper changed. Or did the cats do something bad?" She followed Ronya down the long hallway into the kitchen.

"Oh?" Ronya shrugged and moved to the sink to fill the kettle. "Dale always takes care of that. But he hasn't been around much."

"Why is that?" Dale was her father's gofer, a funny, ageless, balding little man who also tried to keep Ronya's grounds in order. But Dale liked topiary better than weeding and, while the shrubs resembling birds, giraffes and other wildlife were a credit to his creativity, the lawns and flower beds were often overgrown.

"I guess your father's been keeping him busy."

Erica strolled to the doorway of Ronya's studio, next to the kitchen. The big room, well-lit by wall to wall windows on the north and west, was as cluttered as ever with easels, tables and tubes of paint. There was one half-finished painting on an easel and a stack of stretched blank canvases leaned against one wall.

Erica turned to the kitchen and her aunt. "Have you been painting much?"

Ronya's eyes glowed, became alert. "I have a wonderful idea for a new series. I'm doing research right now." She gave Erica a searching look. "What's troubling you, love?"

Matt Nicols! Erica squashed that thought at once. "They discovered a body at the fire site this morning."

"Oh, dear! How dreadful."

"I know. I can't help remembering . . ."

Erica found herself enfolded in Ronya's arms. It was like hugging a warm, soft pillow faintly scented with gardenias. "I miss her, too," Ronya murmured.

"I wonder if I'll ever be able to forget it."

Ronya stepped back, her gaze intent. "Isn't the fire that took Suzanne the very reason you do what you do?"

Erica shifted in her chair. She often used her knowledge of psychology to size up other people but she'd never wanted to probe into her own fascination with arson investigation. "I suppose there might be a link."

The kettle whistled and Benny landed on Ronya's shoulder with a squawk. "Kettle's hot! Kettle's hot!"

Erica rubbed the parrot's head with an affectionate finger. Benny, with his green plumage, yellow face and blue feathers around the beak, not to mention a couple of bright red feathers peeking out from under his wings, always reminded her of Ronya's more exuberant paintings.

"By the way," Ronya said, "I saved you some newspaper clippings about your father. He's developing a new type of shopping center. Malls without walls or something like that. I don't understand a bit of it myself." She set the tea tray down on the battered oak kitchen table. "Now tell me about your holiday. Did you meet any nice men?"

"Not really. Why so interested in my love life?"

"What love life?" Ronya gave an elegant sniff as she poured tea into fragile antique china cups. "Surely you don't want to end up an old maid like me."

"But it's very romantic. You lost your one true love and renounced marriage forever." Erica turned her cup to drink from the side that wasn't chipped. Part of Ronya's charm was that she might use a priceless Spode urn to hold paintbrushes, but drink tea from an old jam jar.

"It wasn't at all romantic," Ronya scoffed. "Any more than that stuffed shirt you date from time to time could be called romantic."

Erica smiled. "Why don't you like poor old Clayton?"

"Reminds me too much of your father."

"Come on. He's not that bad."

"Which one? Your father or young Gallagher?"

"Both of them."

"Your father's never been capable of understanding a woman's needs," said Ronya. "Neither is Clayton Gallagher."

Erica finished her tea and stood up. "My needs are pretty simple right now. A hot bath and an early night. I've got a ton of work to catch up on."

"Fine, dear." Her aunt's eyes were misty. Deep into the memories of her one great romance, perhaps. Erica wondered for the hundredth time who Ronya's lover had been. A married man? Perhaps someone with a shady past?

She found it odd that her father and Ronya were both reticent about the subject. It wasn't unusual for her father to hold back, but she didn't expect it from her aunt.

Well, her own youthful romance and subsequent disastrous marriage were certainly best forgotten, she mused as she soaked in the tub. She suspected now that the main reason she'd married Trevor was because her father had approved of him. He'd approved of so little else that she did.

Stretching out in bed she closed her eyes, but sleep eluded her. The nightmare memories were back in full force. She was six years old, her white cotton nightie billowing in the breeze, crying helplessly for her mother but 'staying put,' as she'd been told. Her heart thudded in terror as the crackling flames devoured her home and the distant wail of the fire engine grew closer.

***

Matt looked at the sad, charred remains of the old theater and reminded himself that today was Tuesday. If the arsonist kept to his pattern, the next fire would be on Saturday. He was desperate for a lead that would let him prevent it. He tipped his head back to stretch the taut muscles in his neck and gazed up at a blue sky that went on forever. The mellow September day would be perfect for riding Black Satin into the hills, perfect for looking at the ranches he'd pass by and living in his dream. But he had a case to solve and little time to do it before the arsonist was due to strike again. Rubbing gritty eyes, he felt in his pocket for cigarettes that weren't there.

The site had yielded no further evidence but he'd wanted one last look before returning it to the custody of Phoenix Properties.

A car door slammed and Glenn ambled toward him. "Still looking?"

"Yeah," Matt grunted. "Waste of time, I guess."

At the sound of another car door, both men turned.

Matt felt his shoulder muscles tighten again. "What's she doing here?"

Glenn eyed Matt for a moment. "I called to tell her the barricades were coming down. She probably wants another look, too."

"What for? She won't find anything." Matt angled his head away to avoid Glenn's gaze. Sometimes his partner could read him too damn well.

"Professional courtesy," Glenn said. "Is there something I ought to know about?"

Matt didn't answer. Erica walked toward them, black hair swirling about the small, exquisite face. He'd nearly out-bluffed her with that kiss, a ploy he'd just as soon forget. It had backfired on him big time. Her lips had been warm and exciting, raising more long-buried memories of Lynne.

Good thing his tenants had interrupted. Otherwise he might still be kissing her—or advancing to something far more intimate.

"You really expect to find anything?" His thoughts made his words so clipped that he winced at the way they sounded.

"Not if your men have been as thorough as usual, Lieutenant." Her tone was level and controlled.

Matt caught his partner's speculative glance shifting from him to Erica and back again. "Glenn, what did you find out about the caretaker?"

"His landlady says he's a lush. He started drinking Friday and she hasn't seen him since."

"If he passed out in the theater," Matt reflected, "the perpetrator probably didn't know he was there."

"Manslaughter instead of murder," Glenn said, echoing Erica's words of the day before, "but the poor bastard's just as dead."

"Well," Matt said, "no point speculating about Hilliard until there's a positive ID."

The breeze wafted Erica's hair across her face and Matt watched one stubborn strand cling to her lips, resisting her efforts to push it out of the way. He wanted to reach out, let his fingers graze the moist softness of her lips, explore the dark tangles of her hair.

He glanced at Glenn, but his partner also seemed to be staring at Erica's kissable mouth as she spoke.

"Is the autopsy finished? I'd like to review the report and the x-rays. If that's all right with you, Lieutenant?"

He could hardly refuse. "While you're at it, take care of some of our crank calls. Thirty-two and counting."

Erica pressed her lips together in what looked to be a gesture of sympathy. Why the hell did he keep looking at her mouth? Nice, sure. But not that great.

"Charlie told me those calls eat up a lot of your time."

"Has to be done, though." Glenn squinted at the brilliant sky, then removed his glasses and polished them on the hem of his shirt. "Once in a while a call pays off."

A new voice spoke. "What the hell happened here?"

Matt swung around. The middle-aged man's khaki shirt and pants were neat but he had several days growth of beard. His nose was a mass of tiny, broken veins. "Who are you?"

The man scowled at him. "Who's askin'?"

"Lieutenant Nicols. San Francisco Police Department," Matt said, flashing his badge.

"That so?" the older man said, with a slight sneer. "Well, I'm the caretaker here. Name's Hilliard."

Matt blinked. If it wasn't Gus Hilliard's body lying in the morgue, then whose was it? "When did you last check the place?"

Hilliard squinted up at the sky, then back at Matt. "Uh, woulda been last Thursday."

The Phoenix Properties manager had told him the caretaker was responsible for several of their buildings. "What were your duties with regard to the theater?"

"Have a look around, check the doors." He shrugged. "The place don't get used, so there's nothing much to do."

"Did you check the locks on Thursday?"

"Yeah, sure. I just told you. Everything was okay." Hilliard stared at the blackened rubble, shaking his head. "Damn shame. It was a classy old place."

"Did you keep any cans of gasoline around the place?"

"Gasoline? What the hell for?"

"You tell me. That's how the fire got started."

"Jesus! I thought maybe it was the wiring or something." He hooked his thumbs in the waistband of his pants. "Nope, I didn't keep no gas here. Little can of oil for fixing squeaky hinges and such. No gas."

"How about cloth?"

Hilliard looked confused. He must have a doozy of a hangover, Matt thought, brain cells fried to cinders.

"Cloth," Hilliard repeated. "Yeah, stage curtains. They was rolled up and stacked in the ladies' room."

Matt frowned. "Are you sure that's where they were kept?"

"Sure I'm sure," Hilliard blustered. "Ain't nobody says I don't know my job."

"How many keys to the building?"

"Keys?" Hilliard blinked. "Uh, three. Front door and two back doors. Only ever used the back doors if I had to get somebody in to fix something. If you gotta park in the alley, it's easier to use the back door."

"Let's see."

Hilliard took from his pocket an enormous ring of keys attached to his belt with a thick chain. He fingered through the keys, mumbling to himself. "No, that ain't it, that's Turk Street and this here's Grant Avenue." The ring slipped out of his grasp and he began again.

Impatient, Matt asked, "You ever get copies made?"

"Copies? What the hell for?" He riffled the keys around again and crowed, "There's them little suckers!"

Holding three keys between thumb and forefinger, he held the ring toward Matt, adding, "You see that code on 'em? That says they can't be copied."

All that meant, Matt knew, was that Hilliard might have had to bribe somebody to copy them.

"You ever loan those keys to anybody?"

Hilliard clenched his fists, though it was obvious to Matt that the man was too shaky on his feet to try hitting anybody. "You sayin' I let some bastard in to burn down my building?"

"I'm not suggesting anything, Mr. Hilliard." Matt's voice was cool. "I'm asking you a question."

"Jeez!" Hilliard glared at him. "I never got no copies made and I never loaned nobody no keys."

"Where have you been since Thursday?"

Hilliard's eyes shifted. "I had the 'flu."

He's lying, Matt thought. He likely drinks on the job and doesn't want his boss to find out. Or does he know something about the fire? "You ever let any of your buddies in here to spend the night?"

"No, goddam it!"

"Who else has keys to the place?"

"The office, I guess. Sure. Grant coulda gave somebody a key. He told me they were gonna sell the place. That's it for sure, Lieutenant. Grant gave somebody a key." Sweat was beading on his forehead.

He's scared out of whatever's left of his mind, thought Matt. Or else his hangovers included sweating as well as the shakes. "Don't plan on leaving town."

He walked as far as the alley and swung his arms to ease the tension in his shoulders again. Erica followed him. Matt wished she hadn't.

Erica wrinkled her nose as a breeze stirred the ashes at her feet. "Hilliard seems nervous. Do you think he's lying about being in the theater this weekend?"

Shoving his hands in his pockets he rocked back on his heels. "Too many things don't add up. For some reason the curtains were moved. And they'd be damn heavy. Plus there's the gas cans."

"So we're dealing with murder?"

"Our job is to deal with arson."

"But there's a link," she said.

"We don't know that for sure." He swiveled his head to look down at her. "Get your car fixed all right?"

It was his first acknowledgment of yesterday and Erica felt her face grow warm. "It seems to be running just fine now."

"Get it serviced," he said, his voice gruff. "No telling where it might let you down next."

She repressed a smile. "Yes, Lieutenant. Have you seen the pathologist's report yet?"

"No. But it should be on my desk by now."

"I'd like to read it."

"Feel free. I'll send Glenn with you, in case you have any questions."

She glanced up at him. His face radiated tension. "You're not coming back to the office right away?"

"I'll be along." He raised his voice. "Glenn!" His partner ambled over. "Take Ms. Johnson to the station and go over the path report with her. Better grab a wrench from my tool kit. Her car has a mind of its own."

"Where are you going?"

"Phoenix Properties. I want the list Grant promised us of people who had keys to the theater."

The sergeant settled himself in the MG with a minimum of fuss. His lean, lanky frame reminded Erica of the bendable Gumby figure she'd played with as a child. To her discomfiture, he kept staring at her. When a traffic light turned amber she slowed to a stop and swiveled to face him.

"You're staring, Sergeant."

"Sorry. I was just trying to figure out what happened yesterday between you and Matt."

"Why would you think something happened?"

Glenn slid low in his seat, his bent knees against the dash. "I know Matt pretty good. Light's green," he added.

Erica drove on. "And?" she prompted.

"Matt can be grouchy sometimes. But he's different around you. I don't recall ever seeing him quite so much on edge."

"He resents my involvement in the investigation," Erica said. "That's all it is. He's afraid I'll show him up."

"Kinda natural, given the circumstances."

"What circumstances?"

"Office pool. Bets are you'll beat Matt to busting the arsonist."

"Why are you telling me this?"

Glenn crossed his arms over his chest and grinned a Cheshire cat grin. "Got a big mouth, I guess."

Erica smiled in spite of herself. "Bull! You don't let a thing slip by without examining it from every angle."

"Think you got me pegged, do you, Ms. Johnson?"

"It's Erica. I think you've appointed yourself the lieutenant's unofficial big brother."

Glenn grinned again. "Just don't let him find out."

"Our secret."

The comfortable silence between them was broken by Glenn as they parked outside the station. "You gonna satisfy my curiosity, or do I draw my own conclusions?"

"About what?"

"What happened yesterday."

Erica exhaled impatiently. "Nothing happened."

Glenn gave her an owlish look from behind his glasses. "Don't ever play poker, Erica."

She followed him into the station at a leisurely pace, thinking about what he'd told her. So, there was a bet going around the office, was there? The lieutenant wouldn't like that one bit. And Charlie's shoes, scuffed brogues or not, would be mighty tough to fill.

She reminded herself to forget the amateur psychology. One of the hazards of majoring in psych was this tendency she'd acquired to categorize everyone she met, to ferret out their reasons for acting as they did. Sometimes it could be useful but Matt Nicols was a challenging case. One she'd be well advised to walk away from.

At the door of the Special Investigation Squad room, she pasted an unconcerned smile on her face. With luck she'd be gone before the lieutenant even showed up.

Glenn was pulling a second chair up to Matt's desk. He pushed a cup of coffee toward her. "Black, right?"

"You remembered," she said.

"Part of police training," he said with a grin.

"Sure!" Erica retorted. "Is it supposed to be a secret you're a nice guy?"

"Lay off, Erica," said one of the junior officers. "Glenn's married. Unlike some of us."

"Nobody'd have *you*," replied another. A heated debate ensued and Erica spoke in low tones only Glenn could hear. "The nice guys are always taken."

Glenn cleared his throat noisily and brought the pathologist's report up on the computer screen. "You familiar with these?"

"It's been a while," she admitted.

"Okay," Glenn said, pushing his glasses up the bridge of his nose. "The main section consists of cut and dried facts. The end is where they give opinions."

Erica started to skim the report. The body was that of a male Caucasian judged to be in his fifties, with third-degree burns to ninety percent of the body. No skin, so no fingerprints. Soot in the air passages. Blood tests revealed an absence of alcohol, drugs, or poisons.

"No alcohol," she said. "Pretty much eliminates any chance of him being the caretaker's buddy on a drunk."

Cause of death, carbon monoxide poisoning. "What does this mean?" Erica said, reading aloud, "... significant carbon monoxide saturation of the blood?"

"It indicates the deceased was alive, though not necessarily conscious, during the fire," Glenn said.

Old fears swept through her mind, seeping into the crevices like the smell of smoke. She forced her mind back to the present.

X-rays revealed no bullets, shells or negative metals. "It says the victim was wearing a gold chain," Erica said. "Why wouldn't that have burned?"

Glenn grimaced. "Human flesh tends to swell during burning. In this instance the swelling would have actually protected the gold from the fire."

Erica swallowed with difficulty. "I see."

He reached across the desk and squeezed her hand. "We see a lot of bodies in Homicide. I don't think it ever gets any easier. What helps is to reduce it to facts, to a sort of scientific puzzle that needs solving."

"It says here that heat tends to destroy evidence of pre-mortem trauma."

Glenn released her hand. "Means you can't tell if there were cuts or bruises. For example, if he was knocked out before the fire was started."

"So all we know is that he died of smoke inhalation. Not much to go on, is it?"

"What about dental work?" She suddenly had the distinct impression she was being watched and glanced up to see Matt standing behind her. How long had he been there? Had he seen Glenn touching her hand? And why should it matter if he had?

Glenn vacated Matt's chair. "Luckily, this guy had a mouth full of metal. It's our best chance to ID him."

"Let's get on it, then." Matt sank into his chair and took a cigarette from his desk drawer. He tapped the end with his thumbnail, turned it around, looked at it with longing, then put it away. Erica observed the ritual without comment. Only afterward did she realize there had been a noticeable drop in the noise level upon Matt's arrival. Was the lieutenant disliked? Respected? Feared? Glenn alone appeared to be unaffected by the presence of his superior officer.

"Anything else, Erica?"

"No, thank you, Glenn. You've been very helpful."

His mouth turned up in a grin that was impossible not to respond to. "Anything else, just ask."

"You're on." As she met Matt's eyes and became aware of the suddenly strained atmosphere, she felt her smile wobble. "Any luck chasing down keys to the theater?"

Matt blew out an impatient breath. "Not much. Grant says only he and the caretaker had keys. Funny thing, Grant can't find his. It wasn't signed for and no one admits giving it out."

"Could it have been stolen?"

"It's a big office. Lots of people coming and going, no security. Anything's possible."

"What now?" Erica said. "Check the dental records? What if he had the dental work done in a different city?"

Matt leaned across his desk. "Ms. Johnson, I believe your specialty is arson investigation. Why don't you stick with what you know and leave the body to the homicide boys?"

Erica sucked in her breath and slowly rose to her feet. "Thank you for the subtle reminder, Lieutenant. I'll do just that." She pressed a card into Glenn's hand. "My pager number, in case you need to reach me." She left with her head high, convinced that all eyes were boring into her back as she escaped through the doorway.

***

The phone rang only once before a hand reached out to pick it up.

"You seen the paper this morning?" The words seemed loaded with some kind of emotion.

"Yes, I have. What about it?"

"Listen, you promised there'd be nobody in that place. You said nobody'd get hurt. This'll end up being a murder rap."

Best to be conciliatory. "I never meant anything like that to happen. It was an accident. How could I know there would be someone in an unused building?"

"Maybe you didn't check close enough. Maybe you were thinkin' too much about the dough you're gonna make. I don't know. All I know is I don't like it."

"Neither do I. But it can't be helped now."

"Well, I'm not settin' any more fires."

"We made a deal. You can't back out now. There are only two, maybe three more jobs to do. I can increase your share of the money. There'll be a bonus, if things work out." A pause. "I've got Saturday's fire planned. The place is empty. You can check it out for yourself."

"Whereabouts?"

"I won't give you details on the phone. Don't let me down now. We've known each other too long to let an accident get in the way."

A long sigh. "Yeah, I guess. But I'm taking all the risk. No more bodies or I'm blowin' the whistle."

The voice was cold, brittle. "If I go down, so do you."

"Yeah, okay, okay. Same place?"

"Yes. I'll call and give you the time."

Chapter Five

The road forked several times, each silver-gray ribbon winding up and over rolling green hillside, but Erica could have found her mother's grave blindfolded. She doubted her father ever came here and while Ronya was the one who had first brought her on that long-ago Mother's Day, it was a sojourn she preferred to make on her own.

She couldn't erase Glenn's words from her mind. 'Human flesh tends to swell during burning.' Had her mother suffered hideous painful burns, or gone swiftly as smoke filled her lungs? Did she struggle and fight for freedom with her last choking breath, or simply go to sleep in a carbon monoxide induced dream?

The burial park was well-watered, a haven of leafy green in a dry, brown countryside, a cool and tranquil link between the living and the dead. Erica parked her car and picked her way among the weathered headstones until she reached her mother's final resting place. Kneeling, she pulled a handful of grass that had grown over the can of water and arranged the spray of carnations she'd brought. They were pink, which she imagined as being her mother's favorite color.

She sat on the grass, hugging her knees to her chest, her chin resting atop one bent knee. A faint but steady breeze rustled the leaves on the live oaks dotting the hillside. When she was younger, she'd often held her breath and listened intently, hoping to hear her mother's voice amid those whispering leaves. It should be easier here, she'd always thought, to dredge up the few precious memories she had of her short time with the woman who had given birth to her.

It was never easy and her memories were vague and faded. She often wondered if they were real or if, as a child, she had imagined them so often that they seemed real. Only one memory was vivid; she'd wanted the white nightie with embroidered pink rosebuds so much that her mother had bought it at once instead of waiting for her birthday. And she could remember Suzanne's laugh. She had the impression that Suzanne had laughed a lot.

Erica raised her head, eyes damp. She really had no memories of her life before the moment her mother had plunked her on the lawn and gone back into the burning house; only feelings and impressions.

The past drifted through her mind like wraiths of fog. Living in her father's apartment with a succession of nannies, boarding school, summer camp. Her first pony. Her first boyfriend, who later became her husband for a brief and disillusioning year. Her father, always unsmiling, in the background.

According to Rony, Eric had sent her away to boarding school because she reminded him too much of Suzanne. She liked to imagine that he'd been so much in love with her mother that he'd never recovered from the loss. He hadn't remarried. And if he ever sought the company of other women, he was so discreet that no one ever mentioned it, not to her, anyway.

Her happiest memories were of the pony and the times spent with Ronya. Though her father didn't appear to be fond of his sister-in-law, he must have seen the need for a woman's influence. Around Ronya she could stop pretending to be the prim and proper little princess her father expected. She could roll in the mud, chase the cats through the garden and best of all, talk to Ronya about her mother.

"Would we be friends?" She was conscious of the wistful tone in her voice. "Surely you, of all people, understand why I chose this career. I'm so afraid it was somehow my fault that night." She squeezed her eyes shut, almost able to feel the tight, urgent arms that had carried her out of the house to safety. She knew, without knowing how she knew, that the arms were those of her mother.

"Why did you go back inside?" she whispered through dry lips. "What was so important in the damn house that you went back for it?" Most important, why did she feel that she'd been somehow instrumental in that decision? A decision that had cost her mother her life.

Straightening up, she wiped away the two single tears sliding down her cheeks. Much as she longed to have a good cry once and for all, this was the best she'd ever been able to do.

***

Erica took her coffee onto the patio and sucked in a deep breath of heady morning air. She'd been wakened early by the roar of the lawnmower and the fresh smell of cut grass that always reminded her of childhood summers spent with Ronya. Dale had been coaxing that relic of a lawnmower to life back then, too. She wandered over to where he was trimming an overgrown boxwood shrub.

"I hear father's been keeping you busy," she said, leaning on the crumbling cement lip of the wall separating her patio from the rest of the grounds.

Dale slanted a suspicious look at her. "What's that supposed to mean?" Dale had always been like that, as if he were looking over his shoulder, expecting the worst.

"Rony said you weren't around much while I was away."

"Can't be in two, three places at once," Dale said. "Though folks seem to expect it."

Erica reached up and rubbed his bald head. "You've been shining your scalp again. Trying out a new brand of wax?"

Dale swiped her hand away, but Erica glimpsed the smile that touched his eyes. "You're too grown up to be teasing an old man," he said.

"You're hardly old. Though if working for my father all these years hasn't aged you, nothing will."

"I've seen fifty come and go. And I remember you toothless and in diapers. How was your vacation?"

"The best," Erica said, "absolutely the best. I swear one day I'm going to move to the mountains and never come back. Spend all my time sitting on a horse."

Dale snorted. "You'd get bored. Too much of your old man in you for sitting still. Always gotta keep moving, finding new things to do."

"You might be right." Erica heard the ring of her iPhone. "See you," she called, turning away to answer it before the voice mail cut in.

"Erica? It's Glenn. Sergeant Davenport. SIS."

"Yes?" She knew almost before he told her.

"There's been another fire. I'm at the site now. Same MO, but it's about three days early."

A sudden rush of fear made her voice sharp. "Was there anyone inside?"

"No. No fatalities this time."

"What's the address? I'll be right there," she said, adrenaline and relief sending her pulse rate up. "Fillmore St. I'll text it." He sounded hesitant. "I know this isn't your problem, but I haven't been able to reach Matt."

"Oh?" She was positively gleeful at the thought of beating him to the fire site.

"He's supposed to be having a day off. I'm thinking maybe he left his phone at home."

"And what does that have to do with me?"

"Like I said, it's not your jurisdiction, but I think he's gone out to a stable in Mill Valley."

Erica's mind was already making the connection. Mill Valley was only a hop, skip and a jump from Sausalito. "A stable. What's he doing there?"

"He boards his mare. Says spending time with her is the one thing that helps him unwind."

"Maybe he should make a habit of it," Erica said, her tone dry.

"I said as much yesterday and for a change he must have listened."

"Can't you call the stable and leave a message?"

"I already tried. No one's answering."

Erica wavered. What was she? A taxi service? She wanted to get to the fire site right away. But he had fixed her car, she reminded herself. She owed him for that. "Tell me something, Glenn. Would you have called me if you'd managed to reach Matt?"

"Your office would have been notified."

"But I wouldn't have been called personally, would I?"

"I doubt it."

Erica paused as his words sank in. "I admire your honesty. I'll stop at the stable and leave a message for the lieutenant."

"Thanks, Erica. He'll appreciate it."

"We are all working on this together."

On any other day there was nothing she'd have enjoyed more than a drive along winding roads through sunlit wooded hills, the breeze playing with her hair. But part of her was impatient to get back to San Francisco and the fire site. The other part, squashed as soon as it surfaced, was an eagerness to see Matt.

Before she'd even parked the car, Erica saw Matt. She couldn't miss him. With his height and those shoulders, he must have played football in his younger days. What had brought him to police work? she wondered. Despite her vow to forget amateur psychology, she found herself drawn back again and again to Matt Nicols. The scant glimpses of the man behind the facade had only served to heighten her curiosity and her desire to learn more. Homeowner and landlord. Renovator of charming old houses. That could be where he'd got the money to afford a Hollis Hearne painting. And now, watching him with his mare, she saw a man who loved his horse.

At first she'd thought he might be buying paintings for resale and profit. Hearne's work was a good investment.

Ditto the house. And a Thoroughbred horse, in particular a good brood mare, could signal big returns. Yet it was obvious the man before her did not view his animal merely in terms of dollars.

The mare was a rare, beautiful midnight black and, even at this distance, Erica knew what kind of breeding had produced the proud, elegant head, the long, slender racing legs, the slim flanks. The horse whinnied, tossing her head in the early morning breeze, pointed ears standing straight up. Matt pulled something out of his pocket and fed it to the mare. Sugar lumps, thought Erica, as she noticed a second man approaching Matt and his horse.

Erica knew Matt was speaking to the mare, although she couldn't hear his voice. The horse's tail flicked once and she lowered her head as if listening to what Matt had to say. Erica watched his big hand rub the horse's satiny nose, saw the way she seemed to relax against him. Perfect trust between animal and master, Erica thought. If only humans could learn to trust each other like that.

At that moment, Matt looked up, straight at her. Their eyes locked across the dusty paddock. He thrust the reins at the other man and strode toward her. Erica felt foolish, as if she'd been caught spying on him. Why hadn't she left a message at the stable office and gone on her way?

Matt's booted feet raised faint plumes of dust as he neared the fence that separated them. Without missing a step, he vaulted over the rail, landing beside her. Erica felt her voice catch in her throat.

"What are you doing here?"

"Your mare. She's beautiful," Erica said.

"I asked what you're doing here."

"G...Glenn called and asked me to pass along a message. Seems you forgot your phone."

"What's the message?"

Erica moistened dry lips. Why was she suddenly so conscious of everything around them? The sun's heat on her back. The faint breeze. The call of wild birds. The whicker of a horse from the nearby barn. "There's been another fire."

"What!" Matt gripped her shoulders. For one crazy second she thought he was going to pull her toward him. Her knees felt as if they might buckle. "Why didn't you say something instead of standing there spying on me?"

"I was not spying," she said. "And if you treated people half as well as you treat your horse you might find the world a nicer place."

"The world isn't a nice place," he said, from between thinned lips, releasing her abruptly. She steadied herself on the fence behind her. "If it was, we wouldn't need cops or arson investigators. Now, where's the fire?"

"A house on Fillmore, near California Street."

He looked as if there were several things he'd like to say. "Matt," she said, unaware until later that she'd used his first name. Or that it had sounded so natural on her lips. "He said it's the same MO. But it's ahead of schedule."

Chapter Six

Matt dove into his car and slammed the door. It bounced open. He swore, slammed it again and vowed that he'd get the damn door hinges replaced this week for sure. He probably should do something about the rusting dents in the fender, too, but who had time for non-essentials? The engine, on the other hand, worked better now than when it was new. Monkey-wrenching it to a state of perfect efficiency often gave him a sense of peace, and always a lot of satisfaction, something he wasn't getting from the job these days.

The Dodge responded like a racehorse at the starting gate, tires spitting dust and gravel as the car gained speed. The ruts in the narrow road seemed deeper than usual. An empty hamburger carton bounced off the passenger seat and two empty pop cans clanked across the floor. Matt looked at the speedometer, relaxed his shoulder muscles and braked to the posted speed.

Why the hell was he in such a lather? Was it that important to get to the fire scene in five minutes? Or was he trying to get away from Erica? As he pulled onto the highway, he glanced in the rear view mirror, but she was nowhere in sight. Likely hanging back, waiting for his dust to settle.

The fire would be under control and Glenn was quite capable of running the show. A few minutes one way or the other wasn't crucial. Wrapping the Dodge and himself around a tree wouldn't help anyone; it would just create more problems.

He pulled off the highway onto another side road and parked at one of his favorite viewpoints where he could see both the city skyline and a glimpse of the Pacific sparkling in the sunlight. He poured coffee from his thermos, lit a cigarette and leaned back, concentrating on relaxing every muscle in his body.

It had taken Glenn, pushing him to take a day off, to make him realize just how much he needed a break. Now his break had vanished, literally, up in smoke.

And Erica, damn her, had intruded on his privacy, seen a part of his life that he didn't share with anyone. Worse, every sight of her was a poignant reminder of Lynne. The guilt he thought he'd succeeded in burying chipped away at his heart.

The memory of the last time he'd seen Lynne still raked his gut like a knife, no matter that he'd been barely eighteen at the time. Even moving to the other side of the continent hadn't dulled the clarity of that day's events. Nervous but determined, he'd taken the subway from the Bronx to the upper east side of Manhattan and the luxury apartment where Lynne and her family lived.

He was wiping his damp palms on his Sunday-go-to-Mass suit when Lynne's father opened the apartment door. The older man was wearing a cashmere sweater, casual slacks and leather slip-ons. Matt felt overdressed, uncomfortable, out of his depth.

"Come in, Matthew." Bob Stannard appeared not to notice the hand Matt had extended. Matt dropped his hand, reminding himself to be patient. After all, they didn't know yet that he wanted to marry Lynne. They probably figured he was going to shirk his responsibility.

Across the room, Mrs. Stannard sat on a couch beside Lynne, who was stiff and upright, her dark hair like a cloud around her face. She was very pale and she'd been crying. He started toward her, wanting to hold her and comfort her and make her smile.

"Matthew!" said Stannard, in a voice so strident it stopped Matt in mid-step. "Keep your hands to yourself. If you had, my daughter wouldn't be in this situation."

"Bob, please don't." Lynne's mother looked pale, too. "You promised."

Matt drew himself erect, trying to shoulder the weighty duties of adulthood. Meet Stannard man to man. "Neither of us meant for this to happen, sir. But since it has, I'm going to do the right thing. I love Lynne."

Stannard moved to the mantel and busied himself filling and lighting his pipe. "I doubt you're aware of the magnitude of responsibility that comes with parenthood, Matthew. It's even heavier for one so young. Lynne tells us you plan to attend university. On a sports scholarship, right?"

"Yes, sir. But that doesn't matter."

"That's where you're wrong, Matthew. Education matters. So does a good job. Marrying your own kind. Those things last a lifetime."

Matt glanced at Lynne. She refused to meet his eyes and a nameless fear brought a shakiness to his voice that he couldn't control. "I don't understand, sir. Lynne's having a baby and I mean for us to..."

"I called you here to tell you we've arranged to take care of things. And to make it clear that you're not to see Lynne ever again."

The blood thundered in Matt's ears. Sweat was pouring from him, despite the room's frosty atmosphere. He straightened his back and swallowed. "What do you mean, 'take care of things'?"

"We've arranged to terminate the pregnancy."

Matt felt as if the wind had been knocked out of him. The room spun around. "An abortion, you mean. You want to murder our baby!"

"Now, Matthew. Once you calm down you'll realize it's for the best."

"You can't do that!" Matt shouted. "It's a mortal sin."

Stannard leveled him with a fierce glance. "So is fornication. Unless the church has made some recent changes in doctrine that I'm unaware of."

Tears rolled down Lynne's pale cheeks and her mother, as dark as Lynne but already greying, put a protective arm around her.

Matt rushed over to Lynne and dropped to his knees in front of her. "You can't let them do this. You can't let them kill our baby. I love you. I want to marry you."

He felt himself yanked to his feet and shoved toward the front door. Stannard's voice had a definite sneer in it. "Your Irish Catholic upbringing doesn't give you much of a handle on reality. I'll have you arrested if you so much as look at my daughter again. Is that clear?"

Stunned, he stormed out. Every footfall was a thud of anger but by the time he was back in home territory, he'd cooled down. Lynne's father couldn't force her to have the abortion, so he'd have to let them get married.

But she didn't call. And she hadn't been at school. She never answered the phone and the senior Stannards hung up on him. He took his frustration and pain to the gym and pounded the punching bag until his fists hurt.

Two weeks after his visit to the Stannards, his mother, face somber, put her arms around him and hugged him hard, then handed him the newspaper. Good old Ma. She'd known something heavy was going down but she'd never pressed him for details.

The paper was folded to the obituaries. The words jumped out at him, stunned him into a grief that brought tears. "Lynne Arlene Stannard...died suddenly on...memorial service...Episcopalian Church...grieving parents Robert and Anne..."

Matt's hand shook a little as he finished his coffee and put the lid back on the thermos. It had been years since he'd allowed himself to think about those bitter days. Lynne had died from complications after the abortion. At the service the old man had accused him of causing Lynne's death and, eaten with guilt, he'd stumbled away, wishing he could die, too. He couldn't help thinking that if only he'd been stronger or smarter somehow, she'd have refused the abortion and still be alive.

Instead, he concentrated on school, football and work. And discovered that sex was easy to get without love, without making promises.

As he lit another cigarette, he concluded that he wanted to see the back of Erica more because she reminded him of

Lynne than because she might solve the arson cases before he did. He started the engine and backed the car around. He'd foist her off on Glenn, who seemed to like her. Thank God Francie would be back from her convention tonight.

In a few moments he was crossing the Golden Gate bridge. He recalled Stannard's comment about his Irish Catholic upbringing and wondered if he'd ever get free of it. The Gilbey case should have cured him if anything could. Yet he still found it almost impossible to believe that a priest would burn down churches.

Matt turned onto Fillmore and pulled into a space just vacated by a fire truck. He looked at the smoke-blackened house and repeated aloud the remark he'd made to Erica half an hour earlier. The world was not a nice place—not when there was even one dedicated fire-setter on the loose.

Erica's red MG was across the street. Then he saw her standing on the sidewalk with Glenn, surrounded by the vultures of the press with their cameras and microphones. A good thing, after all, that he hadn't hurried to the scene. As far as he was concerned, San Francisco's media circus was a time-wasting irritant. The more they pressed him for juicy headline-grabbing quotes the more he balked. Cooperation was not his long suit. And when it came to the press, he'd been burned a few times too many.

As the reporters melted away and he started toward Glenn and Erica, he reminded himself that the watchword from now on was professionalism. Cool professionalism. He'd make sure everything was strictly business—no personal revelations, no relaxation of the armor.

"What a shame I missed the news hounds," he said. "Nobody dying out there today? Things must be really slow if they're reduced to checking out a house fire."

"Arson is always news." Erica's words were tart, her glance withering. "Sometimes those so-called news hounds come up with a credible lead."

He gave her a long, cool look. "At least I don't have lip marks on my ass." He turned to Glenn. "What's the story?"

"I've seen worse," Glenn said. "The house was unoccupied and unfurnished. Nobody inside."

Matt tilted his head to look at the blistered paint. "From the outside it doesn't look too badly damaged. Did the firefighters find anything?"

His partner nodded. "They found a 'trail'—probably rope—and the place stinks of gasoline. Also, there's a burned-out gas can, same as in the theater."

"The trail makes for a slow burn in the beginning," Erica said. "Gives the arsonist time to get away before any flames or smoke are noticed."

Matt felt his irritation returning. Did she think she was telling him something he didn't know? He said to Glenn, "Did you get a sample of the 'trail'?"

"Yep. Also the ashes at the point of origin. Looks to me like cloth but maybe some paper, too."

"Why would there be paper in an unoccupied house?" Erica asked.

"Maybe to protect the carpets," Glenn said. "The house is for sale so I imagine plenty of people have been tramping through it."

"Any signs of forced entry?"

"Back door was jimmied but no tools left around. The boys are checking for fingerprints right now."

"Good," Matt said, his nod abrupt. "I'll go take a look." He was about to get his gear from the Dodge when he remembered something Glenn had said earlier. "You said the place was for sale. How do you know that?"

"There's a lockbox on the front door and a realtor's sign on the grass over there. I haven't looked yet to see who's got it listed."

Matt walked across the lawn to the sign that had been knocked face down by firefighters. The name on it stopped him cold. The listing salesperson was Frances Cameron of City Realty. What the hell was going on? Could Francie be mixed up in some rip-off game involving arson?

He called up the facts they'd gleaned on the other five fires. Nothing there pointed to Francie. And while Francie wasn't above selling her own mother to make a buck, he couldn't believe she'd do anything illegal. Or criminal. She was too straight. Wasn't she?

Come on, Nicols! He might know the lady in the biblical sense and he'd heard her opinions on damn near everything, but what did that mean? He didn't actually know what went on in her head. He'd find out, though. She'd be back this evening. He'd make sure he was the first person she saw.

Matt walked back to Glenn. From the corner of his eye he saw Erica hauling her boots and overalls out of her MG. Striving to keep his face impassive, he said, "Place is listed with City Realty. Francie Cameron, to be specific." Glenn knew he was seeing Francie. As did half the guys in the squad room. He could hear the talk already.

"Small world," was all Glenn said.

"Small town," Matt muttered. He knew, without Glenn saying a word, exactly what the other man was thinking. Father Gilbey, coming back to haunt him. He drew his lips into a determined line. "I'll talk to her tonight." He eyed Glenn. "You wanna be there?"

Glenn grinned. "Hell no, Superman. I'm sure you've got your own special way of dealing with the lady."

Matt bit back the automatic retort. Glenn could afford to be smug, having found the one perfect woman to be his wife. "You still living vicariously through my bachelorhood?" he said, acid from his short temper leaking into his tone.

"That's right," Glenn said in an exaggerated drawl. "In juicy detail." He flipped open his notebook. "The fire was reported at seven this morning by a neighbor out walking his dog. The fire chief figures the fire was set not more than half an hour before that."

"The guy was taking a chance," said Matt. "Lots of people up and about at that time in the morning. The others were set between midnight and four."

Erica returned, wearing her overalls and boots and carrying her hard hat. "The rest of the MO looks the same, though. Door jimmied, gas can, fire set with material on the premises."

"Could be a copycat artist," Matt mused. "The press has been really playing up the fact our perp isn't high-tech. Just good old gasoline and crumpled up paper or whatever."

"The fact that it's only been two days since the last fire backs up the idea that it might be a copycat," Glenn said.

Erica spoke up. "The fire was set around six-thirty this morning. Why was the perpetrator taking such a chance? The house was empty; he could have done it any time."

"What are you getting at?"

"Just a thought. Maybe the guy wants to get caught."

Matt snorted. "If he wants to get caught he's being damn coy about it."

"Just a suggestion, Lieutenant," she said and walked toward the house. Matt watched her go, wondering whether his 'cool professionalism' was working as well as he'd intended.

"You gonna tell her you know Francie?"

Matt groaned. "Davenport, for a man who's been married so many years, you don't know squat about women."

"What's that supposed to mean?"

Matt blinked. What *did* it mean? That he knew women were prone to jealousy? But Erica had no reason to be jealous of Francie.

"Nothing, I guess. Just me mouthing off." But he knew now what had happened. His errant emotions had identified Erica with Lynne and Lynne would have had plenty of reason for jealousy.

He wouldn't make that mistake again. Lynne was in the long-dead past. Erica was an entirely different person.

Chapter Seven

Erica mentally reviewed the facts on the Fillmore fire as she drove to her office. Assuming that all six fires were the work of one arsonist, the latest indicators were that something had changed. The arsonist wanting to get caught was just one possibility.

She sighed. Someone, somewhere, had to gain from the fires. But what? The prime motivating factor was usually money, with revenge a close second. Ranking somewhere below that was the frightening possibility that the perpetrator was setting fires for fun, which meant he—or she—would have to be caught in the act to make a charge stick. And, so far, Matt and his SIS were coming up empty.

Erica pulled into the basement of her downtown office and parked. Matt Nicols, like the arsonist, was proving quite the enigma. And because he was never far from her thoughts, he had the power to disrupt her entire investigation. She couldn't let that happen.

Not so long as her life revolved around slamming fire starters behind bars.

And how long might that be? she asked herself, an unexpected exhaustion overtaking her and slowing her pace as she headed for the elevator. It hadn't taken first year psychology to figure out what drove her. Every unchecked arsonist was a threat against all that she held dear. Life, love, and the pursuit of happiness, including maybe one day finding that one special man. If he existed.

Talk about irony. Most men she met were clones of the lieutenant. With walls erected that Batman himself couldn't scale. Yet none of them kept reappearing in her mind the way Matt did. Erica shook her head and dismissed the implications, wrinkling her nose at the smell of smoke clinging to her hair. There was just something about him that got to her. Maybe it was youthful lust. The same thing her college classmates had experienced, only a decade late.

She vowed again to banish him from her mind and walked into the reception area of the San Francisco office of California's Insurance Crime Prevention Bureau.

"Erica," the receptionist said, "I've been trying to get hold of you. There's been another fire."

"Fillmore Street?" At the receptionist's nod, she said, "Old news. I've just come from there." The sudden rush of adrenalin dissipated.

Becky sniffed the air and laughed. "I should have known. You smell like smoke. How did you find out before we did?"

"Grapevine," Erica said, taking the fistful of messages Becky held out to her and glancing at the top one. "When did Clayton Gallagher call?"

"Only every hour on the hour since you got back from vacation. Persistent devil, isn't he?"

"That's how he got to be Chief Executive Officer."

"Well, I don't think he believed me that you weren't in when he called. What's *he* like?" Becky asked.

"You've met Clayton."

"Not Clayton," Becky said. "Charlie's replacement. That *is* the grapevine you're tapped into?"

Erica leaned on the reception counter and dropped her voice as if to add fuel to a conspiracy. "Becky. He's an absolute hunk."

"Oh, wow," Becky breathed. "Lucky you."

"Yeah," Erica murmured as she went into her office and shut the door. "Lucky me." Clayton Gallagher was of medium height, impeccably dressed, graying and distinguished. A younger version of her father? Then the image blurred. The shoulders broadened. The Brooks Brothers suit turned into jeans and a sweat shirt, the face became that of Matt Nicols. She scowled. The man had the most annoying habit of popping into her mind.

She'd seen that Matt had great strength, inward as well as physical, but her work brought her in contact with lots of strong, impressive men. Something else drew her to the lieutenant in a way she didn't understand. Was it his eyes, the hint of despair she'd glimpsed once or twice? The set of the firm lips that suggested some great tragedy in his past? Maybe that was it. If he'd lost someone near and dear to him, as she had, maybe their souls were communing on some plane she didn't know about.

Sure, Erica. The surly lieutenant is really a sheep in wolf's clothing, a wounded soul in torment. And you're the one who can free him from the burden of the past. Make him whole again. Why don't you concentrate on the arsonist instead of a fantasy?

She headed to her closet-sized washroom, complete with glass-enclosed shower, a luxury that was one of the perks of the job. One of the few perks, she amended, stepping beneath the stinging spray. A woman investigator poking around fire sites was still a rarity, but she was good at her job, one of the best, in fact. It was unfortunate that she still had to spend too much time and energy proving the fact. She recalled what Glenn had said about the police station bet pool. The guys at the station believed in her abilities but it wasn't surprising that Matt never looked very happy to see her.

Donning the change of clothes she always kept at the office and scraping her wet hair back into a pony tail, she flopped into her chair and punched her personal security code into the Bureau's computer files. After entering the information on the Fillmore Street fire she waited while the circuitry accessed other data bases, checking for cross references. The computer beeped and the real estate board's listing appeared on her screen.

Erica pursed her lips as she scanned it. "So, the house was listed a mere two weeks ago," she murmured. "With Frances Cameron of City Realty."

Pushing more buttons linked her to the Property Insurance Loss Register. She gnawed her bottom lip, frowning, not sure exactly what she was looking for. Any sort of common denominator would be welcome. When none appeared, she scanned back to the real estate listing. Frances Cameron must know something about the vendors.

She dialed City Realty. "Frances Cameron, please." The voice at the other end informed her that Ms. Cameron was out of the office until tomorrow.

"All right, I'll call her then. Oh, could you tell me if she's been out of town long?" The secretary's voice betrayed a mixture of envy and enthusiasm. Ms. Cameron was at a convention in Denver, receiving a top achiever award. "I see. Thank you."

She sat back in her chair. The listing sales agent was obviously a go-getter. And if she didn't get the asking price? Arson? Erica shook her head. Burning houses down wouldn't earn Ms. Cameron any sales commissions. And if she was a top achiever, she wouldn't have time to go around setting fires for fun. Erica decided to start a comprehensive market comparison of homes in the Fillmore Street area. It had to be done, in any case, before the adjuster submitted his recommendation.

Once that was done she'd trot down to the station and take another look at the police photographs of the fires. If Lieutenant Nicols didn't continue his irritating habit of getting in her way. Maybe he'd be filling his face at McDonald's and she'd be lucky enough not to see him.

She paused at reception on her way out. "I'm not sure when I'll be back, Becky."

"Oh, Erica. Don't forget about the International Association of Arson Investigators meeting. I know you don't want to miss it. Any truth to the rumor that you're running for California chapter President?"

Erica wagged her finger at the young woman. "You know you shouldn't pay attention to gossip."

Becky rolled her eyes in an exaggerated fashion. "What else do you think keeps me going?"

Erica laughed as she turned to push the elevator button. She'd known for some time that her name was one of those being bandied about for the presidency. The token female candidate? As little as a month ago she would have been all for it. Along with increasing her visibility, it was a logical career step and would make her boss at the Bureau happy. But would it make *her* happy?

Watching Matt Nicols with his beautiful black mare this morning had reminded her how much she enjoyed being with her own mare, Missy, and Missy's exuberant colt, Merlin. She felt a pang of guilt at the thought that she hadn't been to the stables to see them since before her vacation. Erica shook her head. Often enough she felt guilty for not working longer hours. Now all of a sudden, the guilt was because she was working too much?

She marched into the SIS room, hating the impulse she had to move on tiptoe so she could turn around and tiptoe out again if Matt Nicols was looming behind his desk. She'd never felt this way when Charlie was in charge, and she had every right to be here studying those photographs.

"Hey, Erica. Heard there was another fire."

"The grapevine lives." She scanned the room. Matt's desk was unoccupied. So was Glenn's. Perhaps Matt had hightailed it back to the stables. Shame he couldn't bring his horse into the office. It would probably be easier on everyone around him.

She stopped short. She was doing it again. Allowing the insufferable Matt Nicols to invade her mind. She flashed the earnest young police officer her most beguiling smile. "Would you happen to know where I could find the police photos from the recent fires?"

"Sure," he said, flexing the powerful torso under his tight T-shirt just enough to be sure she'd notice as he bent across Matt's desk and handed her the file.

"Thanks a lot." The enlarged black and white photos had been catalogued and separated into individual fires. At least someone in SIS was a little organized. Wasn't likely to have been Nicols. She'd seen the sad state of his apartment.

Enough of Matt Nicols! She pushed the lieutenant from her mind and took her time sifting through the photos. The warehouse fire had been first. August twenty-eighth. Photos taken between three and four in the morning. An industrial area, very few onlookers. Mostly truckers from the looks of them. Fire number two had been the Chevron station on Sunday, September second. In spite of the hour—between four and four-thirty a.m.—the fire had attracted a fair-sized crowd.

The third fire was Friday, September seventh, at the clothing boutique, between one and two a.m. The crowd was large, which accounted for the great number of pictures taken from all different angles. The photographer had tried for accurate shots of as many people as possible. One blurred face in the background looked vaguely familiar, but Erica dismissed the idea as ludicrous.

Wednesday, September twelfth, was the fourth fire and again the photos were shot between one and two in the morning. The site was on the Embarcadero near China Basin and it was probably safe to assume the big crowd witnessing the damage to the boat repair shop was made up of passing motorists as well as boaters.

"See anything interesting?" Erica started at the voice close behind her shoulder. She should have been relieved that it was the young officer and not Matt. So why the wash of disappointment?

"Not really." But as she studied the photos, her hand trembled. The blurred face she'd seen in the boutique photo was too familiar.

Afraid of what she might find, she went back through the earlier fires. Nothing from the warehouse site. But at the service station, standing off to one side.... Erica went back for another look at the boutique fire. It was hard to tell. The face was heavily shadowed.

She looked up. "Can you bring this photo up on the computer for me?"

"Sure thing." The officer managed to brush her shoulder while he did so, but she ignored him as she used the software's zoom function to look more closely at one area of the photo. The face was blurred, but the woman wore something fastened around her neck. Erica's breath caught in her throat as the magnifying glass slipped out of her hand. She'd recognize that pendant anywhere. It belonged to her aunt.

***

Chill tendrils of evening fog rolled in off the Pacific, curling around apartment buildings and blurring street lights. Matt reached into the Dodge for his black leather bomber jacket. The damp autumn air reminded him of the crowd's roar after a touchdown, of crackling fires and hot buttered popcorn. But the homey fireside scene wasn't something he'd get at Francie's. Not what he'd come for, either.

A taxi stopped and Matt watched Francie deal with the driver, her sleek blonde hair gleaming under the street light.

No sentimentality about Francie—she knew what she wanted and went after it. She liked rolling around in the sheets as much as he did, but her career was her life and she wanted no commitments. Perfect. Neither did he.

With a dozen long strides he was beside her, reaching for her garment bag. "How was Denver?"

The taxi slid away and Francie smiled up at him. "Great! I'm ready to go out and sell everything in the city."

"I thought the conference was on for the whole week."

"It is. But you know me. I couldn't stay away that long; I might miss out on a sale."

The elevator doors closed and he slid a hand under her suit jacket at the back, loosening her blouse. Her flesh was smooth and firm. She was in good shape for her age, whatever that was. Not that it mattered, but he'd always wondered how many years she had on him.

She circled her lips with the pink, wet tip of her tongue. "Easy, big boy. I've been traveling for hours and I'm going to have a shower before I do anything else."

Matt poured drinks while she riffled through her mail. "Come on, Francie, your mail can wait. What I have to tell you is important."

"Important? You want to list your house?"

"No. But this concerns one of your listings—the house on Fillmore. There's been a fire."

"Oh, my God! Why didn't you tell me right away? How bad is it? Have you been in touch with the owners?"

"Of course. And it's bad but not a write-off. Minor rebuilding. Repainting inside and out."

"Damn! That means the house will be off the market for at least a month, maybe longer."

"I got the impression the owners are anxious to sell."

Francie nodded. "They need the money out of the house as soon as they can get it."

"Bad enough to torch it for the insurance?"

She looked shocked. "Arson?"

He nodded.

"This is an official interview?"

"Semi-official."

She leaned back in her chair and looked at him over the rim of her glass. "This is a new Matt I'm seeing."

"You've never been involved in one of my cases before."

"No, just your sex life." She tossed down her drink. "Get me another, will you, sweetie? I'll call the Burtons. I might still manage to pull off a sale."

While she was on the phone, Matt gazed out at the fog-shrouded lights of the city. He'd once mocked the sentimental songs about San Francisco. Now he sometimes caught himself humming one of them.

Hearing Francie hang up, he asked, "Who gains from the fire?"

"Only the bank," she said. "Who else? The Burtons have bridge financing. They'd get more from a sale than from fire insurance."

He sloshed his remaining scotch around the melting ice cubes. "This case is beginning to drive me nuts. Six fires during the last three and a half weeks."

"Six? It was four last time I talked to you."

"There was another one early Monday morning. Very early. An old theater owned by Phoenix Properties."

She gasped and put her drink down. "That's my listing, too! Not in writing, mind you, but I'd have had Phoenix signed in another week." She gave an angry kick and her shoe landed on the other side of the room. "Damn it. I had a buyer for that theater, I know I did."

"You've shown the theater?"

"I gave the key to a client Sunday night."

At once Matt was on his feet, every muscle taut, his mind churning. "Who did you give that key to? When? Did you get it back?"

She stared up at him. "You're scaring me. I didn't burn down that stupid old theater."

His voice was ragged. "A man died in that fire. We haven't been able to ID him yet."

"Oh, my God!" She looked stunned. "Philip Mandell! I gave the key to him Sunday night before I went to Denver. Could it be him?"

Matt forced himself to sit down. "Why didn't you show him through yourself?"

"I didn't have time. I had a plane to catch. Besides, Philip likes to do his looking on his own."

"Your plane didn't leave until midnight," Matt pointed out. "Surely to God he wouldn't go looking then?"

"How would I know?" she retorted. "I had dinner with another client Sunday night. He drove me to the airport. I can't be in two places at once."

He knew Francie was fond of her bankbook; if it was possible she would have cloned herself to make more sales.

"All right, so you gave Mandell the key. You didn't get it back?"

"No. I told you..."

"Okay, okay, you had to get to the airport. You said Mandell wanted to check the place out solo. Why?"

She pressed her lips together in a thin line. "Do you know who Philip Mandell is?"

"Don't use that tone with me. Like you, I can't be in two places at once and I've had my mind on arson lately. He's something to do with live theater, right?"

Francie sniffed. "Sarcasm doesn't suit you. Philip Mandell is the director of Peninsula Players, the most prestigious repertory theater group in the west. He's been profiled by half a dozen national magazines."

"Get to the point, Francie."

She shrugged. "Well, he told me he liked to spend a lot of time visualizing what a building would look after it was renovated, how it would feel to work in it. He said the atmosphere was important."

How long had it taken Hollis Hearne to visualize the painting that hung in his living room? "Okay, I can grasp that. What time did you give him the key?"

"Seven-thirty. What time did the fire start?"

"The alarm was turned in just after three a.m."

She topped up her drink. "I'll call Philip and ask him about the key. Also see if he's interested in building on the site if the old theater is beyond renovation." After two minutes she hung up. "No answer. That doesn't mean anything, though. He never answers if he's working on a play."

Matt paced to the window but the lights were now mere ghosts in the heavy fog. The scotch tasted sour in his mouth. Identifying the body in the morgue wouldn't bring the poor bastard back to life. And if the body turned out not to be Mandell, he could talk to him tomorrow, find out about that key.

Wait a minute. Ron Grant at Phoenix Properties had told him he'd never given the theater key to anyone. His staff backed him up on that. So how did Francie get it?

An image of Erica, black hair blowing in the breeze, sprang to mind. What would she make of the situation? She'd sure as hell react different from Francie. But he'd always known Francie had dollar signs in her eyes. He had a sudden urge to see Erica, to share this latest finding.

You're losing it, Nicols. He sat down. "I could do with a cigarette."

"I thought you quit. Going to bed would be a lot better for both of us." She leaned forward, allowing him a generous view of her breasts, bare beneath her blouse.

Strangely, it had no effect on him. A sudden image of Erica supplanted Francie and his body stirred in response.

"You're probably right," he said. The physical release he'd come for no longer seemed important. "How did you get hold of that key in the first place?"

Francie smiled. "Used my powers of persuasion to talk one of Phoenix's office flunkies into giving it to me. He said he wasn't supposed to, but I convinced him it would benefit the company in the long run."

He could just imagine what kind of powers she'd used. "Did you ever let that theater key out of your possession other than to Mandell?"

"Never."

"How well do you know Mandell?"

"Just what I read in the papers." She caught his expression and added, "I'm not sleeping with him, if that's what you mean. He's a client, that's all."

"So was I at one time." And they'd celebrated in her bed the night the deal closed on his house. He wondered how many other clients were given the same privilege.

"Who'd you have dinner with Sunday night?"

Her eyes narrowed. "Is this really necessary?"

"I'm afraid so."

"I don't want my clients hassled by cops!"

"Calm down, Francie. Since when is asking questions harassment?" And since when had he been relegated to the role of cop?

She subsided into her chair. "Oh, all right. His name is Rawlins. He's an architect, a real estate developer, a patron of the arts and, above all, a real gentleman."

"I've seen his name. I know he's a big wheel."

"Matt, I've spent a lot of time getting next to him. I don't want him pissed off with me because I got him involved in something like this."

"Why should he be? The fires aren't your fault." What was she so antsy about? Then it hit him. She was sleeping with Rawlins.

"Where did you have dinner?"

She glared at him. "Fourneau's."

"Nice place," he said. "Real nice. I remember the roasted red pepper salad dressing we had the time you and I went there. The guy's got good taste. What time did he pick you up?"

"Eight-thirty. We left the restaurant at ten-thirty and he drove me directly to the airport."

"And you caught the midnight plane to Denver?"

"Of course I did! You can't possibly believe I'd be involved in anything illegal." She moved to the arm of his chair and massaged the back of his neck with supple fingers. "Matt, if you care about me, please keep my name out of this. I've spent years building my reputation and contacts with the right kind of people."

If she cared about him, would she be sleeping with Rawlins? For a second he thought about dumping her on her ass, then remembered it was his idea that they weren't supposed to care about each other. "I can't promise, Francie. But you shouldn't worry." He managed a derisive smile. "After all, I'm a suspicious cop and I believe what you tell me."

She nibbled his earlobe, murmuring, "Let's leave the shop talk and get relaxed. Want to join me in the shower?"

It was tempting. Why not? There was no question he could use the release.

But his mind wouldn't shut up. And for the first time since he'd known her, his body wasn't really interested in what she had to offer. He rose. "Let's leave it for tonight. I'm going to work for a couple of hours."

Her smile was forced. "Okay, tough guy. You know where I live."

Yeah, in her bankbook. "See you, Francie."

Alone in the elevator he thought about what she'd told him. At least the puzzle of the missing key had been solved and maybe he was finally on the way to identifying the body in the theater.

Outside, he filled his lungs with cool, damp air. Where now? Back to the office or home to his lonely bed? His rumpled unmade bed came to mind and Erica was there, smelling of lilacs, her long dark hair fanned across his pillow.

Chapter Eight

For the first time since she'd moved into the carriage house five years ago, Erica was reluctant to go home. But she could no longer avoid asking Ronya about the fires. She found her aunt in the studio, doing rough charcoal sketches on a large drawing pad.

Sliding her hands into her jeans pockets, she paced the studio. "So," she said with forced casualness, "you didn't tell me how you amused yourself while I was away."

Ronya looked up, eyes bright and inquisitive. "Since when have you been interested in how I fill my days?"

Her aunt was sharp as a tack when she wanted to be. The bemused air of confusion Rony often put on was a pretty convincing act. Or was it an act? Maybe she had good days and bad days. Or maybe all artists spent half their time in a world no one else could see.

Erica took a breath. "Actually, it was the early mornings I was interested in." There was a flutter of wings as Benny landed on Ronya's shoulder. Her aunt turned her head to give the bird a kiss. Erica smiled as Benny kissed her aunt back. Old Benny knew where his next meal was coming from.

"Bad bird, bad bird," he recited before he scrunched his vivid green neck feathers and hopped down from Ronya's shoulder, then strutted away to harass a tabby cat sleeping under the table.

"I don't ask how you spend your night hours, Erica."

Erica watched Ronya put away her brushes and paints. They were the only possessions her aunt bothered to keep in any sort of order. "Well, I'm afraid your nocturnal wanderings have become my business. I saw your face in the crowd photographed on site at two of the recent fires around town."

"I beg your pardon?"

"I've seen the police photos, Rony."

"Certainly I was there." Her aunt bristled. "Is everyone who happened along a suspect?"

"Of course not. But I did wonder why."

Ronya's smile was bright. "Have I told you about my new idea for a series focusing on San Francisco?"

"Are you changing the subject?"

"Not at all. In fact, it was the first fire I saw, the service station, that prompted the idea. I'm planning a series on fires."

"Go on," Erica said.

"I didn't set out with the intention of going to a fire. Philip and I were walking back to his place from a gallery opening and then dinner, with some wine and a chat about the old days." She sighed and Erica wondered if the memories had been happy or sad. "When we heard the sirens we followed them. It was Philip who said, 'San Francisco and fires, Rony. Now there's a hot topic.'"

Erica grimaced. "Philip never could tell a good joke."

"It started off as a joke. But then, after the next fire, the ideas came so fast I couldn't wait to get home and start sketching." Her expression softened. "You didn't really think your old aunt was out there, single-handedly burning down the city, did you?"

Erica shook her head. "No. I just...I don't know." Her voice caught. "I wish I could remember the night she died, Rony. Why can't I remember?"

Ronya stroked Erica's hair. "You were so young."

"Not that young. I remember the sirens. The flashing lights. The smoke and flames. Even the way the yard smelled that night."

Her aunt's look was sympathetic. "Are you sure you remember all that? Or have you romanticized those things in your mind over the years until they seem real?"

"I don't know." She tilted her head. "I remember you, though. And Philip and Catherine. Father I don't remember until later."

Ronya closed her painting case and straightened up. "He's never been an easy man, your father. He loved Suzanne but didn't understand her. He wanted to put her on a pedestal, out of reach, so no one else could touch her. He even tried to keep her away from me after they were married. I suspect he resented her having friends or interests other than himself."

"He didn't treat me that way. He seemed quite eager to marry me off to Trevor."

"We all disagreed with him on that point. Trevor was too immature for the depth of love you're capable of."

Erica made a deprecating face but Ronya nodded. "It's true. Even as a little girl, you had all this love pouring out of you. You'd come here and gush over the cats and dogs, goldfish even. Anything that might return affection."

"You make me sound pathetic."

"Poor little rich girl?" Ronya said. "Perhaps. Still, it almost broke my heart. You tried so hard to be what your daddy wanted, even when those things were contrary to your nature."

"I know he loved me. He's just never had an easy time showing his affection."

Ronya nodded. "He was the same with your mother. She tried to teach him to give and receive affection but she failed. And believe me; she was used to getting whatever she set her mind to. You're very like her in that regard."

"What I've set my mind to right now is catching this arsonist. Rony, what kind of God lets crazies run around loose lighting fires?"

"It's society you ought to be questioning, Erica."

"That sounds more like Clayton's department."

"Clayton Gallagher?" Ronya gave a pained sigh.

Erica wagged a finger at her aunt. "I know what you're thinking."

"You haven't the slightest idea."

"You think Clayton's a father figure. That I'm looking to him for the affection my real father didn't give me."

"You're the one with the psychology degree, not me."

"Well, you're wrong. I happen to prefer mature men."

"I may not know much about psychology, but I think you're overcompensating for Trevor. Is Clayton still pressuring you to get married?"

"I think he's given up."

Ronya sniffed. "You hope. More likely he's reworking his strategy. He'd stifle you the same way your father stifled your mother."

"I have no plans to marry Clayton Gallagher or anyone else. I like my life just fine the way it is. How about you and Philip?" she teased, turning the discussion from herself to her aunt.

Ronya's eyes clouded. "We're the best of friends and always will be. We understand each other; we both lost the one we loved most."

"Am I ever going to hear about these great tragedies?"

"Oh, perhaps one day."

There was a knock at the door and Ronya, the look on her face betraying her relief at being off the hook, hurried to answer it. "Come on in, Dale."

He stopped just inside the doorway. Erica focused on the tattooed snake curling through the reddish hairs from his wrist up to his elbow. Its forked tongue had fascinated her ever since she'd been little.

"I just wanted to tell you to stay off the lawn for a couple days. I put some stuff on it. And keep the animals off it, if you can."

Benny fluttered onto Dale's shoulder and nuzzled his beak against Dale's jaw. "Good boy! Good boy!" the bird squawked. Dale took a small handful of sunflower seeds from his shirt pocket and began feeding the parrot.

"You're spoiling that bird rotten, Dale," Ronya said, "and he loves every minute of it." She smiled. "All right, we'll remember about the lawn. Won't you be around?"

"Depends. Boss might be sending me out of town."

"Since when has free travel been one of the perks of working for my father?" Erica teased.

"Never know," Dale muttered. "The old man might be giving me a one-way ticket."

Erica rubbed his shining pate. "None of us could get by without you, Dale. You know that. Isn't that right, Rony? How would we manage without old Dale?"

"You're absolutely right," Ronya said, the smile she beamed at Dale full of affection. "We couldn't."

***

"I don't like to disturb Mr. Mandell. He's a private, moody fellow, but a good tenant these past twenty years." Matt and Glenn followed the apartment manager into Mandell's living room. One wall was lined with books, another covered with play posters and publicity shots of actors. A third wall had large windows facing the green ocean of Golden Gate Park and beyond it, the blue Pacific.

The manager checked the other rooms. "He's not here. The refrigerator is well stocked and his car is in its usual spot. Your best bet is the rehearsal hall. It's only a few blocks and he often walks."

A telephone sat on the massive antique roll top desk, an address book beside it. Matt riffled through the book while Glenn telephoned.

"He's not at rehearsal, either," Glenn said, hanging up. "The assistant director says they're starting rehearsals for the new season. He can't understand why Mandell isn't there."

Matt turned to the manager. "What about girlfriends?"

"From time to time, I've seen him bring a lady with long, graying black hair in, but I doubt very much if she was a girlfriend."

"Okay," said Matt. "Thanks for your help. If you hear from Mandell give us a call right away."

Reaching his car, Matt turned to Glenn and handed him a note. "The address book listed these two doctors. See if one is Mandell's dentist and get the ME onto him. I'm off to interview Rawlins."

Glenn grinned. "Be nice to him, Superman. You don't want to get Francie mad."

Matt gave him a withering look.

Riding the elevator up to Rawlins' office in the financial district, Matt thought about Francie's description of the man and the scraps of information he'd picked up from the papers. Architect and real estate mogul, Rawlins had his photo taken with celebrities and made well-publicized donations to various charities.

'Rawlins & Associates' was lettered in matte brass on oak double doors. The receptionist informed him that Mr. Rawlins was busy. Would he care to wait?

He wouldn't, but he had to follow up every possible lead. Besides, he wanted to know what a 'gentleman' had that a well-educated, occasionally bad-tempered cop didn't. But, knowing Francie, it was probably the money.

"I'll wait." He sank onto a fat leather settee. Several boring minutes later he took out his cigarettes.

"I'm sorry, Lieutenant. This is a non-smoking building."

That figured. He put the crumpled pack away and ate a sugar lump. Twenty minutes crawled by while he drummed his fingers. Then a tall man came down a hallway and stopped at the reception desk.

"Sorry about the wait, Lieutenant. I'll be with you in a moment." Watching Rawlins walk away, Matt cursed under his breath. Another twenty minutes? But Rawlins was back in less than two, motioning Matt to follow him.

The window in Rawlins' spacious office framed the city north to Fisherman's Wharf and the Golden Gate. A large glass desk, brass-edged and almost bare, dominated the room. It was as different from his own scarred and battered desk, Matt thought, as Rawlins was from himself. Elegantly spare and graceful, Rawlins wore an expensive suit and his graying brown hair and pencil mustache looked as though they'd been styled by an expert. Was that what separated the gentlemen from the working stiffs?

Deep in his soul, Matt was aware that little had changed since his interview with Lynne's father a lifetime ago. He might be eons older and wiser. He'd never be 'one of them.'

Rawlins' icy blue eyes moved from a black leather appointment book to his Rolex and finally to Matt. He said, "What can I do for you, Lieutenant?"

Matt observed Rawlins while he provided a brief outline of the theater fire. The man's voice and movements seemed studied and mechanical. If this was what Francie liked in bed, he'd misjudged her in spades. His hackles rose as Rawlins said in a bored voice, "All very interesting, Lieutenant, but I don't see how I can help."

"Let me put it another way. Ms. Cameron says she dined with you Sunday night. Can you confirm her alibi?"

"Alibi! Surely Ms. Cameron isn't a suspect?"

"We have to follow every lead."

Rawlins, looking offended, smoothed his moustache with one finger. "Ms. Cameron and I dined together Sunday evening at Fourneau's on Nob Hill. I picked her up at her apartment around eight-thirty and, as I recall, we left the restaurant about ten-thirty. I then drove her to the airport."

"Did you stay until she boarded?"

Rawlins shrugged. "No, I didn't wait. She had some reading to do for the conference, so I left."

"Did Ms. Cameron mention the theater?"

Rawlins fingered a gold pen. "She may have. She had telephoned to postpone our dinner date and I agreed to pick her up an hour later than we'd previously arranged."

"And did she name the client?"

Rawlins hesitated. "I believe so. Not strictly ethical on her part, perhaps, but she was excited and optimistic about the deal."

"Was the name familiar to you?"

Rawlins' eyebrows arched just a trifle. "I am a devotee of live theater, Lieutenant. Philip Mandell is well known as a director and..."

"We're aware of his professional reputation," Matt interrupted.

Rawlins frowned and leaned back in his chair. "I had met Mandell a few times, years ago, but I didn't know him well. He was a friend of my deceased wife's family."

Interesting! "Have you spoken to him recently?"

"Oh, no. I should think it's twenty years at least since I've had personal contact with him." Rawlins appeared to hesitate. "However, I do believe my sister-in-law remained in touch, despite a serious dispute some years ago. Shall I have my secretary give you her name and address?" Rawlins stood as he spoke.

"Thanks," Matt said, struggling to keep his tone civil. Why did he dislike the man so much? Jealousy? Or Rawlins' subtle way of indicating that all men were not equal?

Francie was welcome to him.

In the SIS office, he brought Glenn up to date and said, "I'm going to see the sister-in-law. You coming?"

"Yeah. By the way, Mandell's dentist and the ME are getting together this morning."

The bridge traffic was light and Matt had no trouble finding the Sausalito address Rawlins had given him, but the run-down Victorian mansion and its odd shrubbery wasn't what he'd expected. Rawlins was a suave man of the world; this place looked as if it might be inhabited by a witch.

The woman who opened the door looked the part. She had long, wild, graying hair and wore several layers of clothing, complete with beads, woolly socks and Birkenstock sandals.

"Miss Germaine, I'm Lieutenant Nicols of the SFPD and this is Sergeant Davenport. May we come in?"

Her smile was gentle and somewhat vague. "Of course. Would you like some coffee or tea, perhaps?"

There was an unmistakable odor of animal excrement in the dusty, cluttered front room. "No thanks," Matt said.

"We don't want to be any bother," Glenn added.

"It's no bother. I don't often have visitors." The woman brushed a strand of hair away from her face and looked at them as though she couldn't quite remember how they'd got there. "Why don't you just come through to the kitchen?"

As they followed her down the hall, the odors altered to include the sharp tang of oil paint and turpentine. In the room beyond the kitchen Matt saw several canvases in various stages of progress. "Sorry if we interrupted your work. We have some questions about Philip Mandell."

"About Philip? That's odd." She filled a kettle at the sink. "What's Philip done?"

"Nothing that we know of. Do you know where he is?"

"Now let me think. I talked to Philip—when was it? Not long ago." She nodded. "He called me. On the telephone. He does that sometimes."

"Would you happen to recall what day that was?"

She kneaded the area between her brows. "Oh, dear. I don't pay much attention to clocks and calendars."

Matt battled his impatience. "It would really be a help to know the day. Do you recall the conversation?"

"Conversation?" The whistling of the kettle almost drowned her out. "I have herbal tea," she said, smile bright. "Or Postum."

"Oh, tea sounds just the ticket!" Glenn said.

She plunked a used tea bag into an oversize cracked mug and set it in front of Glenn. "And for you, Lieutenant?"

Matt bit his lip to keep from laughing at the look on Glenn's face. "Nothing, thanks. If we could get back to Philip Mandell for a minute."

"Oh, he was very excited," she said. "Just like a little boy. He was off to inspect a theater he was interested in buying.

That's always been his dream, you know. A permanent home for the Players."

"So the call might have come on the weekend?" Matt prompted.

"That's right." She beamed as if he'd handed her a winning sweepstake ticket. "Sunday. I remember because my niece was due back that night and I knew how pleased she'd be if Philip..."

"There was a fire Sunday night," Matt interrupted. "In an old theater just off Market."

Her eyes widened. "So there was. Poor Philip."

Matt stiffened. "Why do you say 'poor Philip'?"

"That was the theater he was hoping to buy. He must be disappointed." Her gaze grew keen as she glanced from Matt to Glenn. "Has he heard about the fire?"

"We don't know. We can't seem to locate him."

"Oh, dear." Shaking her head, she spoke into an intercom. It looked out of place in the old-fashioned kitchen. "Could you come over here for a minute, dear?" The kettle caught her attention. "Oh, yes, I was making coffee. Or was it tea you wanted, Lieutenant?"

"Nothing, thanks."

Their hostess looked disappointed, but Matt wasn't taking any chances. He'd seen *Arsenic and Old Lace*. The odd thing was that he liked the old girl.

"I've called my niece. She knows far more about these things than I do."

Matt exchanged glances with Glenn who quirked an eyebrow and gave an almost imperceptible shrug. A moment later the back door opened and Erica Johnson walked in.

Matt felt his jaw sag. "What are *you* doing here?"

Chapter Nine

"I could ask you the same thing." Erica stood in the doorway, trying to hide her dismay at finding the two SIS men in her aunt's kitchen. She saw Matt's jaw tense and knew there was precious little chance she'd get any information from him.

"I asked first," Matt said.

"I live here. Ronya is my aunt." Ignoring Matt, she glanced at Glenn. "Perhaps you'll tell me what's going on, Sergeant."

Glenn said, "We're investigating the theater fire."

Erica's glance shifted from one man to the other. If they'd spotted Ronya in the police photos, they weren't wasting any time. And it wouldn't matter to them that she was convinced of Ronya's innocence. Doing research for paintings of San Francisco area fires likely wouldn't satisfy them as a valid reason for Ronya's presence.

"Have there been some new developments?"

Matt, with a quick glance toward Glenn and Ronya, said to Erica, "Is there some place private where you and I could talk?"

Erica hesitated. Did she really want to invite the lieutenant into her home? But, looking at Ronya's vague expression, she knew she must protect her aunt as much as possible. She owed her that. "This way."

Trying to ignore her intense awareness of Matt walking close behind her, she led him along the path to the carriage house. She was also aware of Dale, seemingly absorbed in clipping a shrub and pretending it wasn't unusual for her to take a man into her home. Dale never asked personal questions but the curiosity in his eyes was almost as hard to deal with.

The original space in the carriage house had been opened up so that the kitchen, living room, and dining area were now one high-ceilinged room. The furniture was white wicker with touches of blue in the cushions. She glanced at her bedroom door, wondering why she was so relieved to see that it was closed.

"Very nice," Matt said as he looked around. He walked over to the french doors and looked out at the flagstone patio edged with white heather and decorated with pots of brilliant red geraniums.

Erica leaned against the kitchen counter, crossed her arms and focused a critical gaze on Matt. He seemed more exhausted and surly than usual. She schooled herself not to notice. Not to care. He also looked decidedly out of place in her country chintz decor.

"Funny," he said, pausing to pick up a piece of sculpture, "how much your house tells me about you. Makes me wonder; what did you get being at my place?"

The delicate ivory carving of a white dove looked trapped in the lieutenant's large, sun-browned hand. Erica recalled the feeling of that hand against her face, fingering through her hair, breaching a more personal privacy. "More than I wanted," she said. "I'd like to forget what happened last time we were alone. Why are you questioning my aunt?"

Matt replaced the dove and gave her a direct look for the first time since entering the room. "You mean my kissing you? You kissed me back as I recall. Is that the part you're hell-bent on forgetting?"

So they were back to this! Erica fought against the color she could feel rising in her face. She'd like nothing better than to forget about that disturbing kiss, the feel of his powerful arms around her. "You're changing the subject, Lieutenant."

"You raised the incident, Inspector."

She forced herself to meet and hold his gaze. "This isn't getting us anywhere."

"I agree." He went to her refrigerator. "Any chance there's a beer in here?"

She raised an eyebrow. "Aren't you on duty?"

"Lady, these days I'm always on duty." He opened the fridge and stared at the bag of mixed vegetables she'd pulled from the freezer that morning. "You eat frozen vegetables?"

"No, Lieutenant. I cook them first."

"Frozen vegetables when there are fresh available anywhere in the city?" He shook his head and peered further into the depths of her refrigerator. "I should have known. Nothing but the best, right?" He pulled out a long-necked, green bottle of European brew and twisted off the cap, tossing it into the spotless sink. "This is your last one. Want a hit?"

"No, thank you," Erica said, hoping her formal tone would convince him to get back to business. "I don't drink beer." What was going on? He seemed more antagonistic than usual. He was mad at her. No. Bothered by her. Something, anyway.

Matt took a long swig. "But someone in your life does, right, Princess? Boyfriend, maybe?"

"This is verging on the ridiculous, Lieutenant. Besides, your partner is probably going out of his mind right about now. Ronya has that effect on people."

"Glenn's a pro. He'll be all right."

"Listen, if you're not willing to tell me what you've discovered, I'll . . ."

"You'll what? Go running to your friend the police commissioner?"

As he lounged against the sink drinking her beer, Erica was struck by a sudden, ludicrous notion that he needed her, whether he knew it or not.

Right, Erica! Wasting time on fantasies again. Get a grip on yourself.

Unlike Clayton Gallagher, there was no danger of the lieutenant putting her on a pedestal. Down the road is where he'd like to see her. Far down the road.

"I was going to say I'd talk to Glenn. Maybe he'd offer me the professional courtesy of a few answers."

Matt stared at the bottle for a few seconds. "All right, here goes. The real estate agent handling the Fillmore Street house also had a kind of exclusive listing on the theater. She gave the key to a prospective purchaser on Sunday evening."

"You've spoken to Ms. Cameron?" Erica said.

Matt nodded and took another pull on the beer. "The guy she handed the key to hasn't been seen or heard from since."

"Our John Doe," Erica said, excitement mounting. "But that doesn't explain why you're questioning Ronya."

"There's more," Matt said, his words abrupt. "When I checked out Ms. Cameron's alibi, her date said he put her on the plane to Denver that night. He also said that Miss Germaine is a good friend of the guy with the theater key. The guy who might be taking up space in the morgue at this moment."

"Who?" Erica asked.

"There's no positive ID yet."

"Tell me."

"Philip Mandell."

"Oh, my God!" Erica grasped at the bar stool as her legs threatened to give way. Matt crossed the room and stood poised as if ready to catch her should she pitch forward. Her grip tightened on the stool.

"I take it you knew him, too."

She glanced up, trying to hide her shock, her fear for Philip. "How soon will you have anything positive?"

"Not long. We found Mandell's dentist."

"Does Ronya know?"

Matt shook his head.

The implications of this new information were unsettling. No. Frightening. "Who told you Ronya and Philip knew each other?"

"Cameron's boyfriend. Some big-time developer. Name of Rawlins." Matt stared at her. "*Now* what is it?"

Erica suspected she'd gone as white as the walls. She blinked against a wave of dizziness as the floor undulated beneath her. None too gently, Matt took her chin in his hand and forced her head up so her eyes met his. "You're acquainted with Rawlins too, I take it?" His lips thinned. "Is that who you keep the Heineken on hand for?"

A bubble of near-hysterical laughter lodged in Erica's throat. "Yes, but it's not the way you think."

He released her, turned his back and strode away as if he wanted to put a mile of space between them. "It doesn't matter what I think. I'm interested in what you know." He swung back to face her. "Or maybe I should say, who you know."

Erica took a deep breath and steadied herself. "Philip Mandell has been around all my life. He's...he's like an honorary uncle."

"And Rawlins?" Matt ground out. "He another 'uncle'?"

"No such luck," Erica said. "He's my father."

An odd look swept across Matt's face, too fleeting for her to identify. "Did you think he'd been two-timing the real estate lady with me?"

"I don't know what I thought." He thrust a hand through his disordered hair. "And it doesn't matter. Your father. Damn!"

"Is there a problem with that?"

"I'm not sure, yet. I need to think." He looked up. "Johnson must be your married name."

"Brilliant deduction."

He scowled. "This case is getting complicated."

"Don't they usually?" She forced herself to stop thinking about Philip. Matt had said they weren't sure yet, and Philip often disappeared for days at a time. It could be someone else. She had to concentrate on the job. "More to the point, what did you learn from Ms. Cameron about the Fillmore house?"

"She said the owners were in a big panic to sell."

"Maybe they opted for insurance instead."

"Francie said they'd do better from a sale. In fact, she was annoyed about the fire stalling things. She's sure she'll have no trouble getting a buyer."

Erica noticed he referred to Ms. Cameron by her first name. Must have been quite the discussion they had. When? Early this morning? Though Erica had left several messages at City Realty, Ms. Cameron hadn't returned her calls.

"Where does that leave us?" she asked, her voice failing as thoughts of Philip returned.

He swung around and slammed the empty beer bottle on the counter. "I'll tell you where it leaves *you*. If that's Mandell in the morgue, it leaves you too damn close to this business. It's called conflict of interest. Which means you're off the case."

"You're not being fair."

"I don't have to be fair. I won't have your personal feelings hampering my investigation."

"I'm hardly stupid, Lieutenant. Or naive. It's been obvious right from the start that you want me off this case."

His jaw clenched. "I've already got one partner."

"You've also got one heck of a mess on your hands. Whether you want to admit it or not, you need me."

"Ms. Johnson, I've never needed anyone. And I'm not about to start at this late date."

Her eyes met his, probing, finding nothing. He actually believed that. Once again she wondered what had happened in his life to leave him in such a vacuum. "How sad." She turned away.

He grabbed her arm and hauled her back to his side. "Don't waste your sympathy on me, Princess. I'm immune."

She refused to struggle. His breath fanned her forehead. She detected the faint odor of beer. "Did you ever stop to wonder just what it is you're trying so hard to be immune to?"

Before he could answer, some inner devil prompted her to rise on tiptoe and press a light kiss on his lips. Her body reacted instantly to his musky, outdoor scent and his tightening grip on her. Shocked, she realized she wanted him to kiss her back.

And just as she acknowledged that realization, his arms moved to enclose her. With a primitive groan, he gathered her against him. His mouth opened over hers, hungry, eager, luring her tongue inside the hot recess to duel with his, hostage to his need. His hands roamed over her back as though she belonged to him, alternately kneading and molding, fitting her to his length. Her arms circled his neck as her fingers brushed through his hair and his breath quickened. She thought she heard him moan deep in the back of his throat.

He rubbed against her, the evidence of his arousal straining at his jeans. An answering surge of heat flooded through her. She arched toward him as he bent over her, his mouth abandoning hers to forge a pathway of wet, hot kisses down her throat. Tunneling both hands through the fullness of his hair, she exalted in the strength of the arms that held her. Then she felt him unbuttoning her blouse.

Cool air danced across her bare skin in delicious contrast to the hot exploration of his tongue snaking over her bra to her belly. In one swift movement, he hoisted her onto the counter, positioning his hands to unsnap the waistband of her jeans.

The sudden shift jolted her from mesmerizing sensual excitement to the reality of her kitchen. Ronya and Glenn were drinking tea only a few hundred feet away.

"Wait. No." He didn't seem to hear her and her hands grappled with his, which were tugging with single-minded purpose at the top of her jeans. "I said no."

His movements slowed. Then halted. "I'm sorry," she said, unable to meet his eyes. "I didn't mean for things to get out of hand."

His breathing was harsh in the silent room. He braced his weight on his arms, one on either side of her. "Mind telling me what in hell you did mean?"

She slid to the floor and tried to button her blouse, conscious of the way she was trapped against him. "I said I was sorry." She ducked under his arm and kept moving until she'd put half the length of the room between them.

He turned to face her. "Oh, I get it. You thought I was like the society dudes you're used to dating, happy with a goodnight kiss at the door."

She tilted her chin up as she met his gaze. "I didn't expect you'd climb all over me."

"Who was climbing on who?"

Before she could respond, the intercom from the main house buzzed, followed by the sound of Glenn's voice.

"Matt, are you there? The pathologist just called. We got a positive dental match on the body."

She watched Matt tuck in his shirt. Had she done that? Untucked it and caressed the warm, smooth expanse of his back? His eyes met hers and she could swear he was reading her mind.

"If you'll excuse me. I have police work to attend to."

Chapter Ten

The door slammed behind Matt and Erica forced herself to focus on Glenn's announcement. The dental match must mean that Philip... She squeezed her eyes shut against the sudden onslaught of hot tears. Philip, the kindest, gentlest man she'd ever known. Burned to death. Just like her mother.

Rony! She had to be there when Matt and Glenn broke the bad news. She gave her face a hasty splash of cold water and ran a brush through her hair. It wouldn't do for Ronya to know she'd been crying.

Or kissing Matt Nicols.

She marched into her aunt's kitchen armed for battle. Matt had threatened to get her dismissed from the case. She must make him understand that because of this disaster it was more important than ever that she be part of the investigating team.

Ronya, looking bewildered, huddled in her favorite chair. Glenn squatted beside her, speaking in low tones, and Erica felt grateful for his concern. Nicols, on the other hand, was talking on the phone, his back to them. She put a comforting hand on Ronya's shoulder and said to Glenn, "They're sure it was Philip?"

"Positive." Glenn glanced at Ronya, who stared into her lap and pulled a tissue to shreds. "We need to notify Mandell's next of kin. Do you think your aunt...?"

"I know the family very well," Erica said. "They own a winery in Napa Valley." She worried at her bottom lip.

"Philip's father is ill; they think he's dying. This news might well finish him off."

Glenn straightened. "Matt!" He glanced down at Erica. "Why don't you go out there with Matt? They might take it better from someone they know."

"I don't see how that..." Erica paused. It could prevent Matt from tossing her off the case. "You're right, I should be there." She bent down to put an arm around her aunt's shoulders. "You okay? Would you rather I stayed here?"

Ronya gave her elbow a reassuring squeeze. "You do what you have to do, dear. Go to Auguste."

Matt replaced the receiver and turned toward them. "What did you say, Glenn? I couldn't hear."

"Erica knows the Mandell family. She's agreed to drive you there. I'll head back to the city and start talking to the actors Mandell worked with."

Hands on hips, a scowl on his face, Matt rocked back on his heels. "And just who made these plans without bothering to consult me?"

"A little country air will do you good."

"Let me remind you I'm still senior officer, Sergeant."

Glenn winked at Erica. "The lieutenant's pissed off. I'd better get out of here before he hits me with a direct order."

As the door shut behind Glenn, Matt said, "I meant what I said about conflict of interest."

"I've no doubt you did, Lieutenant, but I happen to be your best source of facts. You need me. And my car." Erica turned on her heel.

Matt glared at her retreating back. She was upset about Mandell—her eyes had been red when she came storming back. It would be tough for her if she stayed on the case. Not to mention tough on him, he thought, recalling her fragrance, the silken texture of her hair. The feel of her skin. Her lips.

He turned to Ronya, still slumped in her chair. He said, "Are you sure you'll be all right?"

Ronya heaved herself to her feet, scattering a lapful of tissue shreds on the floor. "Don't worry about me, Lieutenant; I've got my cats and Benny to look after. And I have to make lunch for Dale soon. You go along now."

Dale? Must be the guy working on the shrubbery. He felt a bond of sympathy with Dale. The poor bastard was probably going to get ersatz coffee and soup out of a can. That is, if she kept her mind on what she was doing long enough to remember where she kept her can opener. Still, he had to admit there was something he liked about Ronya Germaine. He just couldn't figure out what it was.

Erica was revving the engine of the MG. Scrunching himself into the passenger seat, he said, "It's my job to notify the next of kin, not yours."

She gave him a tight smile. "So nice of you to try and spare me. But these people are my friends."

"If that's what you want."

She blinked, obviously not expecting him to give in so fast, then pressed her lips together and turned her attention to driving. The tenseness of her shoulders and jaw told him she was taut enough to explode.

He'd been ready to explode, too. Erica coming onto him, then pushing him away, Glenn usurping his decisions, not to mention Francie's greed and the weeks of fruitless investigation, had almost pushed him over the edge. But somewhere in his head was a safety valve that kept him from actually going over, the same one that had kept him straight when Lynne died. For a short while at least he'd be able to relax, be detached, gather his strength.

He watched Erica covertly as she maneuvered the MG onto Highway 101. What game had she been playing this morning? Did she want him as much as he wanted her? She'd sure acted like it. Or was she trying to get his goat because he'd been irritable with her?

She was a distraction he didn't need, yet part of him was glad she was along. He could handle looking at death and burned-out buildings, but informing a family that one of its members had cashed in his chips was a part of the job he'd always hated.

Matt cleared his throat. "How about giving me a run-down on the family? It helps to know who I'm talking to."

She ran one hand through her silky dark hair. His hand itched to do the same and he looked away.

"There's Auguste Mandell, Philip's father, who is almost eighty and in a wheelchair. He's frail and I'm so afraid this news will kill him. Philip was the apple of his eye." Her tone became wry. "Auguste is an old-fashioned papa and all his dreams are—were—centered on his eldest son."

Matt grunted, remembering growing up in the middle of eight kids. "Go on."

"The younger son, Justin, runs the winery. He's a typical farmer, patient and quiet. And his wife, Cheryl."

"Kids?"

"No."

"Was Mandell ever married?"

"Only to the theater."

"Who inherits the winery when the old man dies?"

Erica frowned. "I'm not sure, but it would probably be Philip, since he was the eldest son."

"What's your aunt's connection to the family?"

"The Mandells and Germaines have been friends for years and years. When they were young, Ronya and my mother used to hang out with Justin and Philip and Catherine."

"Haven't heard you mention your mother before."

Erica gave him a sharp glance. "Why should I? Anyway, she died years ago."

"Sorry." He should have remembered Eric Rawlins mentioning his deceased wife.

They circled San Pablo Bay and headed north. The September sun was warm on the rolling, wooded hills now that the cooling influence of the Pacific was behind them. He'd leave Erica in peace, let her think her own thoughts.

The MG's engine still sounded rough; too bad she didn't keep her car in shape. Too bad Captain Bailey thought she was God's gift to SIS, too. Although, with any luck, this conflict of interest thing would get her off his case and out of his life.

Off a side road near Napa, Erica turned between massive stone posts under a sign that said 'Mandellini.' The half mile long winding driveway was a brute—tight switchbacks, loose gravel and a steep bank. At the top sprawled a long, low brick house, almost hidden under masses of ivy. The sign on the carved double doors spelled out, again, 'Mandellini.'

The reception area was cool and dim. Erica stepped up to the polished walnut counter and rang a little brass bell.

A short, plump Mexican woman in a white apron appeared, her grin almost splitting her face when she saw Erica. "*Querida!* It is so long since we've seen you!" She clasped Erica's hands.

"Too long," Erica said. "Dolores, you look worn out."

"The grape harvest, *querida*. You remember. Day and night we work. Every year I think it will be easier, but every year I am older." She eyed Matt. "And who is this, little one? The boyfriend?"

That caught Matt's ear. So Erica had talked about a boyfriend, had she?

"Hardly."

What did she mean by that?

"This is Matt Nicols, a police lieutenant from San Francisco. We've come with sad news."

The smile vanished. "Ah, no! Philip? What happened?"

"*Muerto.*"

"*No!*" Dolores gave a long, drawn-out wail, and Matt looked on as Erica put a comforting arm around the woman. After a moment, Dolores stepped back and dashed the tears from her face with the back of her hand.

Matt frowned. Breaking the news was his job, even if he didn't like doing it. He'd expected Erica to support him as he did so, not the other way around.

"This is bad," Dolores said. "Very bad. Mr. Auguste is dying. This news will make his last days a bitterness. How did it happen?"

"A fire," Matt said. "We're still investigating."

Dolores looked up at Erica. "And you, too, are investigating? You will find out?"

"Yes, I am." Erica directed a pointed look toward Matt. "And I *will* find out who did it, I promise."

"The department has a special squad on the case twenty-four hours a day," Matt said.

The woman was silent for a moment. "That is good. Erica, you take this policeman to Mr. Justin's office." She wiped her hands on her apron. "I will make a lunch. You will stay?"

"I'm afraid we can't."

Dolores nodded. "Yes, much work. The padrone will not die in peace but it is better he knows the truth. You come and say goodbye before you leave?"

"I will." Erica motioned Matt to follow her. "The office is this way."

Matt was beginning to wish he'd come alone. With Erica almost part of the family, it was only natural they'd look to her for answers, but he didn't have to like it.

"Erica! It's wonderful to see you." The next member of the household also greeted Erica with a hug. Justin, perhaps fifty, looked the part of a farmer in his denim bib overalls and red plaid shirt, while his squint and dark tan indicated an outdoor life.

Matt imparted the news in a couple of sentences, intent on gauging Justin's reaction.

There was no doubt the younger Mandell was surprised. His face paled and he sagged into his chair. "Mother of Mary," he said. "Poor Philip. And things were going so well for him." He looked up at Matt. "How did the fire start?"

"All we know is that it was deliberately set."

Justin gasped and his hands clenched and unclenched as though in torment. "You mean Philip was murdered?"

"We don't know yet. It's possible your brother was just in the wrong place at the wrong time."

Shaking his head, Justin said, "This will be rough on my father." He paused and added, "There are days when I think he's hung on these last few months just to see the grapes brought in one more time."

Justin rose. "My wife will be bringing the padrone to the den for his glass of wine. The doctor doesn't approve, but my father takes orders from no one. I think we'll all need a drink today."

Matt agreed. He wasn't looking forward to breaking the bad news to the senior Mandell.

A dusty bottle of red wine stood on the sideboard. Justin said, "One of our best vintages. Dolores has been spoiling the old man shamefully since he came home from the hospital. I'll get her to bring up another bottle."

As Justin left, Matt looked at Erica, noting her pallor. He cleared his throat. "You're doing fine."

She looked so startled that Matt mentally kicked himself for acting like such a bastard that civil words from him surprised her. He walked over to the fireplace and looked at the pictures on the mantel. "Is this Philip, here with Justin?"

"Yes." Erica's lilac scent teased his nostrils.

"This is your Aunt Ronya, right?"

Erica craned her neck rather than get too near him, Matt noticed. "That was a long time ago."

The years hadn't been kind to Ronya, he thought. "I've seen her somewhere before."

"Of course," Erica said, her words coming almost on top of his. "This morning."

"No, before that. I just can't put my finger on it."

"Her picture's in the newspapers whenever she has a show. That may be where you've seen her."

"Could be. Who's this with her?"

"That's Catherine, sister to Philip and Justin. She and my aunt were roommates at one time."

"Where is she now?"

"She died in the Sixties. A drug overdose, I've been told."

Matt stepped back, the image of Ronya's young face still niggling at him.

Justin returned and was pouring the wine when a well-dressed woman with red hair, heavy makeup and a petulant expression came in pushing a wheelchair. The old man in it, bald, sunken-jawed, his flesh wasted, looked every bit of eighty years old.

"Erica." His voice was hoarse and barely above a whisper. His eyes swiveled to Matt. "Who's this?"

"Lieutenant Nicols, San Francisco Police. Auguste, I'm afraid I have some bad news."

The alert intelligence in the rheumy eyes belied the frail body. "San Francisco police," he wheezed. "Bad news, eh? Something's happened to Philip."

Matt told him.

Mandell's head dropped to his chest and his veined and wrinkled hands twisted in his lap.

Matt looked up, surprised to see a smile on Cheryl Mandell's face. When he caught her eye, she rearranged her expression and said in a brittle voice, "Oh, my God."

Erica knelt and held one of the old man's hands. "I'm so sorry, Auguste." He reached out to touch her cheek.

"Who would kill Philip? He was a good man, a good son." The old man lifted his hands and dropped them in a gesture of despair. "Woman, take me to my room. I want to be alone for a while."

Cheryl pushed the wheelchair into the hall. The click of her high heels faded, then a door opened and shut.

"Lieutenant, Erica, will you take a glass of wine?" said Justin.

"Thanks," said Matt. "Mr. Mandell, can you think of anyone who might want Philip out of the way?"

"It's been on my mind since you first told me, but no, I can't."

Matt sipped his wine. It slid over his tongue with a delicious smoothness that surprised him. Granted, his experience was limited mostly to the Catholic Church gallon jug vintage, which he hadn't tasted for so many years that Father Mac was likely rolling in his grave. "Was your brother wealthy?"

Cheryl, returning, answered. "He would have been soon. The winery was to go to Philip on Auguste's passing."

So, Matt thought, here's a couple who will benefit a great deal by Philip's death. Maybe the theater fire would turn out to make sense after all. He turned to Justin. "Mr. Mandell, how did you feel about Philip inheriting?"

The eyes that met his gaze were candid, unflinching. "Philip had no interest in the vineyard. I knew it would be mine to manage for the rest of my life."

Cheryl's voice held bitter sarcasm. "My husband doesn't care about money, Lieutenant. All he's interested in are his goddam grapes."

"That's not true," Justin said, his voice quiet and a little tired, as though he'd heard this comment many times before.

Matt drained his wine. He didn't have time to listen to marital spats. "We have to get back. Mr. Mandell, I'll let you know when your brother's body can be released."

Justin hugged Erica again. Matt was surprised by the annoyance he felt at seeing another man touch her.

"This way," she told Matt, out in the hallway. "I promised Dolores I'd say good-bye."

Matt smothered his impatience and followed her into the kitchen where Dolores must have been waiting for them. "Mr. Auguste?" she asked.

"He's a tough old boot, Dolores. He may outlive us all yet."

Dolores gave an eloquent shrug. "The old, they don't show their tears."

"Cheryl took him back to his room."

"That one!" spat Dolores. "I would not ask *her* how he is. Now that Philip is gone, she will wait for the padrone to die so she can spend his money."

Matt recalled Cheryl's smile upon hearing of Philip's demise. She had good reason to be pleased. When the old man kicked off, leaving everything to her husband, community property laws meant she'd get half of the vineyard.

A dark-skinned little boy ran in the back door. "Gramma, you said I could ride the horse after lunch."

"Oh, Felipe, don't bother me now," Dolores said.

Matt stepped forward. Dolores might spill something interesting to Erica with him out of the way. "I'll take you, kid. Where's your horse?"

The youngster's eyes lit up. He grabbed Matt's hand and tugged him toward the door. "I show you, mister."

Matt looked at Erica. "You won't be long?" She gave her head a shake, but her eyes lingered on him as if she knew what he was up to.

"What's the drill?" Matt asked the youngster, wondering what breed of horse awaited.

"You put me on, then you lead him around," said the little boy. Felipe's eager little face exuded joy.

The 'him' was a sway-backed chestnut mare with a benign expression and a long, tangled tail. Her halter rope was tied to the porch railing.

"What's her name?"

"Dolly. She's a real good horse."

Matt stroked her silky nose and examined her teeth. She was twenty if she was a day. Dolly nuzzled a sugar lump from his palm, smacked her lips and snuffled hopefully at his pocket. "Don't be a greedy girl."

He lifted the boy up to straddle the mare's broad back. "Hang on tight to her mane, now." He undid the rope and looked around at acres of trellised vines. "Which way?"

"Down the rows. But we can't get too close to the vines or Mr. Justin will get mad."

"You're the boss," Matt said, setting off, the mare plodding behind.

Chapter Eleven

On the back step, Erica stopped short at the sight before her. Matt was coaxing old Dolly along with a sugar lump while Felipe clung atop her back and drummed her ribs with his bare heels.

"I see you got Dolly's number," Erica said, as the unlikely threesome stopped beside her.

"More like she's got mine," Matt muttered. "Okay, ride's over, short stuff." His tone was brisk, but Erica noticed the gentle way he set Felipe on his feet, then snatched the boy's peaked cap, turning it around and setting in on backwards.

Felipe grinned up at him. "Thanks a lot, mister. Come on, Dolly." Clucking to the mare, he grabbed the rope and tugged the horse toward the fence.

Erica hoisted a covered basket behind the driver's seat of the MG. "What's that?" Matt asked.

"Dolores's maternal instincts are working overtime. She took one look at your scrawny frame and packed enough lunch for an army. She says you're to eat every crumb."

Matt stood by her door, leaning one hand on it as if he'd forgotten all about rushing back to the city, and scanned her length while she settled behind the wheel. "Sure it wasn't your scrawny frame she was talking about, Princess?"

Erica flipped her sunglasses into place. "I'll have you know I'm the perfect weight for my height. One hundred and fourteen pounds."

Matt laughed as he climbed into the other seat. "And Dolores said *I* look scrawny."

She gave him a thoughtful glance. "What she actually said was that you look tired and overworked. I couldn't argue with that."

He leaned over and turned the rear view mirror toward himself. "I don't look that bad, do I?"

He didn't. Not to her. Truth was, he was starting to look too darn good. Erica straightened the mirror. "I'd say you've had a rough couple of weeks." The engine caught and she accelerated with a spray of gravel.

Matt tossed a sugar lump in his mouth. Erica cringed as he crunched it to bits. "How can you eat those?"

"Got to keep my blood sugar up. What else did your friend Dolores have to say?"

Erica kept her gaze on the road as she guided the car down the sharp switchbacks. More than one car had smashed in the rocky weed-choked ravine. "Nice try," she told him. "But no go."

"What nice try?"

She aimed a quick grin at him and returned her attention to the road. "I'm getting you figured out, you know. When it comes right down to it, you're quite obvious. So spare me the injured-innocent look. I know you beat a hasty retreat from the kitchen so Dolores could tell me privately if she had any suspicions about Philip's death."

He grinned back. His face had the look of a little boy caught with his hand in the cookie jar. "Well, what did you get?"

"I thought you wanted me off this case."

"I do."

Braking to a stop at the main road, she swiveled to face him. "Do you usually get what you want?"

"Not very bloody often," he admitted, leaning back and popping another sugar cube into his mouth.

"Too bad," she said, her voice husky. "I always get what I want." She guided the car onto the highway.

"Save the small talk and tell me what Dolores said."

"Okay. But you're not going to like it."

"Try me."

"She held her hand over her heart and said you have the eyes of someone who experienced a grievous loss long ago, and that the wound still festers."

Matt snorted. "Not much of a revelation. Show me one adult in the entire state she couldn't say the same about. What else?"

"Nothing. There's no love lost between her and Cheryl, but then no one in the family has much use for Cheryl."

"Not even her husband?"

"I never could figure them out," Erica mused. "They're two such different people." Yet they'd been together for a good many years, in spite of Cheryl's apparent dissatisfaction with Justin.

Her mind filled with memories of Philip taking her and Rony to Mandellini. Of old Auguste before his stroke, showing her the different vines, explaining how to tell the right moment to pick the grapes. She'd learned to ride there, when she was Felipe's age. Later, she'd learned the proper way to taste the wine, swirling it in her glass and leaning forward to capture the bouquet. Taking a sip, she'd swish it around the inside of her mouth, feeling the flavor burst against the back of her throat, before inhaling sharply to get the full effect of the finish.

After several miles she stopped the car on the side of the road. "I'm starved. Okay if we stop here to eat?"

"I thought you were kidding about the food."

"I never joke about food. Besides, I was afraid you might want to stop at McDonald's." She caught Matt's expression. "What's wrong?"

He was scowling, but it was a little-boy look. "I want to get back before Glenn solves this case all on his own."

"What's another hour?" She climbed out, taking a blanket and the picnic basket. "Dolores was right. You look wiped out."

"Give me that, then." Matt took the picnic basket from her and kept pace as she followed a dusty footpath that led off the road and ended a few hundred yards later in a shady clearing.

With a flick Erica spread the blanket. Matt stood watching her. "This not to your liking?" she asked.

His eyes were wary. "I'm puzzled. Why the tête-à-tête? Earlier you didn't want to be alone with me."

"I promise to behave if you will." She continued, "You're hungry. I'm hungry. We'll eat and talk about the case." He went on watching her. "Listen, I realize you're not just a dumb cop who got lucky and made lieutenant. You've probably got a criminology degree. I also recognize that you've got a very strong sense of justice. Philip Mandell was a dear friend and I want to see justice done. I know arson and I'll help as much as I can, but as for the rest of it . . ."

She squatted down and delved into the basket. "I knew it! I knew good old Dolores would throw in a bottle of wine." She tossed Matt a corkscrew. "Make yourself useful." He took the bottle and sat down next to her.

"That wasn't bad wine we had. Is this the same kind?"

"Not bad?" she echoed in disbelief. "You can't *buy* a wine like this."

"Can't afford it, you mean?"

"I mean it's not for sale. Auguste only produces enough for his own private stock."

Matt fumbled with the corkscrew. "I'm afraid I'm a scotch drinker, myself. I've never had much experience with wine."

"I suspected as much. Here, I'll do that. You dish up the food." She took the wine bottle and opener, catching his look of amusement. "I knew how to uncork a bottle long before I was old enough to appreciate the contents."

She filled two glasses and watched as Matt laid out cold chicken, cheese buns, sausage rolls, sliced ham, potato salad, homemade pickles and a triangle of Brie. "No pie?" she asked, disappointed. "Dolores makes wicked pie."

"There's something in here wrapped in foil. Who's going to eat all this food?"

"You are. I promised her."

"You should learn not to make promises you can't keep."

She took a slow sip of wine, her eyes on him over the rim of her glass. "I'll bear that in mind."

Matt filled his plate and started to eat. Stubborn man really ought to have someone to look after him, she thought.

No one can exist for long on McDonald's, cigarettes, and sugar lumps.

She reined in the thought. Things had changed a lot since she was a little girl. Nurture was out. Self-sufficiency was in. So why did this nurturing instinct rear its head every once in a while? Maybe her biological clock was starting to do weird things. She'd heard that could happen near thirty.

Matt drank wine like a trucker drinking coffee. Erica winced.

"Don't gulp it," she said. "Sip. Let it roll around in your mouth. Smell the bouquet. That's the only way you can appreciate a good wine to the fullest."

He did as he was told. "I have to admit it makes a difference. The taste is a nice contrast to the food, too."

"I can tell it's not you that uses those copper pans hanging in your kitchen," she said. "Any good cook knows that food is complemented by decent wine."

"Wrong." He lifted his jaw in a stubborn tilt. "I know about food. In fact, I'm one of the best cooks I know. Liquor is something else. Never thought all the fuss about wine made any sense."

Matt could cook? Unbelievable. Maybe he thought being able to sear a steak qualified him. She'd have to teach him something about that, and about wine, if she got the chance. Wait just a minute. Was she sure she wanted to get that close to him?

"Tell me what they were like when they were younger." Matt took a bite of Dolores's apple pie. The Mandells, I mean. And your aunt."

Erica shrugged. "I don't know much. From what I've heard, though, the five of them grew up together. My mother and Philip were into theater. Ronya and Catherine both wanted to be artists and studied in Paris, then roomed together until Catherine died, as far as I know. Ronya doesn't like to talk about her."

"Was your aunt into the drug scene as well?"

Erica smiled. "She's kind of eccentric, I admit, but that wasn't caused by drugs. My grandmother was just the same."

"And your mother?"

"She died when I was six. I don't remember her."

Matt sounded thoughtful. "So, when they were growing up together, Justin was the odd man out."

"I don't think so. I'm told they were one big happy family." She saw Matt's change of expression. "What?"

"I come from a big family. And the big, happy family myth is just that. A myth."

Erica filed away this first scrap of personal information Matt had offered her. "How are things now?"

"I don't know. I haven't been home in a while."

"Where's home?"

He raised an eyebrow. "You mean I finally lost the Bronx accent?"

"Gee, and I thought it was Queens. More wine?"

"No. Damn stuff's making me sleepy." He shot her a warning glance. "You'd better not, either. You're driving. I swear this stuff is overproof."

Erica forced the cork back into the bottle. "It doesn't affect me. But if we get pulled over I'll let you do the talking."

Matt stretched out and pillowed his head on his hands. "You were right about Dolores's cooking. She's damn near as good as I am." He gave her a self-mocking grin. "I could go for a nap right about now."

"Getting back to the real world lose some of its urgency?" she asked, kneeling on the blanket to pack up the remnants of their lunch.

"Some. Ever wish you could hide out from the rest of the world? Let the crazies take care of themselves?"

"All the time," Erica said. She gave his leg a gentle nudge with the toe of her boot. "On your feet, soldier."

He groaned, but rolled to his feet. She saw him wince as he stood up. "What's wrong?"

"Nothing. Old football injury."

Another piece of personal information. The good food and the wine were working miracles. And she'd guessed right about his having played football. "You looked like you were in real pain."

"I told you, it's nothing. Damn knee just gives me a jab once in a while." He folded the blanket.

They were halfway back to the road when Erica realized something was wrong. Up ahead, both car doors stood open. She broke into a run.

"What is it?" She heard Matt close on her heels. Grabbing her arm, he pulled her to a stop. She pointed to the car.

His gaze skimmed the surrounding woods even as he reached for his gun. "Stay back!"

He approached the car as if it was a bomb set to explode at any minute. Slowly he circled it, then called to Erica. "Did you lock the doors?"

She caught up and stood beside him. The contents of her glove box had been emptied on the ground. "I never lock the doors. Saves me a fortune in broken windows." Stooping, she picked up her insurance and registration forms.

"Are you missing anything of value?"

Erica surveyed the interior of the car and shook her head. "They were probably hoping for a DVD player or a phone. When there was nothing to steal they just dumped everything out in frustration."

"Don't touch anything," Matt told her. "We'll get it dusted for prints."

"Don't be silly," Erica said. "It was just some kids looking to make an easy score."

The look on Matt's face suggested otherwise.

As soon as everything was stowed back in the car Erica turned the key. Nothing.

She tried again. Nothing.

She shot Matt a sideways glance. "Maybe they tried to steal the car and gave up when it wouldn't start."

"Only an idiot would steal this car. I seem to recall telling you to get a new starter."

"This only happens when I'm with you. You must be a bad influence or something."

Matt gave an exaggerated sigh. "Unlatch the hood."

Erica watched as he bent over the motor, wondering if the car acting up would make the careful truce they'd struck a thing of the past, with Matt redoubling his efforts to get her dismissed from the case.

He beckoned. "I want to show you something."

Joining him, she looked down at the intimidating jumble of belts and hoses connected with rusty-looking metal parts. Matt slapped a tool into her hand. "This is a wrench. Buy one. Don't leave home without it." He leaned inside and pointed. "This gizmo here is your starter motor. Connected to the armature. Can you see where I mean?"

Erica stood on tiptoe. "Uh huh," she stated, with a confidence she was far from feeling.

"Now watch. No, wait." He took hold of her shoulders and positioned her directly in front of him, trapped between him and the bumper. "See that little square part sticking out toward us? You want to grasp it with the wrench."

Erica leaned forward. His breath stirred the hair on top of her head. She was getting goose bumps. His hips cradled her bottom as he put his arms around her and took her hand in his, positioning the wrench where he wanted it. "Contact. Feel that?"

How could she concentrate on a lesson in mechanics when his powerful body hugged hers at every juncture? Erica tried to nod. The top of her head connected with his jaw. She felt a few strands of her hair snag on his whiskers.

"Give it a tiny little nudge. Fraction of an inch."

Erica did as she was told. "Okay." He stepped back without warning. Her legs felt limp without his support. "Now try it."

She turned, moistening her lips. "Try what?"

"The key," he said, with a trace of impatience. "It should start."

On cue, the engine turned over and caught. Matt closed the hood and got in next to her. The motor idled like a purring cat. A purring cat with bronchitis, Erica amended, but she made no move to put the car in gear.

"What are you waiting for? Let's go."

"Why does it only act up once in a while?"

"What you've got, Princess, is the game of starter roulette. Once in a while it stops on a dead spot. You move it forward a titch and no problem. Until next time."

"How do I fix it?"

"You invest in a new starter."

"They don't make parts anymore."

Matt shrugged. "Factory rebuilt. Same thing."

"Why didn't you show me that last time?"

"I assumed you'd get a new starter, like I told you."

She shrugged. "It never did it again until today."

"Believe me; it'll keep on doing it."

She nodded. "Thanks. For showing me what to do, I mean. I'll make sure and buy a wrench."

"No," he said. "Make sure you get a new starter installed. Have them do a tune-up at the same time."

"I will," Erica said. "As soon as the arsonist is behind bars. As soon as I know why Philip had to die."

He blew out an impatient breath. "Have you heard even one word I've said? You're too close to this case to be effective."

She threw the car into gear with a lurch. "Let me be the judge of that, Lieutenant."

"You're not in any position to judge." He slapped his open palm against the dash for emphasis.

She wasn't going to waste time arguing now. That could come later because, if he wanted her off this case, he had one hell of a fight ahead of him. But he was quiet for the rest of the drive into San Francisco, leaving her free to think up strategies to counter any reasons he might toss out to get rid of her.

Glenn was walking across the station house parking lot when they drove in. He squatted by the passenger window, a smile spreading across his face as he saw the picnic basket and half-empty bottle of wine. "Have a nice drive?"

Matt wrenched open the car door and almost sent the other man flying. "Yeah, great. Where are you off to?"

"The rehearsal hall. I just got off the phone with the assistant director. And get this. He says he knows for a fact Mandell was being followed."

Chapter Twelve

"Wait for me. I want to be in on this." Matt shot out of the car, bashing his knee on the door and swearing as he strode toward the station.

The same knee he'd injured at football? Erica wondered. He'd seemed reluctant to talk about it to her and she'd bet he wouldn't want to show any weakness in front of a man, even Glenn. Typical male pride.

Glenn looked at Erica and nodded toward Matt's car. "You tagging along?"

"Sure," Erica said. "Why not?"

The 'why not' was Matt Nicols, but neither voiced the answer. She'd just slid to the middle of the front seat, Glenn beside her, when Matt wrenched open his door. Erica held her breath, half-expecting him to order her out of his car, and exhaled when no explosion was forthcoming.

Matt swerved onto the street, throwing Erica hard against him. She righted herself, wondering if this was his way of showing his annoyance at her presence. No, he wasn't that subtle, just in a hurry.

Settling back, she felt a lump and fished out a Big Mac container. Laughing, Glenn tossed it into the back seat where it joined a muddle of newspapers, coffee cups, sneakers, one lone sock, and a crumpled tie.

"When it gets to the ceiling Matt drives to the dump with a shovel," Glenn said. Erica wasn't totally convinced he was kidding.

"The rehearsal hall is only a few blocks from the service station fire," Matt said.

"Probably doesn't mean anything," Glenn said.

"I'll run our new computer program on it," Erica said. "It correlates fire sites to pinpoint the probable area where the arsonist lives." Neither man commented and she fell silent, conscious of unspoken undercurrents.

After several minutes, Glenn pointed. "Up ahead."

Matt aimed the car at the curb and it shuddered to a halt, one front tire on the sidewalk. Glenn winked at Erica, slid out and turned to give her his hand. Matt was already half way across the street.

The rehearsal hall was upstairs over a warehouse. They climbed the narrow staircase to find a large, high-ceilinged room with lines on the floor to mark off the stage area. Half-opened doors at the far end of the area led to smaller spaces. The dusty windows set far above head height were closed, rendering the big room hot and airless.

Erica swallowed as memories surfaced of Philip sitting in Rony's cluttered living room or out at Mandellini, face intense over a glass of wine as he talked about his latest play. It seemed eerie that though she'd seen some of them on stage, she knew nothing of the twenty or so people who milled about the room, people who had been a major part of Philip's life. Now he was dead. Could someone here be involved?

For a moment she felt out of her depth. Maybe Matt was right and she shouldn't be here.

No! She squared her shoulders. She was part of this investigation and neither Matt nor anyone else was going to change that.

"Erica." She hadn't noticed Glenn return to her side. "Here." He put a chocolate bar in her hand. "You look like you could use a hit of caffeine."

"It's been a long day."

"A very long day, Princess. For all of us."

When Matt called her Princess it sounded like a slur. From Glenn it sounded warm and friendly. She bit into the candy, the bitter-sweet chocolate melting against her tongue and sliding down her throat, the dark taste promising to sooth her jangled nerves.

Across the room, Matt was talking to a youngish man with glasses perched on his chubby face, speech punctuated by exaggerated gestures. After a moment Matt turned away and came over to Erica. She held out half the candy.

"No thanks." She cringed as he popped a sugar cube into his mouth. "We're just waiting for the stage manager. The place is overrun by rumors."

"Who's the cherub?" she asked.

"That's Zeigler, the assistant director." Matt scowled. "A real know-it-all."

The stage manager arrived and Erica watched as he assembled the cast and crew. When Matt announced the demise of Philip Mandell, almost every face registered shock and two or three people began to weep. Zeigler didn't seem surprised, but Glenn's earlier phone call had no doubt prepared him for the news.

When Zeigler came into the small office they'd taken over for questioning, she noted he was sweating profusely. The heat of the room or nervousness? If she had to choose one word to describe him it would be 'fussy.' He fussed even as he sat, dabbing at his forehead with a lace-trimmed hankie.

Matt said, "You say you believe Mr. Mandell was being followed. How long had this been going on?"

Zeigler crossed his legs, adjusting the crease in his pants. "Oh, at least two or three weeks." His voice was nasal, with rounded vowels no doubt cultivated at some exclusive eastern school.

"I understand you're assistant director."

"Oh, no, no, much more than that." Zeigler's hands fluttered up to adjust his glasses. "I'm doing my doctoral thesis on the Peninsula Players. I have *so* admired Philip and his work over the years."

"Describe the person who was tailing Mandell."

"I'll do my best. It was a woman, tall, about my height. Dark-skinned, maybe Latino. Dark hair under the most unattractive head scarves. Always carried a shopping bag." He leaned forward, and lowered his voice. "I suspect she had a change of clothing in that bag. She appeared somewhat wrinkled. Not pulled together, you know." Zeigler eyed Matt. "Much like yourself, Lieutenant. Why, someone with your proportions would cut quite a figure in the right outfit."

Erica choked back a laugh.

"I'll bear that in mind," Matt said, his tone dry enough to suck water out of a glass. "How often did you see this woman?"

"Oh, perhaps two or three times."

Matt let thirty seconds go by in silence while Zeigler squirmed. "Did you know Mandell before you started to work here?"

"Only by reputation."

"With Mandell gone, who'll take over as director?"

Zeigler buffed his nails on his pant leg and exhibited a smug smile. "I'll be doing that, I'm quite sure. I know of no one else who would be capable of following in Philip's footsteps."

"Were you aware that Mandell was searching out a permanent site for the Players?"

"Philip and I weren't as close as I would have liked. He didn't always confide in me."

"When was the last time you saw or spoke to Mandell?"

"That would have been here, last Friday."

After Zeigler was dismissed, the other members of the company came in, one by one. Everyone questioned spoke of Mandell as a demanding but respected director and a reserved man for whom the power of the play was everything. All denied having contact with him outside of work or of having seen him since the previous Friday. None could offer any motive for his murder.

The last person was a tall, black woman who identified herself as Leila Atkins, the wardrobe mistress.

"How long have you been employed by the Peninsula Players?" Glenn asked.

"Close to eight years. Best job I ever had."

"I understand Hans Zeigler is a recent addition."

"Came here in May. No one likes him much. Him and Philip had some awful set-tos. Thinks he knows everything, that one."

"Because he's working on his doctorate?"

"I guess. But book learning is nothing. Practical experience is what counts. I heard Philip tell him that often enough."

"I understand you believe someone was following Mr. Mandell?"

"Yes, sir, I think so. I was coming to work on the bus, worried because I was kinda late, and I saw Mr. Mandell. He always walked to work, see. I thought if I was lucky maybe I'd still get here before him. That's when I saw her."

Erica leaned forward as Matt said, "Go on, please."

"She was about a block or so behind him, trying real hard to look like she was minding her own business. And I'd seen her once before, close to quitting time, standing across the street here. She saw me watching and took off real casual like."

Matt asked her for a description and it tallied with Zeigler's.

"Any other time you noticed her, Ms. Atkins?"

"Just those two times. Hans joked about it. Said maybe Philip had a jealous girlfriend. If you ask me, Hans was the jealous one."

"Why do you say that, ma'am?"

"Why, it's as plain as the nose on your face! Hans was in love with Philip."

Five minutes later, Erica and Glenn followed Matt down the stairs to the car and climbed in.

"What are the chances that Zeigler made passes at Mandell and probably got rejected in front of the cast," Matt said, as he started the Dodge. Erica noticed the engine purred to life at once. And, unlike her MG, the purr was smooth as butter.

"Not much of a motive for murder," Glenn said.

"Maybe Mandell was gay. A crime of passion."

"No," Erica said, "that can't be right. Philip wasn't gay." Both men turned and looked at her.

"He never married," Glenn pointed out.

"Neither has the lieutenant here. Do people go around making assumptions about his sexuality?"

"I dunno," Glenn drawled. "Zeigler was certainly giving him the eye today."

Erica giggled, more a release of tension than amusement. Matt glowered.

"Since there was no sign of forced entry at the theater, either the arsonist had a key or Mandell let him in," Matt said. "And if Mandell let the perp into the theater, he must have known him. Or her. First thing tomorrow we'll check out Mandell's apartment, see what we can find out about his personal life."

Glenn shifted in his seat to look at Matt. "It's after six. Mind dropping me at home? For a change I'd like to see my kids before they're asleep."

Erica turned. "How many do you have?"

"Two boys and a girl." Even in the fading light she recognized the proud look of fatherhood. "Good kids."

"You're very lucky," she said, trying not to sound wistful.

"Yeah, well, their mother gets a lot of the credit. It's not easy being married to a cop."

Matt interrupted. "It's frustrating the hell out of me that there's still only one thing we know for sure about the theater. The fire was deliberately set."

"What I'd like to know is whether all six fires were set by the same loony. That would help," Glenn said. "The theater fire fits the pattern, yet it doesn't. It was the only one with a fatality."

"Somebody could have set the earlier fires to make the murder look like an accident." As he spoke, Matt stopped in front of a house in the Golden Gate Park area. "Door-to-door service. Say 'hi' to Penny for me."

"I will, Matt. Thanks for the lift. 'Night, Erica."

Matt flicked on the car's headlights and lit a cigarette. In the brief flare of the match his eyes looked bleak. Erica found herself wishing she could erase that exhaustion, bring a smile to his eyes. Years ago, she'd given her father shoulder massages when he came home from work, the closest they'd ever come to affectionate touching. In spite of the wall Matt had built around himself, she had no doubt he'd be a lot more demonstrative.

Matt put the car into gear and it lurched from the curb into the sparse traffic of the residential street. He took a deep drag and exhaled. "If you don't slide over I might get the idea you like sitting next to me."

She hadn't noticed that most of the front seat was available. She slid toward the passenger door, annoyed with herself. The leg that had been pressed against his felt cold. "Sorry."

"You don't have a thing to be sorry for."

A strained silence ensued until Erica asked, "What's Glenn's wife like?"

"Keeps a great house. Raises wonderful kids. Doesn't whine about being unfulfilled. The type of woman every mother wants her son to marry."

"Including yours?"

"Ma wanted me to enter the priesthood."

Erica repressed a smile. "Father Matthew. In your own way you are a crusader. You just picked a different pulpit, that's all."

He flicked his cigarette out the window. "My mother will be thrilled."

Erica fell silent, wondering if her own mother would be thrilled with what she was doing. "Matt, I meant what I said earlier. If Philip was murdered, I want to see his killer get what's coming to him."

"You're not the only one, Princess."

"Why do you call me that?"

"What, 'Princess'? 'Cause that's what you are. A white, Anglo-Saxon princess."

"You make an accident of birth sound like something to be ashamed of."

"That wasn't my intent. Know anything about horses?"

"Yes. As a matter of fact..."

"You saw my mare. She's a Thoroughbred, therefore a princess. Would you object to my calling *her* 'princess'?"

"I wish you had as good a sense of people as you do of horseflesh, Lieutenant Nicols."

"I'll give you one thing. Horses are a hell of a lot easier to be around. Though I could probably keep a whole stable of mistresses for what that mare costs me."

Erica changed the subject. "You're convinced Philip was murdered, aren't you?"

Matt glanced at her. "You're something, you know that? The way your mind jumps from subject to subject without a break. Yeah, I think someone killed him. Wish to hell I knew why. He have any romance in his life?"

"None that I know of."

"Not even your aunt?"

"Definitely not my aunt."

A jarring squeal of brakes cut Erica off before she could say more. Horns blared, then a sickening crunch of metal against metal. Matt braked the car to a bone-rattling stop and got out.

Then he was gone, running toward the accident, weaving between the stalled vehicles.

Erica followed, elbowing her way through the gathering crowd. At the intersection she stopped, appalled.

A Volkswagen had its nose buried in the side of a black Lincoln. Gasoline poured from the Lincoln, inching its way under the Volkswagen to the still sputtering motor.

"Get back!" Erica screamed at the people pressing close behind her. "It's going to explode!"

"My baby!" a woman wailed. Erica's stomach gave a sickening lurch as she saw the back of a child's car seat through the Volkswagen's rear window.

Before she could blink Matt was there, reaching inside the car, emerging with a crying infant in his arms.

An explosion cracked and flames enveloped both cars, screening Matt from her view. She pulled away from restraining hands and ran, skirting close to the blazing vehicles. Intense heat seared her face, bringing tears to her eyes. She brought her arm up to shield her face.

Matt lay face down on the pavement, the infant sheltered beneath him. She sank to her knees beside them. The crowd surged forward.

Matt pulled himself to his feet. The baby in his arms whimpered and then went quiet, eyes staring at the flames. The mother struggled through the crowd, white-faced in the glow of the street lamp. As if it were happening in slow motion, Erica saw Matt pass her the child, saw the mother's head bend low as she nuzzled the precious bundle. Erica felt a lump form in her throat and her eyes fill with unshed tears. Sirens howled in the distance, rapidly coming closer.

A woman's throaty purr came from Matt's other side. "That was an incredibly brave thing you did."

Erica tensed.

"I just got there first, is all."

"I'm from the Chronicle. I'd love to interview a real live, modern day hero."

Erica saw Matt's eyes go cold. "Amazing the way reporters manage to arrive before the emergency crews."

The woman shrugged. "How about that interview?"

"Sure," Matt said, turning away. "Soon as you and your colleagues study first aid so you can help out in disasters, not just document them."

"Hey, Lieutenant Nicols," yelled a man with a TV camera on his shoulder. "Not your usual type of fire. You guys branching out?"

Matt ignored him. An ambulance and a fire truck wailed to a stop. The flashing red lights throbbed through Erica's over-tired brain. Feeling an arm circle her shoulders, she glanced up to see a concerned look on Matt's face. "You okay?"

She fought the temptation to lean against him, to burrow into the sheltering warmth of his broad chest. She blinked back her tears and somehow found her voice. "That was the bravest thing I've ever seen."

"No big deal."

Erica caught his hands in hers, thrilling to their rough, capable strength. To her amazement he didn't pull away. Her heart was pounding, adrenalin soaring, the feeling of noisy, carnival unreality heightened by the pulsing of emergency lights across Matt's face. "That baby wouldn't be alive if you hadn't risked your life to rescue it." She rubbed her cheek softly across his swollen knuckles.

Matt freed his hands, his touch as gentle as it had been with the baby. "Somebody else would have got him out." More police cars and another fire truck arrived. "Looks like everything's under control. Let's see if we can get out of this mess." He turned toward her and for a moment Erica thought he might touch her again. Instead he buried his hands in his pockets and headed toward his car, only to be stopped by another reporter.

"Hey Lieutenant, who's the looker?"

Erica hoped the camera hadn't filmed that little exchange between Matt and herself. It felt too private, too intimate to be flashed across millions of TV screens.

"My colleague, arson investigator Erica Johnson. Call her tomorrow at the Insurance Crime Prevention Bureau. I'm sure she'll be happy to answer your questions." As he spoke, Matt bustled Erica ahead of him into the car.

"Now I'm going to be fending off the press."

"Better you than me. Besides, you're more photogenic."

In what seemed like mere minutes the brightly lit police station came into view. Matt parked in front of Erica's MG and killed the motor.

"Tell me you're not going inside to work?" she said.

"I just want to review a few things."

For a moment she hesitated, then laid her hand on his arm. "You're going to burn yourself out."

His muscles tensed beneath her fingertips. His eyes remained straight ahead, but she saw the telltale tightening of his mouth. He took a long deep breath and Erica knew that her touch was bothering him a lot more than it should. Slowly she withdrew her hand and eased out of his car.

Even after she was safe in the MG, with the engine idling, he still hadn't moved.

Chapter Thirteen

"How did you and Erica get on last night?"

Matt wasn't fooled by Glenn's casual tone as they unlocked the door to Philip Mandell's airless, silent apartment. "Meaning?"

Glenn's features were the essence of innocence. "I happened to catch the late news. Saw you and Erica."

"Saw us *what*?"

"Nothing." Glenn threw his hands in the air. "I'll take the bedroom."

"Good idea. I'll start in here with the desk."

The old oak swivel chair creaked under his weight but felt as comfortable as though it had been custom made for him. And the big roll top desk, with its carved curlicues and cubbyholes, would look perfect in his dream home; a sprawling rancher with cedar shake roof and siding and a veranda running around three sides. The house would be set on a low rise amid clumps of trees and surrounded by fenced green fields where a dozen horses grazed. If he could find the right stud for Black Satin, her foals just might earn enough money to make the dream a reality.

The dream had been giving him problems the last few days, though. It was being invaded. Invaded by a woman standing in the shade of the veranda, a woman with long dark hair and kissable lips.

Damn! Matt's gaze skimmed Mandell's crammed book-shelves, more books spilling over the coffee table and onto the floor. Framed photographs stood everywhere, Erica

149

and her aunt in several. Every place he looked, everything he touched, brought him back to Erica. He tightened his lips and turned to the task at hand.

At the end of an hour, with only one drawer left to search, Matt concluded that Mandell had lived theater twenty-five hours a day, eight days a week. Other than a few telephone and garage bills, every scrap of paper concerned the Peninsula Players.

The last drawer produced pay dirt. Mandell's will. "Look at this, Glenn," he called.

Glenn came out of the bedroom, gave the document a quick scan, then let out a low whistle. "Who'd have thought?"

Matt tapped the document with his ballpoint pen. "Who indeed? Why would Philip Mandell leave everything he owned to Ronya and Erica instead of to his brother? It doesn't figure. Especially when he must have known his old man would leave him the winery."

"And if you were the brother, would you be happy with only a life tenancy and a salary for running the place? I doubt it somehow."

"What if," Matt said, "Philip didn't care for his sister-in-law, Cheryl? Didn't cotton to the idea of her getting her hands on any of it?"

"Yeah," mused Glenn. "If she knew what was in the will, that would have given her a reason for murdering Philip before the old man kicks off. With Philip out of the way, the winery will go to Justin and she's entitled to half the property."

"Unless she signed a pre-nup." Matt tilted the chair back. "I wonder how Erica and her aunt would have felt about ending up with the winery? Even with the provision for Justin, they could still have realized a fair chunk of cash out of the place."

Glenn took his glasses off and polished them, giving Matt a myopic glance as he did so. "I don't suppose it matters now. Erica wouldn't have benefited under this will unless old Auguste died before Philip. And he didn't. He's still alive."

"We don't know that she wouldn't benefit!" snapped Matt. "Philip Mandell could be loaded. Maybe the winery doesn't even come into it. This will makes Erica a suspect. As of now she is off the case."

"Bailey won't like it."

"Captain Bailey is going to have to face facts," said Matt, his face grim. He drummed his fingers on the scarred surface of the desk. "I wonder who else knows about this will?" He pulled more papers from the bottom drawer. "Theater and more theater. Wait! What's this?"

Glenn looked up from reading the will in detail. "Find something useful?"

"An IOU for five thousand dollars, signed by one Dale Todd. Dated three months ago. Due and payable yesterday."

"Man or woman?" Glenn wondered.

"Could be our killer," Matt said. "People have killed for a lot less."

Glenn stared out the window for a moment. "Motive is one thing, but who had the opportunity? Who knew Mandell was going into the theater that night?"

"Francie and Rawlins knew. Ronya might have known. I'd bet Zeigler knew, too. Mandell was obsessed with getting a theater; he likely talked it up."

"When did Rawlins join our suspect list? I know you don't like the guy, but..."

"He could have his reasons. Justin and Cheryl could have known where Philip was going to be that night, too. Philip might have talked to them on the phone about it. Or Ronya." Matt reached for the old album Glenn had brought from the bedroom. "Let's have a look at those pictures before we go."

The faded snapshots of young Mandells and Germaines on the beach, at picnics, around swimming pools and tennis courts, brought a wave of nostalgia for the past. For his family. One picture was of two young women, an attractive Ronya and the other, incredibly beautiful, must have been her sister, Erica's mother; the resemblance was startling. He remembered photos of his own mother as a sweet-faced girl and slammed the album shut. This was no time to start feeling sentimental.

Glenn spoke up. "What do you suppose Philip would have done with the vineyard if he'd lived to inherit it?"

Matt shrugged. "Who knows? He might have sold it. Especially if he needed the money for his theater. Doesn't look like he was interested in anything else."

"Leaving Justin out in the cold."

"Maybe. Maybe not. Justin told me that if Philip inherited, he'd still have the job of running it. For the rest of his life. The will backs that up."

"I think it's important," Glenn insisted. "What if, under a sale agreement, that provision for life tenancy and salary couldn't be enforced? What if the new owners kicked him out as soon as the deal closed? If Justin figured there was any possibility the winery might be yanked out from under him he might have felt desperate."

"Desperate enough to kill." Matt finished the thought. "You could be right. His wife did say all he cared about was his quote, 'goddam grapes' unquote."

Glenn picked up the album again. From a back pocket he pulled out photos that Matt recognized as copies of the portraits he'd seen at Mandellini. Matt pointed to one with Ronya. "I've seen her somewhere before but I can't figure out where."

"Other than yesterday morning, you mean."

"Yeah. It'll come to me." He rose. "Come on. Let's go see Bailey, though I can think of a lot of people I'd rather see right now."

Glenn raised his eyebrows. "Oh?"

Matt snorted. The implication was written all over his partner's face. "No, not Erica. I'm not ready to confront her with this will stuff yet."

"When?"

He clapped his partner on the back. "Trust me. When the time is right, I'll know it."

An hour later Matt finished giving Captain Bailey the latest facts on the case and leaned back while the Captain picked up his half-smoked cigar and rested his burly fist on the desk.

"So you think this is a murder case, do you?"

"Yes, sir." Matt knew the captain well enough to mistrust that particular tone of voice.

Bailey squinted at Matt through the cigar smoke. "All right, give me one good reason why I shouldn't turn this whole damn case over to Homicide. Your men deal with arson, not murder."

"I'll give you two, Captain." Matt sat forward and mentally crossed his fingers. "First, it's possible the six recent fires were set to make the murder look like accidental death. SIS is handling the arson evidence; that evidence is what will give us the perp and a conviction."

"Yeah? Go on."

"Second, you know Davenport and I spent fifteen years in Homicide. We've got the experience to deal with a murder."

Bailey puffed on his cigar and the smell of the smoke, rank as it was, made Matt ache to light up a cigarette. After a tense minute, Bailey put his cigar in the ash tray and nodded. "Okay, you got it."

Matt exhaled. If the captain knew how much he wanted to keep the case, how badly he needed to solve this one, he'd probably change his mind. And this wasn't the time to say he wanted Erica off the case. Bailey liked her so much that the request might just make him sore enough to retract his decision.

"We'll track down the woman tailing Mandell," Matt said. "Chances are she works for a local PI firm so it shouldn't take long."

"After that," Bailey said, "you've got to convince her to say who hired her." Matt didn't like the captain's knowing grin. "You deal with her, Nicols, you're popular with the broads."

Matt refused to be baited. Bailey had a big mouth; probably every man on the force knew about him and Francie by now. "Sure, Captain." He stood up.

"Sit down!" Bailey snapped. "I'm not through yet. For now you can carry on. But lay off Eric Rawlins."

Matt opened his mouth but Bailey cut him off. He waved a stubby finger in Matt's face. "Hear me out. Rawlins is a prominent citizen. He's respected. Mandell's money is peanuts to a guy like him."

"And he makes big campaign contributions," Matt grated, before he could stop himself.

Bailey's eyes were like ice. "Just solve the case, Nicols. I'll deal with the politics."

"Sir," Matt said, rising from his chair.

"Don't get your tail in a knot," Bailey said. "If you prove Rawlins is a suspect, you can have him for breakfast. Otherwise, leave him alone. Understood?"

"Yes. Sir. Anything else?"

"Get your ass in gear pronto. The mayor's gonna erupt like a volcano if we don't give him an answer pretty damn soon."

Back in the SIS room, Matt gave in to frustration and smashed both fists on his desk, the shock jarring his arms right to the shoulders.

Glenn gave him a telling look. "I must say, celibacy doesn't do much for your disposition."

"Neither does Bailey."

"He didn't take us off the case, Matt. And he could have."

Matt rubbed his knuckles. "I'm doing my damndest to be grateful."

But, though he tried to concentrate on the files in front of him, Matt couldn't stop thoughts of Erica invading his mind. He'd intended to have her removed from the case, but Bailey hadn't left much room for maneuvering. Besides, he wanted to check on something first, something that might clinch his argument.

As he leafed through the fire photographs his mind continued to tease him with images of Erica from the first day they'd met, from the time they'd spent at Mandellini, from the picnic under the trees. Present or not, she'd left her mark on him and he didn't like it. Determined to forget her, at least for the moment, he forced his attention back to the photos.

Nothing at the boat basin, nothing at the warehouse. He picked up the photos taken at the boutique. There! Ronya Germaine, slick as silk, watching the building go up in flames. He nodded in satisfaction as he spotted her again at the service station fire. Satisfaction faded and became weariness. He pushed the photos aside.

Damn Erica! She knew. And she'd been covering up for her aunt. Why? Who was she trying to protect? The old girl or herself?

He'd liked Ronya, for some reason he couldn't identify. But finding her at two of the fires reinforced his decision that emotion was something he didn't need in his life. Just because he liked Ronya didn't mean she couldn't have been out there setting fires.

Matt chewed on a hangnail and thought about how to bring this to the attention of the captain.

No.

No, there was a much better way to deal with it.

Erica was in this thing up to her beautiful aristocratic neck. So why not keep her around, pump her about the rest of the family? And watch her. If she knew anything, this was his best chance of finding out. He couldn't imagine her being guilty of setting fires or committing murder, but he hadn't been able to imagine Father Gilbey guilty of setting fires either.

***

Erica propped her foot on the bottom rail of the paddock fence and admired the stallion's antics, wondering if he and Missy could produce another colt as beautiful as Merlin. "You don't fool me," she murmured. "Matter of fact, you remind me of someone I met not so long ago. Someone who's almost as good-looking, and every bit as proud and stubborn." The stallion tossed his head as if he'd understood every word and found it unthinkable that anyone could come close to him in looks.

"Are you planning to add to your collection?"

"Daddy!" Erica whirled, the childhood greeting tumbling out before she could stop it. She saw by his frown that he'd heard it. Her father had never been the 'daddy' type. But, though he rejected any show of emotion, she couldn't forget that he was the one who had taught her, during the months after her mother's death, to overcome her fear of being alone in the dark.

"How are you, Father?" Resisting the urge to address him as 'sir'—he lacked any ability for teasing or playfulness—she brushed a kiss across his close-shaven jaw. He stood still, back stiff, not acknowledging the embrace.

"I'm quite well."

Accustomed to her father's cool reserve, she took his arm and drew him to the fence. "Isn't he a pretty boy?" she said, indicating the horse. "Quite as vain as they come."

He ignored the stallion, remaining, as usual, indifferent to whatever had no direct effect on him. "You might have had the courtesy to let me know you'd returned to the city."

"You always track me down." Erica released her father and hung her arms over the rail, crooning to the stallion who was swishing his tail and pawing the ground with one front hoof as if he disapproved of her sire.

"No mean feat. I was at a luncheon with Gallagher today. He said you hadn't returned his calls."

"Not yet."

He raised one steel-grey brow. "Why not?"

She turned to face him. "You're tapped into city hall. Surely you know there's been a string of arson fires."

"And a disagreeable police lieutenant bumbling around asking meaningless questions," he added, disdain etched into every feature on his face.

"That's right," Erica said. "You've met Ma...Lieutenant Nicols."

His eyes darkened and she knew he'd noticed her quick correction. But he didn't comment, pointing instead at the skittish stallion. "You didn't answer my question about the nag."

Excalibur's ears were laid back as he continued to paw the ground. He must be picking up on the vibes, Erica thought. Horses were intuitive that way. Erica put her finger to her lips in mock warning. "He's a champion Thoroughbred, not a nag, and very temperamental. He's watching you. I wouldn't get too close if I were you."

"That's hardly likely, my dear."

Too true, Erica thought. Her father seemed to have no feeling for animals. "He'd be quick to tell you one doesn't 'collect' animals like antiques or paintings."

Her father whisked an imaginary fleck of lint from his lapel. "Frankly, I fail to understand society's attraction to four-legged creatures. People seem to care more about their pets than they do other human beings. It's a sad statement on the breakdown of civilization when a person is ostracized for eating meat and covering their nakedness with leather or fur."

Erica glanced down at her father's expensive Italian leather loafers. In a way, it was comforting to see that some things, at least, never changed. Right now she was ripe for comfort. "How did you find me?"

"Your aunt, of course. Actually, she's one of the subjects I wish to discuss with you. Dale says she's becoming increasingly vague. With Philip's demise, I really think we ought to explore the possibility of settling her somewhere more suitable."

Erica bit her lip. He'd said the words 'Philip's demise' without a shred of emotion. No apparent regret that a man they knew was now dead. "Don't worry about Rony. She's doing fine."

"I'm not exactly worried. Still..."

"What will people think," Erica finished for him.

His quick frown signaled an intense irritation. "She walks around with that dreadful bird on her shoulder like some sort of sideshow freak. I can't help but wonder what your mother, rest her soul, would think if she was still alive."

Erica turned away. "Well, she's not."

"I'm sorry, darling." He moved to her side and lifted a hand as though to reach out to her, then dropped it. "Would you care to dine with me tonight? Since you're not seeing Clayton, that is."

Erica rolled her eyes. "I promise I'll call Clayton as soon as I get the chance."

"The man is quite smitten with you, Erica. I don't understand why you seem impervious to him."

"What now? You acquire a sudden yen to bounce a grandchild on your knee?"

His face reddened. "You're my only child. Clayton Gallagher does strike me as eminently suitable."

Erica kept her laugh light. "I'll take that under advisement. You came all this way to invite me to dinner? Why didn't you text me?"

"You know how I dislike that form of communicating. Besides, I heard about a new restaurant out this way and thought we might give it a try."

Knowing her father, it would be no less than five stars. And she was wearing her oldest jeans and a pair of scuffed cowboy boots. "They probably wouldn't let me in dressed like this." He did a credible job of looking disappointed, Erica thought. Maybe he really had missed her. "But we could stop at the Mountcrest Inn. The view is sensational."

Rawlins tugged at his shirt cuffs until a half-inch of snowy white was visible below the sleeves of his custom tailored jacket. "Very well. Are you finished here?"

"For now. I just wanted to see Excalibur in the flesh again."

Her father followed her toward the parking lot. "You're still driving that old rattletrap. I don't understand why you won't let me buy you a new car."

Erica skidded to a stop. "I am sick and tired of people nagging me about my car. I happen to like it."

"I'm happy to hear others share my concern."

"I doubt you'd be happy if you knew who," Erica said under her breath, watching her father unlock the driver's door of his gleaming gray Jaguar sedan.

"Mark my words. You'll wind up stranded in the middle of nowhere with only yourself to blame."

"I like living on the edge. Besides, if I buy a new car I'll pay for it myself. I can afford it."

For a change the MG started without quibbling. Thankful that it had given her father no more cause to criticize, she led the way over steep winding roads to the Inn. At the parking lot she had only a moment to glance at the sun sinking into an expanse of silver and peach ocean before he was at her elbow.

Once they'd been seated, at Erica's insistence, on the outside deck, her father opened the wine list. "The selection is most inadequate," he muttered.

"Don't worry about the wine. Enjoy the scenery. See? There's the Muir Woods National Monument."

He gave the Monument a bored glance and immediately returned to the wine list.

Watching him study it, Erica sighed. He'd always insisted on 'the best' as defined by others. The best hotel, the best restaurant, the best wines. The best make of car. He seemed to lack the sensual techniques to determine 'the best' by his own standards. Others were impressed by his good taste, his air of breeding, his worldliness; she alone knew how much research he did to project that image.

She doubted Matt Nicols had ever researched anything except police procedures. She smiled, trying to imagine Matt and her father in the same room. Funny thing was, the two men had more in common than either would be willing to admit.

"Something amusing on the menu?"

Erica gave a guilty start. If her father knew she'd paired him and Matt Nicols even in a fleeting thought he'd be offended. "I was just thinking how seldom we get a chance to do this anymore."

"Well, you do insist on burying yourself in soot and ashes. I'll never understand the fascination."

Erica snapped her menu shut. It was an old argument. And, as always, it struck her as odd that he'd never made the connection between his wife's death and his daughter's chosen profession, that he didn't recognize her need to unravel the mystery surrounding every unexplained fire. Except, of course, the one that concerned her most. But supposing her mother's death had been her fault? How could she live with that?

After they'd ordered he sat back, looking more relaxed than she'd seen him in a long time, and asked about her recent riding excursion in the Rockies.

By the time they'd consumed most of a bottle of local Chardonnay, Erica was feeling mellow. Her father could be charming as Lucifer when he put his mind to it, and she pondered the fact that he'd never remarried. What about Frances Cameron, the real estate agent who was reputed to be her father's sometime companion?

She was dunking her calamari and wondering how to shift the conversation in that direction without being obvious about it when he surprised her by saying, "I was saddened to hear about poor old Philip. I always thought his life was wasted in something as insubstantial as theater. A shame that his family had enough money to indulge him." He paused. "Philip's death is one of the reasons I wanted to discuss your aunt." He seemed almost ill at ease.

"Ronya and Philip weren't romantically involved, if that's what you're wondering."

"I know that," he said, his voice sharp. "What I'm wondering is whether... No. I can't bring myself to say it. It's too far-fetched."

Erica put down her fork. "Can't say what?"

"It's just..." Pushing back his plate he dabbed at his lips with a napkin. "Do the police have any leads?"

Erica shrugged, playing it safe. If Matt had any leads, she wasn't at liberty to discuss them with anyone, even her father.

"Because I can't help remembering... Oh, it was so long ago, I hesitate to bring it up at all. Certainly I wouldn't mention it to the police unless I thought it had some bearing on the case."

Erica crossed her arms over her chest. "Now that you've started you can't leave me hanging."

He sighed as if the memory was particularly painful. "One Christmas, when you were just a baby, Ronya and Philip got into a terrible, nasty row. Ronya swore that one day she'd see he got everything he had coming. As I recall, your mother intervened. She was good at keeping the peace and she cared for them both a great deal."

"What's your point?"

"My point? Isn't it obvious? Ronya's mind is going and she's made good her threats against Philip."

Erica laughed in relief. "That's it? Almost thirty years ago she made an idle threat. Really! If I didn't know better, I'd think your mind was going."

Her father's skin took on a dull red hue which Erica chose to blame on the sunset. "I'm simply trying to be a good citizen and assist the police with their investigation. I have half a mind to give your Lieutenant Nicols a call."

"Don't bother," she said, stabbing a quartered tomato.

"You don't think he'd be interested?"

She raised her eyes to meet his gaze. "The lieutenant has already been at the house questioning Rony. If he thinks it needs to be followed up, he will. He's quite thorough."

"An Irish flatfoot in the true sense of the word?"

Erica flinched at the slur. "The man works day and night. He's as devoted to his profession as you are to yours."

"Ah! But does he make money?" He shook his head at his own question. "Of course not. Still, someone has to protect our good citizens. Might as well be a broken-down has-been football player who can't get a proper job."

"You seem to know quite a bit about the lieutenant."

"I make it my business to find out about people."

"I know you do," Erica said, picking her next words with care. "What do you know about Frances Cameron, the woman you were having dinner with the night Philip died? I understand you're her alibi."

He gave her a mocking look of congratulation. "I see you have your sources as well."

"Never mind that. Tell me about the Cameron woman."

"Erica, really! A gentleman doesn't speak about these things."

"You needn't bother with the intimate details," she said, her tone dry. "I merely want to know if she had reason to harm Philip."

"Ridiculous. Frances was working on a sale and Philip was a lot more valuable to her alive than dead. And believe me; she knows which side her bread is buttered on."

"You have to admit it's a coincidence that she was also the listing agent on the next place that was torched."

"I'd hardly call that a coincidence, my dear."

"What would you call it then?"

Her father eyed her for so long she felt uncomfortable. She sensed that he was wrestling with a dilemma, and knew it did no good to rush him when he was deciding whether or not to reveal a particular tidbit of information.

He cleared his throat. The decision had been made. "I'm going to share something with you that I had intended keeping to myself. Given the circumstances, I feel it's something you should know."

"What's that?" Erica asked, primed to hear about some skeleton in Philip Mandell's closet.

"If you want to know about Frances Cameron, you should be talking to Lieutenant Nicols."

"Why do you say that?"

His smile was unpleasant. Why did she get the feeling he was enjoying this? "Because, my dear, Nicols and the Cameron woman have been carrying on an affair for years."

Chapter Fourteen

Matt Nicols and Frances Cameron!

Erica hardly saw the road as she drove the familiar route from Mill Valley to Sausalito. She passed the turn-off that led to her home and was halfway across the Golden Gate bridge before she admitted to herself just where she was headed.

And Matt Nicols had the nerve to cite *her* on conflict of interest! Just when she'd come to admire him as a crusader for justice, she learned he was covering for his girlfriend.

She'd admired him for other things, too, a little voice in her head reminded her. He'd displayed incredible bravery rescuing that baby last night. And on the drive back from Mandellini... No one had made her hormones hum the way he did. Not ever. Her feminine pride was more than a little piqued. Just how far would he go to protect Frances Cameron?

Erica struggled between anger and second thoughts as she parked outside his house. This could be a total waste of time. The man lived at his desk and it was a wonder he found time to dally with anyone. But the third floor windows were lit; maybe he was up there with Frances Cameron right now.

Telling herself she didn't care if she caught him naked and in bed with the infamous Ms. Cameron, Erica started for the front door. He owed her an explanation. And she wasn't prepared to wait until tomorrow to hear it.

Her anger carried her to the second floor, where she could hear music coming from his apartment. Her steps slowed and stopped. Matt Nicols listening to classical music?

Probably Ms. Cameron's influence. Country and western was a more likely choice for a cowboy like him. Before she could change her mind, she balled one fist and banged on his door.

She waited a moment, then knocked again. And again. Still no answer. Two-fisted, she pounded with renewed determination.

"For cripes's sake! I said I was coming!"

The door was wrenched open. Erica faltered. Matt faced her bare-chested and wearing unfastened jeans that he'd obviously pulled on in a hurry. Droplets of water dewed the dark texture of his hair.

They faced each other in silence for what seemed like the longest fifteen seconds Erica had ever lived through.

"Well, well. If it isn't Inspector Johnson," Matt drawled, folding his arms across his chest.

Erica blinked. He had so much body hair. It formed a thick dark pelt downward from the hollow of his throat, fanning his pectorals before it thinned to a jagged black line that dissected the flat planes of his belly and disappeared inside his jeans. She forced her gaze back to his face. "I need to talk to you."

"Now?" he said, in a lazy drawl.

"Now," Erica said, taking one determined step inside, then another. "Sorry that it's apparently not convenient." She managed to inject just the right amount of sarcasm into her words.

"I'd have got dressed if I'd known you were coming." He closed the door behind her. "Then again, maybe not."

Erica swung around to face him. "Are you alone?"

He leaned against the panels of the door. "Maybe. Then again, maybe not."

"Answer me, dammit! Or is Ms. Cameron lolling in your bed, anxiously awaiting your return?"

He started toward her, walking with the predatory stroll of a jungle cat. She backed up a step but he bypassed her to throw open his bedroom door. The bed was unmade. And empty. "Satisfied?"

She looked away from the intimacy of that rumpled bed. Matt was less than an arm's length from her. Close enough that she could see the individual whiskers darkening his jaw, see a small scar at his temple.

He looked down at her, arms folded again. "Now, would you care to explain that last remark?"

"Oh, you're good." Unable to face him down, Erica pivoted, clasping her hands together to stop them from shaking. Why was she shaking?

Because Frances Cameron wasn't in his bed?

Because the woman had shared his bed in the past?

Or because, for one mad impulsive second, she'd wished he would throw her down amid those tangled sheets, sheets that would have the same distinctive fragrance as his skin? And make love to her the way she'd never been made love to before?

"You're very good," she repeated. "You certainly had me fooled into believing you were a modern-day crusader, devoted to putting the bad guys behind bars."

"I haven't pretended to be anything I'm not." His voice was husky, masculine, compelling, sending a tingling awareness dancing down her spine.

Taking a deep breath, she said, "I know you're covering for Frances Cameron. Who else are you covering up for?"

"I'm not covering up for anyone."

"Is Captain Bailey privy to your relationship with Ms. Cameron?"

"That's none of your business."

"I say different."

He advanced on her. "I'll tell you something he doesn't know yet, Princess. And I wonder what he's going to say when he knows you're in this thing up to your luscious lips, so deep it makes my past relationship with Francie look like a church picnic." His eyes rested significantly on her lips as he spoke.

He'd said 'past relationship.' Meaning what? That the relationship was in the past? Or that it had changed?

What did she care? He was a healthy male with lusty male appetites. Naturally he'd have someone around to satisfy them. An undemanding someone who'd be eternally grateful for his attentions whenever it fit into his schedule. "You didn't tell me you'd been involved with the Cameron woman."

"My choice of partner has no bearing on the case."

"Oh, really? It didn't for one minute cross your mind that the conflict of interest you were so quick to accuse me of was staring at you from the mirror?"

"Nah," he said. "I was too busy trying to figure out why you didn't tell me about your aunt's penchant for hanging out at fire scenes."

Erica recoiled, caught her bottom lip between her teeth. "I forgot."

"You forgot?" He rocked back on his heels, his expression sardonic. "Could there be anything else you 'forgot' to mention? Like who inherits under the terms of Mandell's will?"

"It would have to be Justin or Auguste. They're the only relatives." Light glinted off a gold medallion nestling against his chest. She stared, hypnotized, unable to shift her eyes. It winked, beckoned. She felt weak, shaken. No longer in control.

"And if I were to tell you you're mistaken?"

Erica couldn't seem to stop herself as she stepped closer and scooped the medal, warm from his skin, into her palm. Her knuckles grazed the soft, curling hair on his breastbone. As soon as she made contact the spell was broken. "St. Christopher!" she said. Beneath her hand she felt Matt tense.

"Stop trying to change the subject."

"I'm not."

With a sudden movement he manacled her wrist. "Oh? What would you call it?"

The round gold medallion trailed from her fingertips. She tilted her head back in order to meet his gaze. "You have one in your car, too. Isn't he the patron saint of travelers?"

Matt frowned. "Not any more. The Church stripped him of his sainthood. Him and me." His eyes locked with hers and she could see each individual eyelash rimming his lids. His eyes were true hazel, like slivers of green and brown velvet crumpled together and overlapping. "But I'm superstitious. What if it *was* him that kept me safe all these years?"

He guided his fingers in a gentle, insistent stroke up and down her arm from wrist to elbow and back.

Erica's breath caught. She wanted to look away but couldn't, wanted to move away but couldn't, feeling herself inexorably drawn toward him.

She shouldn't be here. She especially shouldn't be here when he was wearing nothing more than timeworn jeans. She especially shouldn't be thinking about making love to this man who, despite his protests, was something other than he seemed.

The music greeting her arrival had ended. All she could hear was the steady sound of breathing and she was so shaken she couldn't tell if it was hers or his.

"How about it, Erica?"

She outlined her lips with the tip of her tongue. "How about what?"

"How about the will?" The flesh of her underarm was unbelievably sensitive to his touch.

"What will?" He was robbing her of all will, taking and bending it to suit his own needs. And hers.

"Mandell's will." He caught hold of her shoulders and pulled her against him. She had to tilt her head way back to meet his gaze.

"Damn you!" he said in a soft menacing tone that intensified her sensitivity to his maleness.

They stood locked in a kind of mental combat, hipbone to hipbone, thigh to thigh, the seconds stretching longer and longer, the tension tighter. She felt the stirring of his body, signaling his reaction to her nearness.

"Damn *you*," she responded, almost in a whisper. Her heart was beating triple time. Why did his masculinity have to be so blatant, his touch setting her heart off like a trip hammer?

"You shouldn't have come here tonight." His breath fanned over her face like a warm summer breeze.

"No," she managed, a scant second before his mouth ravaged hers with a need and greed that spoke to the emptiness inside of her. And she was kissing him back, reveling in the rightness of being in his arms.

She wanted this man.

Needed him.

Now.

His skin was satin to her touch. Smooth. Firm. It had been so long since she'd been held like this. No, that wasn't right. No one had ever held her like he did.

The insistent pressure of his body spilled a warm flood of sensation through her, making her feel graceful, delicate, brimming with feminine power, as she drew back and began to unbutton her blouse.

His eyes darkened, the pupils dilating to midnight black. With an elegant shrug she let the garment slip from her shoulders and slide down her arms, flowing over her like a cotton river to puddle at her feet. His eyes followed, then came back to her breasts.

No man had ever made her feel the things that Matt Nicols did.

Her skin tingled with new awareness as her hair brushed the skin of her shoulders, the nape of her neck. Matt raised his hands to cup and reshape her breasts. They were milk-white against his tanned and bruised skin, easily overflowing his palms. She closed her eyes, reveling in his touch.

With a harsh exclamation, he released her. Her eyes flew open.

"Francie wasn't here to warm my bed tonight, so you thought to fill in, is that it? Thought I'd cover for you in exchange for your favors?"

Erica's ears rang as if she'd been slapped. "What are you talking about?"

"The subject you're avoiding. Mandell's will."

"Can't we forget about the case for one night?" She trailed her fingertips down the muscled wall of his chest, thrilling at the warmth of his skin.

"You'd like that, wouldn't you?" Pushing her away, he bent to retrieve her shirt, tossing it at her. "You'd do anything to stop me finding out that Mandell left all his worldly goods to you and your aunt."

"What?" Shocked, she hugged her shirt to her breasts as she searched his face for some sign that he didn't mean what he'd said.

"You heard me. Mandell left everything to you and your Aunt Ronya."

"You're forgetting something." She stabbed her arms into the shirt sleeves and fastened the first few buttons.

"Yeah?"

The buttons weren't lined up but she didn't care. "I wasn't even here."

"Your wacko aunt was, though. You saw those photos."

Erica slumped into a chair. "I've already questioned her. She's researching for a series of fire paintings."

"And picking her subjects, maybe?"

"Seriously, can you see Rony skulking around with a couple of cans of gasoline?"

"Maybe she got that handyman of hers to do the heavy work."

Erica shook her head, her hair swirling around her face. "Rony's got far more money than she could give away in several lifetimes. Besides, she and Philip were old friends; she loved him. You saw her reaction when you told her they'd identified his body."

Matt's eyes were still flinty. "There's something there. I can feel it. And I intend to find out what."

Erica rose. "What about the Cameron woman?"

"Everybody's a suspect."

She could tell from his words that 'everyone' included her. "Tell me something. Do you ever turn it off, stop being a cop?"

"Why the hell would I want to do that?"

Chapter Fifteen

Erica strode through the crowded clubhouse dining room to the table where her father sat alone, eating breakfast and reading the Sunday edition of the New York Times.

"Erica, good morning." He shuffled the newspaper into a tidy heap and set it aside. "What brings you out so early? Let me order you some breakfast. I can recommend the eggs Benedict."

"Just coffee," Erica said, dropping into the chair across from him. "I need to talk to you."

He filled a second cup from the insulated carafe on the table and pushed it toward her. "Regarding...?"

"Something we were discussing last night."

"We discussed a great many things, as I recall. Could you be more specific?"

"Ronya and Philip. The threat she made toward him."

"Shouldn't you be talking to your aunt about this? She's directly involved."

"Possibly. But I want to hear your version first. What happened to make her threaten him?"

Rawlins sat back and made a steeple of his fingers, looking at her with much the same expression as he'd worn before telling her about Matt Nicols and Frances Cameron. She sensed that what he had to tell her now would be equally distasteful. But it would be the truth. He prided himself on having his facts straight and never imparting rumors or half-truths.

"They all grew up together. Philip, Justin and Catherine Mandell, Ronya and your mother. As you are aware, your maternal grandfather was wealthy, with a good family background. The Mandells had money, although not the same social distinction, unfortunately."

He mused over his coffee for a moment, while Erica tried not to fidget. "That information is not important, perhaps, except that family money and influence provided the young people with the time and means to do pretty much as they pleased, which could have been the basic cause of the problem."

Erica resisted the urge to drum her fingers. He'd get to the point eventually. "Philip and your mother were the best of friends. But Ronya and Catherine were lovers."

"I beg your pardon!"

"This was long before such a liaison was fashionable, you understand. The two of them went to Paris together to study art and shared an apartment there as well as when they returned to New York for further studies. No one would have known if they'd been discreet." His lips thinned with disapproval. "Instead, they chose to flaunt their homosexuality. Both families were upset, naturally. But they thought the girls were merely experimenting, so endeavored to keep them apart, convinced things would right themselves eventually."

"How did Catherine die?"

"I'm coming to that. You have to understand that she was the weaker of the two and her family's displeasure made her very unhappy. Philip worked on that vulnerability and convinced Catherine to leave Ronya. I believe he actually went to New York and brought her back to California himself. Ronya was incensed. But by the time she found out where Catherine was and flew west to take her home, it was too late. Catherine had fallen in with the wrong sort. And no one knows whether her overdose was accidental or if she'd decided that life was no longer worth living."

Erica exhaled, surprised to find she'd been holding her breath. "So that's Ronya's tragic secret love." It wasn't the kind of secret she'd imagined, yet seemed all the more tragic because of the circumstances.

"And," he said, "she never forgave Philip for his interference."

"She must have, at some point. They spent a lot of time together these last few years."

"Biding her time, if you ask me," he said. "Can you tell me, honestly, that you always know what she's thinking or feeling? Can you be sure she doesn't cover up her real self beneath that ridiculous 'eccentric artist' facade?"

Before she could voice her retort, his gaze shifted to someone behind her. The flash of impatience in his expression was quickly masked by his usual urbane manner. "Were you looking for me?"

"I have a few questions, Mr. Rawlins."

Erica turned, startled. How long had Matt been standing there? Had he heard her father's story?

Rawlins folded his heavy linen napkin into a neat square. "Actually, I'm already late for an appointment. Please keep it brief, Lieutenant."

"Thank you. I will." Matt sat down in the chair next to Erica, limiting himself to one quick glance.

After she'd left the night before, the memory of her silky skin and enticing curves had kept him roused and restless. He deserved a medal for sending her away. There was no way he'd get involved with a suspect, even if he was convinced of her innocence.

But there was more to it than that. Much more. He didn't want another Francie, another shallow relationship with nothing but sex. That thought had kept him tossing for even longer. What in hell was the matter with him? He was married to his job; he didn't need or want any other commitment.

Forcing Erica out of his mind and concentrating on the case had finally sent him to sleep. Thinking about the case had brought certainty that Rawlins knew more than he'd let on. Tracking Erica's father down had been easy. He hadn't counted on finding Erica with him.

"Mr. Rawlins, you mentioned there'd been a dispute between Philip Mandell and your sister-in-law some years ago. Can you tell me what it was about?"

"Certainly, Lieutenant, I'd be glad to." Matt noticed Erica open her mouth as though to protest.

With dry precision, Rawlins related the story of the love affair between Ronya Germaine and Catherine Mandell and Philip Mandell's part in destroying it. He added, "In the event that you question my sister-in-law, Lieutenant, I would like to warn you that her mental capabilities are deteriorating. In fact, Erica and I have been discussing whether we should make arrangements to put her in care."

This time she spoke up, her tone sharp. "You've been doing the talking, not me. There's absolutely nothing wrong with her."

Rawlins smiled as he rose. "My dear, your loyalty does you credit but it's distorting your objectivity. Lieutenant, I'm afraid I can't give you any more time this morning but if I can help in the future, don't hesitate to give me a call." He turned to Erica. "Shall I walk you to your car?"

Erica's eyes clashed with Matt's for a brief moment. "I have a couple of things to discuss with the lieutenant first."

"As you wish."

Matt leaned back in his chair and watched Rawlins depart. "Has he always been like that?"

"Like what?"

"Like you could freeze ice on his ass."

Her face flamed. "That's my father you're talking about."

His eyes moved over her face feature by feature. "Exactly. And even with everything I know about breeding horses, some genetic accidents still baffle me."

Her fists clenched on the tabletop, knuckles white. "I don't appreciate your vulgar slurs, Lieutenant. I would also request that you keep the information about Ronya's involvement with Catherine confidential."

"What did you think I was going to do? See if I could interest the National Enquirer? Anyway, in this day and age, they're not going to give even an inch of space to a thing like that."

Erica scraped her chair back from the table. "I think my original assessment of you is right on the mark. You're two of a kind, my father and you."

Matt gave a disbelieving laugh. "How the hell do you figure that?"

"Add it up. You're both hungry for power. You both cover up your true emotions. And let's not overlook the fact that you're both seeing the same woman."

And we both push your buttons, Matt thought, his eyes following Erica as she walked away, head high, spine rigid. He'd actually meant the genetic accident thing as a compliment; the improbability of a dry, controlled man like Rawlins producing a daughter with Erica's fire.

He wasn't the only man in the room watching her, Matt noticed, mouth tightening. But he was the one who'd sent her packing last night instead of taking her to bed. He still couldn't believe he'd exercised that kind of self-control. Next he'd be up for sainthood.

She was wrong about one thing. He and Rawlins were nothing alike. Rawlins was smooth on the surface, like this elegant club, but who knew what went on underneath? He'd lost, for the moment, the opportunity to penetrate Rawlins' shell, but he could still have a look at this place, see how the other half lived.

The left side of the long gallery leading from the dining room to the main entrance had floor to ceiling windows which looked out on greens where golfers roamed the sunlit velvety grass, their clubs flashing in the sunlight. Mentally Matt replaced them with sleek long-legged Thoroughbreds and split-rail fences.

Dismissing his favorite fantasy with reluctance, he looked at the right-hand wall, hung with black and white photos of tournament winners. Matt walked the length of the gallery searching for Rawlins' face. Be interesting to know if the man played golf like a pro or if he was just a duffer who liked the prestige of belonging to one of the city's best golf clubs.

No, there he was, with a proud smile, displaying a trophy, beside a younger man holding a golf bag. Matt read the inscription, dated ten years ago. Eric Rawlins, winner of the California Open, with caddy Dale Todd.

Dale Todd, the name on the IOU in Mandell's apartment! If this was the same guy it would save a hell of a lot of tracking time. Matt leaned in for a closer look.

Ten years had wrought some changes and wiped away the man's thinning hair but he was still recognizable. Ronya Germaine's handyman. Todd caddied for Rawlins, gardened for Ronya, and Mandell had known him well enough to loan him five grand. On the surface, there was nothing suspicious.

But, Matt thought, if Dale Todd had been around for ten years or more, he'd know the dirt on both families and could be worth talking to on that score alone. As a suspect, he'd also have to come up with an explanation for the IOU and alibis for the six fires.

An hour later, Matt had gleaned all he could from police records. Dale Winston Todd, now fifty, had spent ten months inside for robbery some thirty years ago. There had been no subsequent convictions. Could have been a single shot at easy money, Matt mused. Maybe Dale was now a model citizen. On the other hand, maybe he'd simply learned not to get caught.

Matt dialed Ronya Germaine. "I'd like to get in touch with Dale Todd."

"I'm afraid he's not here today."

"Can you give me his address or phone number?"

She made little fluttery sounds. "Oh, dear, I'm afraid I don't know either one. Is it terribly urgent?"

"No, but I'd like to talk to him." Matt paused. "Ms. Germaine, if you can't get in touch with him, how does he know when you want him to work?"

"Oh, that's really quite simple. He comes when he has time, that's all. We don't have any sort of schedule; that wouldn't suit either of us."

For a moment Matt felt a stab of irritation. Then again, maybe it wasn't such a bad way to live. "Would Erica know where he lives?"

"I doubt it. Anyway, she's gone out. Lieutenant, why do you want to speak to Dale? Is he in trouble? He's a very nice man, you know, even if he does have a little problem."

Matt tried to keep his voice even. "What sort of problem?"

He sensed her hesitation. "Maybe problem is the wrong word. They say a man with no vices..."

"What sort of problem, ma'am?"

She sighed. "Horses, Lieutenant. Dale bets on horse races."

"I see. Thank you, Ms. Germaine. You've been very helpful." Todd had probably borrowed the five G's from Mandell to bet on a 'sure thing' that came in last.

He dialed again.

"Glenn, I found out who Dale Todd is. Ronya Germaine's handyman and Eric Rawlins' caddy."

There was a pause. "This is turning out to be a real family affair. You talk to him yet?"

"Can't find him. There's no phone listing and, believe it or not, Erica's aunt doesn't know where he lives. He's been working for these people at least ten years, maybe longer; he could be a valuable source."

"I've also picked up some information since I saw you, Matt. I talked to the manager at Phoenix Properties and he says there was nothing up in the theater projection room but old movie reels and a set of plans of the building."

"So," Matt said, "Philip Mandell was up there looking at plans. And those stage curtains were dragged clear across the building so the fire could be set under the projection room."

"I talked to Mandell's lawyer, too. He says Mandell's estate is peanuts. He sunk everything he made back into the Peninsula Players."

"And Erica says her aunt is rich as Croesus. Which makes Mandell's will worth nothing." Both men digested that.

"I also checked on Francie," Glenn said. "She was definitely on the Denver flight the night of the theater fire and she flew back the day the Burtons' house burned. There's no way she could have set those fires."

"Good."

"What are you doing in the office?" Glenn asked. "Thought you were going to try for a day off."

"Can't stay away, you know that. I get withdrawal pains if I don't see these four walls every day."

"Uh-huh, sure you do. Just a minute." There was muttering in the background. "Penny says will you come for dinner?"

"Sounds great. Is she serving Big Macs?"

"She says it's a surprise. She figures you need some mystery in your life."

"Tell your sweet wife it's time she learned a new joke. I'll be around later."

He decided to check the last thirty years of unsolved arson. It was likely a waste of time, but might turn up some new leads. Or at least give him some new ideas to mull over. Insurance was the usual motive so his hunch that the six fires had been set to cover up Mandell's murder could be way off.

He scanned the first fifteen years quickly, familiar with most of the cases. Nothing to help him there. When his eyelids drooped he got a coffee from the machine. The stuff tasted older than the cases he was looking at.

Attacking the previous fifteen years, he was all but nodding off when he saw a name that brought him wide awake and startled him into spilling his cold coffee.

Victim: Rawlins, Suzanne. Could it be...?

It was. Twenty-two years ago. Fire started with gasoline and newspapers. Victim's husband, Eric, cleared of suspicion. No other suspects. No motive.

Matt settled down to read the details. Suzanne Rawlins and her little girl, Erica, had been alone in the house, after canceling plans for an overnight stay with friends. Husband out of town. Firemen found the child crying on the lawn. The mother inside, dead, along with a cocker spaniel puppy. The house was a write-off.

Why hadn't Erica told him all this? Mandell had been a pal of her mother's; couldn't Erica see the two deaths might be connected?

Matt steadied himself. They *might* be connected. It was definitely worth checking. His thoughts turned to the little girl Erica had been when her mother died, the woman she was now. So that was why she was so intense about arson investigation. He looked at the file, face somber. There were worse reasons to become an investigator.

But to lose a mother so young! He'd been crushed when Lynne died, but at eighteen he'd coped. He wondered if Erica had seen this file. She'd only been six when it happened; she'd likely buried everything except the urge to find and punish arsonists.

"And why did you become a cop, Matthew?" said a voice in the back of his head. The answer came so fast and clear it was like a blow. He grabbed a cigarette from his jacket, lit it and inhaled the smoke deep into his lungs.

Robert Stannard was a murderer. He'd murdered Lynne. And Matt's unborn child. He'd never voiced that belief, rarely even acknowledged it. But it had always been there, along with his own guilt, under the surface.

And he'd become a homicide cop because he wanted to punish people like Lynne's father. The idea of being a cop had never entered his head before her death. As gang leader of the Honchos, he'd made a habit of staying as far away from cops as he could.

Matt swung his feet off the desk and headed for his car. Okay, so it was interesting to know why he'd become a cop. Psych lesson over. Finding Mandell's murderer had priority over everything else.

***

The phone was answered almost at once.

"What went wrong yesterday?"

"Nothing went wrong." The voice at the other end was defensive.

"Don't try to con me. There was no report of a fire in any of the papers, yesterday or today."

"That's right. 'Cause there was no fire. I figured I'd pick my own time and place just so we didn't have no more 'accidents.'"

"What are you talking about?"

"You wanted a fire, you got one. Only it was on Wednesday, not yesterday."

"My God! You don't mean the house on Fillmore?"

"Yeah, that's the one. I cased the place and it was empty. No accidents, right?"

The hand that gripped the receiver was white-knuckled, the palm sweating, the voice that finally spoke harsh with controlled emotion. "Right, no accidents. But you could have ruined everything trying to do things your way. Don't you think I know what I'm doing?"

"I kinda wonder at times."

"Well, get this through your head. The sites are important. The timing is important."

"Okay, okay, I guess you got a right to be pissed off. But I don't like accidents."

"Neither do I. I've told you that a hundred times. You've got to do the last one exactly as I say."

"The last one?"

"Right. It's all I need now. Then we're finished."

"One more. That's for sure?"

"Right. Tomorrow, Monday. That's five days since last Wednesday. I told you, the timing is important. I have to decide where, though, so I'll get back to you. There are a couple of possibilities. I'll check them out first."

"You do that. No accidents. No foul-ups."

"No accidents. You have my word."

Chapter Sixteen

Erica parked in one of the spaces marked 'visitor' beside the new condominium complex. She slid from behind the wheel, telling herself that she had no reason to be nervous. Nevertheless, she had to wipe damp palms on the thighs of her jeans as she approached the wrought-iron security gates. She located the number she'd noted down and pressed the buzzer.

A woman's voice crackled over the line. "Yes?"

"Ms. Cameron? Your office told me about the open house."

"Come on up." A click indicated the gate was unlocked and Erica walked in, giving the Japanese-style entrance only a glance. Normally she would have found the sound of clear water bubbling around rocks and pebbles under a small foot bridge soothing, but not today. She glanced in surprise at her clenched fists. Why did she feel as if she was getting ready to do battle?

The woman who opened the door was nothing like she'd expected. But what had she expected? What sort of woman would interest both her father and Matt Nicols?

Not even the skillful makeup and meticulous hair could disguise the fact that the woman had seen forty come and go. "Francie Cameron," the woman said, extending her card and reaching for Erica's hand.

"Erica Johnson," she responded, aware of the assessing gaze that swept her from head to toe. Clad in jeans and a bulky sweater, face devoid of makeup and hair scraped back in a ponytail, Erica felt as unsophisticated as she knew she must look. She found herself wishing she was better prepared for this meeting. If it did turn out to be some kind of battle, she should have come armed: worn a dress, put on some lipstick, prepared herself emotionally.

Ms. Cameron's peach colored jacket looked expensive. The hemline of her black wool skirt was an inch above her knees, revealing great legs. "House-looking, are you?"

"Could be," Erica said. "I saw your sign outside the other day. This is such a nice neighborhood."

Francie ushered her in. "Well, come on, I'll show you through. Whereabouts do you live now?"

"Sausalito," Erica said. Catching the woman's sharp look she added, "I rent."

"And you work in the city?" Ms. Cameron led her to the living room where floor to ceiling windows displayed a fantastic view of downtown high-rises and a sweep of blue sky. Erica faked an appreciative glance. "Note the gas fireplace," Francie said, with a graceful gesture of one manicured hand.

Erica focused on those peach-tipped nails, imagining them sifting through the pelt of dark hair bisecting Matt's chest. She sucked in her breath and glanced up to see Ms. Cameron watching her as if she were under a microscope.

"Where do you work?" The older woman's words were slow and careful, as if she were speaking to a small child. "If this isn't in your price range I have other listings that might be more suitable."

Erica almost laughed, feeling herself regain control. Ms. Cameron must have concluded she couldn't afford the condo. "Money's not a factor," she said, marching ahead to the spacious bathroom that boasted a sunken marble tub and a separate glass-enclosed shower stall.

Ms. Cameron said, "Live alone, do you?"

Erica didn't answer. In her mind's eye the stall became fogged with steam, allowing just a glimpse of naked limbs tangled together, trysting against the slippery glass. She swung about in an attempt to drive the vision from her mind and nearly trod upon Ms. Cameron's imported leather pump. Erica tilted up her chin, met the other woman's eyes. "As a matter of fact, I do."

She felt as if the silent battle waging between them would soon be out in the open. Francie turned and led the way to the kitchen. "Do you like to cook?" she asked. "This kitchen is a gourmet's dream."

Erica followed, taking her time, into the oak-lined room. She ran her fingers along the smooth surface of the granite counter top. "I do like to cook. But I don't often find the time."

Francie gestured at the double sink, then dropped her hand. "Where did you say you worked?"

"I didn't say."

The other woman tucked her hands into her jacket pockets. "That's right. You didn't. And you're not really in the market for a new home, are you?"

Erica conceded with as much grace as she could muster. "No, I'm not."

"What are you in the market for?"

"Information."

"Regarding..."

"I'm investigating a recent fire on Fillmore Street. One of your listings."

The transformation was startling. The woman's nostrils went white, her face tightened, aging her a good ten years. Almost immediately she recovered. "Is that so? I suggest you talk to Lieutenant Matt Nicols. I've told him everything I know. Which is nothing. I was out of town when it happened. A couple of thousand people can vouch for that."

"I know," Erica said.

As she scrutinized Erica, Francie's face softened. Erica could have sworn she was fighting back a smile. "You working with Matt?"

"Sort of."

She nodded. "That explains it."

"Explains what?"

"Why he hasn't been around lately. If you catch my drift."

Erica caught her drift all right. "And does that bother you?"

Francie shrugged. "They say nothing lasts forever. And he's a good enough lay." She eyed Erica thoughtfully. "Really good, in fact. But he's a self-absorbed son of a bitch. I mean, there's no time wasted wining and dining and whispering sweet nothings in your ear." She studied her nails. "A girl has to look out for herself. Nothing wrong with flowers once in a while. Gifts on your birthday."

Was that where her father came in? Wining and dining and velvet-lined boxes from Antoinette's or Shreve & Co.? "Sounds as if you've got your priorities in order."

"Make no mistake about it." Her 'just between us girls' wink set Erica's teeth on edge. "But you're young. You've got time yet to enjoy the best of both worlds." She crossed her arms over her chest. "In fact, maybe I ought to do you a favor and give you some advice."

"What sort of advice?"

"Matt Nicols advice."

Erica's heart started to pound. Her palms grew damp. Did she even want to hear this?

"You have to understand that Matt steers a hundred and eighty degrees from anything resembling a commitment."

"I'd guessed that."

"He's been doing it for so long that it's like second nature. He doesn't even realize he's doing it."

"He's committed to his job," Erica pointed out.

"Obsessed is more like it. He's a one man crusade. Takes it real hard when some criminal gives him the slip."

"Thanks for the tip," Erica said. It was obvious that Francie Cameron, although she might have intimate physical knowledge of Matt, hadn't gleaned any more idea than Erica of what motivated the man.

"Funny thing about his family," Francie added, as Erica reached the front door.

She swung around. "What about them?"

"He doesn't talk about them much. But when he does, you can tell he really cares about them."

"What's your point?"

"I think, deep down, he's afraid to admit just how strong his emotions can run."

Erica shot Francie a startled look. Pretty shrewd insight for a woman who appeared so self-serving and shallow. Francie shrugged. "Meet all kinds in this business. You need to be a sharp judge of character or you won't survive. Take you, for instance. How long before I figured you weren't looking to buy?"

"Not long," Erica admitted.

"How long before I figured you were really here looking for the inside track on Matt Nicols?"

Erica felt herself color. "That's not why I came."

"No?" Her raised eyebrows made it plain Francie didn't believe this desperate fib. "You didn't want to know if he and I were still warming the sheets together?"

Erica worried her bottom lip.

Francie gave her a considering look. "I doubt you're concerned about cutting in on my territory so my guess is that he hasn't taken you to bed yet. And you're wondering why not."

"You've got it all wrong," Erica said, with forced bravado.

Francie laughed. "You're a bigger liar than he is, hon. But trust me, nothing's wrong with that man's sex drive. Shouldn't be long before his zipper wins out over his conscience." She paused. "Shouldn't be long, either, before he forgets about his aversion to dark-haired, upper-crust society girls, like the one who broke his adolescent heart."

She stiffened. "He told you that?"

"Not a chance. But I have ways of finding out what I want to know."

Curiosity got the better of her. "How did she break his heart?"

Francie paused before she spoke, as if savoring what she was about to share. "The ultimate unforgivable act. She died."

Chapter Seventeen

Erica spent the rest of the day at home doing laundry and cleaning, but her vigorous attack on dust and grime didn't dispel the thought fragments chasing each other around in her head. The most persistent was Francie Cameron's disclosure. Now she knew why Matt called her 'Princess' in such a derogatory way.

Erica stopped folding towels and stared at herself in the mirror. Her apparent resemblance to the girl he'd loved and lost revealed a lot about Matt Nicols and the way he acted around her.

The phone rang as she put away the vacuum and her heart gave a ridiculous leap of hope. But the voice on the other end wasn't Matt's.

"Clayton." She tried to sound pleased. "How are you?"

"Quite frankly, I'm feeling neglected. I've missed you, darling. And you haven't returned any of my calls."

"I'm sorry. It's been really crazy since I got back."

"Perhaps we can make up for lost time tonight. When should I call for you?"

"Tonight? Did we have plans for tonight?"

"It's old what's-his-name's retirement party. You asked me some time ago to accompany you."

"Charlie," she said. "Is that tonight already?"

"You sound odd, Erica. Is everything all right?"

She'd forgotten Charlie's retirement party. Matt Nicols was certain to be there. No, everything was not all right. "I'm fine, honestly. I just forgot, that's all. I'm sorry."

"So what time?" A thread of annoyance edged his tone.

"Uh. Eight, I guess. Is that convenient for you?"

"Certainly. I look forward to seeing you, my dear."

Erica was staring into her clothes closet when she heard the doorbell. Again that ridiculous bubble of hope leapt to her throat. She slammed the closet door, realizing it wasn't for Clayton Gallagher's benefit that she was thinking of wearing something sleek and feminine, but for Matt, who had yet to see her in anything other than jeans, coveralls and boots.

Dale stood on her front step, something fluffy cradled in one large freckled hand. A pitiful snuffling noise issued from the ball of fuzz.

"What have you got there?"

Dale shot a furtive glance over his shoulder. "I found her under the shrubs near the road. Poor thing ain't old enough to be away from her mama. She's half-starved."

The kitten's fur was a ginger color almost the same as the hair speckling Dale's arms. He must have had a head of red hair once, Erica thought, but in her memory he'd always been bald.

Erica could feel spindly ribs through the creature's matted fur. The kitten opened her tiny mouth but seemed too weak to meow. "Come on in. I'll call Rony's vet." Dale cradled the kitten against his chest and followed her into the house.

"It's Sunday," he reminded her.

"That's right." She frowned. "If we can't get hold of him it might be kinder to put her out of her misery." At Dale's look of dismay, she said, "Heat some milk, then. She might be able to suck it from a rag."

"Eyedropper would be better," Dale muttered.

She found an eyedropper in the bathroom, gave it to him and went to the telephone. When she returned to the kitchen area, Dale was feeding the kitten milk, one drop at a time, gentle fingers massaging the animal's throat to encourage her to swallow, his voice barely above a whisper as he murmured words of praise the entire time.

"The vet says he'll check her over today," she said, watching the tender scene and feeling almost like an intruder in her own kitchen. "He'll make sure she's not too far gone."

"I'll take her right away," Dale said. "All the poor little thing needs is a chance. Look at her. She's a real fighter."

"I wonder if she wandered away from her mother or if she was dumped here."

Dale shot her a dark and telling look. "Don't make no difference. Them that are meant to survive always do."

***

"Are you certain we're in the right place?" Clayton asked as he parked beside a second-rate hotel on the outskirts of Oakland.

"This is the address the Captain gave me." She followed the sound of music to the semi-detached conference area, noticing Clayton wrinkle his nose and frown at the pall of cigarette smoke and the strident rock music issuing from the doorway.

One hand on Erica's elbow, he guided her inside. "These people look more like street hooligans than upholders of law and order."

She hung back, searching the room with a quick, surreptitious glance. Given his height, Matt should be easy to spot.

Glenn Davenport sat next to a pretty blonde woman at one of the banquet tables. At the front of the long room, which was decorated with a profusion of streamers and balloons, Captain Bailey was deep in consultation with a pony-tailed young man.

There was no sign of Matt. Erica released a pent-up breath. Captain Bailey glanced up, caught her eye and beckoned to her and Clayton.

"We've received a summons from the Captain," she said.

Clayton frowned again as he looked around. "This is very peculiar. Where's the head table? And the VIPs?"

Erica smothered a giggle. "Oh, no. You thought we were coming to Charlie's formal retirement dinner. With the mayor and everyone. Black-tie. Very civilized. I'm afraid this isn't it."

His frown deepened. "Would you mind explaining?"

"This is Charlie's *party*. Thrown by the boys in the squad room. A different affair entirely."

"Erica, I wish you'd made that clear at the outset."

"I thought I had," she said, as they neared Bailey.

The Captain slapped Clayton on the back and beamed at Erica. "Glad you both could make it. You like country and western?"

Erica, knowing Clayton's tastes ran to opera, waxed enthusiastic for both of them. Bailey and Clayton were soon deep into discussing city politics and Erica had to endure it for all of three minutes before she got the opportunity to interrupt. She gave Clayton's arm a gentle tug. "Here's Charlie."

"Erica!" Charlie enveloped her in a fatherly bear hug. Standing back, he gave her a long, hard look and let out a lecherous whistle. "All this and brains, too. The girl's got legs!"

Good-natured hoots erupted from the officers nearby and Erica smiled in acknowledgment. She hadn't worn a dress for so long that the cool seductive length of stockings and the hemline grazing her knees felt strange. She'd chosen a simple turquoise silk sheath with oriental embroidery, slit high on one thigh. In a rare moment of vanity she'd slid her feet into black patent high-heeled pumps, knowing they displayed her legs to full advantage.

"Charlie, I'd like you to meet Clayton Gallagher. Clayton, the city of San Francisco doesn't know what it's losing putting this old work-horse out to pasture."

Charlie guffawed. "Gotta take my freedom while there's still life in the old bones." He winked, pointing at the balloons overhead. Erica looked up and felt herself flush, suspecting they weren't balloons at all, but air-filled prophylactics. Someone had covered them with leering felt-penned faces.

The exchange seemed lost on Clayton as he smiled his politician's smile and checked out the other guests, no doubt making sure he wasn't neglecting anyone he considered important.

"Shall we sit over on that side?" Crossing the room, she stopped at Glenn's table and presented Clayton. Glenn introduced his wife, Penny.

"Would you care to join us?" Penny asked. "We can easily pull up a couple of extra chairs."

Consternation brought heat to Erica's cheeks. When Matt appeared he'd be sure to sit with his partner. "Clayton has already cornered a table," she lied. "But thank you, anyway." She paused. "I hear you have a beautiful family."

"They run me ragged," Penny said, with a laugh. "But some things are worth it."

"Like me." Glenn laid a possessive hand on her knee and leaned over to kiss her cheek. Erica felt a twinge of envy at their easy display of affection.

Clayton deposited her at a small table tucked in an alcove, then joined the line-up for the bar. Erica tried to keep her eyes from straying to the door every thirty seconds. Where was Matt? Surely he wouldn't miss Charlie's party.

Erica was tapping her foot to a rollicking country and western tune when she felt a touch on her shoulder. She whirled, then relaxed. It was Mendoza, one of Matt's detectives, wearing his signature scent, jaws working at the usual wad of chewing gum. "Care to dance?"

She glanced over at Clayton. His dark tailored suit, silk tie and suave demeanor seemed incongruous among policemen wearing jeans and checked shirts and obviously intending to let their hair down tonight. But why should she care? He hadn't attended for her sake. As the mayor's chief executive officer, he needed to be in touch with the pulsing hub of the city. It was just his misfortune that this party wasn't the kind of pulsing hub he'd thought it would be.

"Sure," she said rising. "Why not?"

Mendoza talked her into three fast dances and she was breathless by the time he returned her to the table where Clayton sat glowering.

Reaching over, she tugged at his tie. "You don't look as if you're enjoying yourself."

Clayton shot her a dour glance and sipped from his plastic drink glass. "This is not my type of affair. Yours either, for that matter."

Erica shrugged. "I work with most of these people from time to time. And Charlie really is a pet."

Clayton leaned forward. "That's exactly what I mean. Why *do* you work with these people?"

Erica wished the tepid, too-sweet wine in her glass was Auguste's special label. "You know my job involves close contact with the SIS. Especially with a mad arsonist loose in the city."

"Why do you want to poke around in smoky ruins? With your talent and education you could choose from a dozen different positions."

She set down her glass with care, resisting the impulse to slam it on the table. "I have." The conversation was a replay of an oft-occurring one with her father. The men in her life simply didn't understand her.

Matt Nicols understood her. The thought popped into her head out of nowhere. She banished it. "Come on," she said, rising, "let's dance." The dancers had formed a chain, hands on each other's waists, and were weaving in and out among the tables, clowning, laughing, almost drowning out the music.

Clayton's lip curled. "No, thank you. How long until it's politically correct to leave? I'd like a decent drink in a real glass. And, Erica, darling, I haven't seen you for weeks. I'd very much like to have you to myself in somewhat more appropriate surroundings."

She sat down and took a leisurely sip of her wine. "We just got here. We can't leave yet."

Not before Matt arrives. Where were these thoughts coming from? She aimed a covert glance over her shoulder at Glenn's table, but the chair next to his was empty. What if Matt showed up with the Cameron woman?

Clayton shrugged. "By the way, which is the officer who's been making a nuisance of himself with your father?"

A twinge of guilt made Erica almost spill her wine. "You must mean Lieutenant Nicols." She glanced about the room, pretending she didn't know quite well that Matt wasn't there. "I don't see him."

"The lieutenant would be well advised to steer clear of your father, if he knows what's good for him. Demanding a personal audience was quite unnecessary."

"He's just doing his job! Father was the alibi for a realtor whose listings were torched."

Clayton sighed. "Really, Erica, you're starting to sound just like these people."

Erica was about to ask what he meant when an officer whom she'd met a few times asked her to dance. She gave Clayton a sweet smile and stood. "I'd love to."

After that she hardly had a chance to sit, let alone be lectured. She'd hear about her behavior on the way home, but for now she was having a marvelous time, dancing and laughing and drinking wine. She and Glenn took time out from a dance to watch Charlie open his gifts, which ranged from fishing tackle to bizarre sex-shop items.

"Your date doesn't seem to be a dancer," Glenn said.

"Parties aren't his thing." Erica checked her watch, surprised that it was past midnight. "It doesn't look as if Matt's going to show." She hadn't intended to say the words aloud, but somehow they'd slipped out. She hoped Glenn didn't think she'd been watching for his partner all night.

"Parties aren't Matt's thing, either," Glenn said. "But he did tell me he'd be here. I hope nothing's happened."

"Me, too. Thanks for the dance, Glenn," she added, as he delivered her back to Clayton.

"Are you ready to go?" Clayton inquired, his voice as cool as the ice in his glass.

"Anytime you are." Then, hearing a slow waltz start, some inner imp made her say, "How about a dance first?"

"First and last," Clayton said, rising.

The noise level abated as couples took to the floor in close embraces. Clayton held her lightly, one hand resting on the curve of her waist. His dance style was correct, if a little wooden, and Erica had just closed her eyes to concentrate on the music when she heard his startled exclamation.

"Here! You can't just cut in like that!"

"Watch me." Erica opened her eyes to see Matt nudge Clayton out of the way and step in front of her.

"Funny," Erica said, her throat feeling constricted, "I didn't think you were the type to make an entrance."

"Actually, I've been here a while." As Matt pulled her into his arms the tightness in her throat increased. The warm weight of his hand against her back and the hard ridge of calluses on the hand that caught hers distracted her from the music and her foot landed atop his.

"Sorry." It was impossible to concentrate when she could feel the thudding of his heart in tandem with hers.

"Easy," he murmured, his voice huskier than usual, his breath stirring the hair on top of her head. His hands settled intimately on her hips, slowing her pace to match his. "There, that's the way."

He was a superb dancer and Erica melted against him as he guided her around the floor. His hands slid from her hips to her waist, then curved around to her back. Held against him like this, she felt as if they'd been dancing together forever.

His cotton chambray shirt, incredibly soft under her hand, hugged his broad shoulders in a perfect fit. She'd always been a sucker for western garb like Matt's string bola tie. Damn him, he looked great! With a sigh, she laid her head against his chest and his hands tightened on her back, moving in slow soothing circles.

"Where did you learn to dance?" she asked, wanting to break the silence between them.

She felt Matt inhale, as if speech required extra effort. "My mother made us take lessons. She was determined none of her kids would be wallflowers."

"You're lucky she cared that much." The one thing denied Erica as a child had been the security of having parents who cared for her. She'd been shuffled off to the best boarding school in the country, convinced that her father simply wanted her out of the way.

"Yeah, she's one in a million." Matt rested his chin on the top of her head, his free hand caressing the length of her spine. "You're the belle of the ball tonight. Your friend doesn't look too happy about it, though."

"This was our first dance of the evening."

Matt chuckled. "I couldn't very well cut in on any of my fellow officers. They're liable to get ornery."

She drew back a little, her eyes finding his. "Clayton can be ornery, too."

His smile was lazy, relaxed. "I'm not worried."

The song ended, the music segueing into another slow romantic number. "Thank you for the dance." When Erica tried to step away his hold tightened, imprisoning her against the hard length of his denim-clad thighs.

"It's not over."

Erica saw Clayton standing on the sidelines, arms crossed over his chest, his gaze following her. "I think it would be better if..." She looked up to see Matt's eyes flash a message across the room to Glenn, who leaned over and spoke to his wife. Penny immediately rose and led Clayton onto the dance floor.

"You engineered that!"

He gave a small shrug. "I need to ask you something, but I'm having a hell of a time working around to it."

Erica had a feeling she didn't want to hear his question. "If it's about the case, this isn't the time or the place to... "

Matt interrupted. "What do you remember about the fire the night your mother died?"

Erica gasped and abandoned all pretense of dancing.

His hold tightened, preventing her flight. Once again Matt had anticipated her movements. Before she quite realized what was happening, he'd hustled her out into the soft September night, quiet except for the distant sounds of the freeway.

Erica hugged her middle as she faced him. He stood a pace away, legs apart, booted feet planted on the dusty pavement.

"Why didn't you tell me your mother was the victim in an unsolved arson?" His voice was soft. Could that be sympathy she heard? "How old were you when it happened?"

She moistened dry lips and opened her mouth but no sound came out. She swallowed and tried again. "I was six years old."

"What do you remember?"

"Nothing!" Her voice grew stronger. "Don't you think I've tried? I don't remember a thing but the sound of the fire engines." She shuddered. Her voice fell. "And the smell. I'll never forget the smell."

When Matt moved toward her she drew back. "I'm not trying to hurt you," he said. "It might be important."

"How?" She couldn't believe how shrill she sounded. The way her voice trembled.

He shook his head. "I don't know, but I've got a gut feeling about it. What if you saw something significant that night? And blocked it out as a means of coping."

"I just...want to forget."

"No you don't, Erica."

Matt approached. She continued to back away.

"I tell you, I do." Her retreat came to an abrupt halt against a fence and she stared up at him, knowing how a trapped animal must feel. Her breath quickened to shallow panting as panic tightened her throat.

"If you really wanted to forget you wouldn't be doing this work. Her death must stare you in the face every day, whether you acknowledge it or not." He closed in, legs straddling hers on either side. There was no place to go. No place to look except into his eyes.

In his gaze she saw new understanding, new awareness, coupled with something that rocked her to the soles of her feet. Raw primitive desire. Desire for her. Not fueled by either anger or lust as in the past, but a smoldering chemical reaction, threatening to consume them.

"If you were honest with yourself..."

If she were honest with herself she'd admit she wanted him, yearned for him, in every way.

"...you'd admit there could be a connection..."

There was a connection all right. A connection between them she couldn't pretend to understand.

"...between that fire years ago and the ones we're investigating now."

"What?" He was talking business, she realized. Nothing to do with him and her. "You can't be serious."

"Think about it. The same family. The same MO. No obvious motive. Victim possibly in the wrong place at the wrong time."

"They said the motive was likely robbery. That's what my father thinks, too." Matt's suggestion was too ludicrous for words.

He gripped her shoulders with hands that were firm, yet gentle. "You know fire is rarely used to cover up a robbery. It's too much trouble."

"You're suggesting someone was responsible for my mother's death and that same person killed Philip?"

"I admit it sounds bizarre, but it bears investigation." Party noise erupted from the building, shattering the peace surrounding them. "How long has the boyfriend been on the scene?"

"Clayton?" She shook her head. "He's been in San Francisco for maybe fifteen years. He and my father conduct a fair amount of business together."

His fingers tightened. "What's he to you?"

"That's none of your business."

"Wrong again."

They were both breathing hard, the air ripe with tension. Behind Matt someone started a car and, for a moment, the headlights spotlighted them against the fence, blinding Erica with the glare. She looked away, but not before she saw the look in Matt's eyes smoldering with intensity.

"You can't do this to me."

"What?" His hands gentled, moved from shoulder to elbow and back again, caressing the sensitive skin of her upper arms in a way that made her shiver beneath his touch.

But his hands, his scent, his nearness were combining to warm her from the inside out. "This?" He lowered his mouth to hers. "Or this?"

After token resistance she kissed him back, hard and deep, arms around his neck. And though their lips were no longer strangers, the texture of this kiss was different.

Gentle. Caring. It reached into her soul, plumbing the depths of who she was and how she was made. She moved against him, trying to get closer. Immediately she felt his response. Heady knowledge. That she possessed the power to whip him into equal frenzy.

She plowed her fingers through his hair, angling her head, reaching for more. He groaned, gathering her closer. His hands splayed her backside, tilting her against him in a provocative way, his desire obvious.

Erica's head reeled as he pushed aside the slit in her dress, his hand exploring the stockinged length of her thigh, moving to where stocking ended and firm female flesh began. At the back of her thigh his fingers found the elastic leg of her panties and lingered there in a seductive teasing movement that went on and on until Erica thought she might explode from the building pressure.

They both heard it. Matt groaned against her lips, echoing her sentiments. "Yours or mine?" he asked, his mouth releasing hers with great reluctance.

"Yours," she said, trying to catch her breath. "My phone's inside in my purse."

"Damn it to hell," he said, his voice thick with need, his lips fluttering against hers. "Times like this I swear I hate my job."

"I know." She pulled him back for one more kiss.

He broke the contact and swore again, rubbing his thumb over her swollen bottom lip. He swallowed, took a breath. "We'll get back to this."

She tingled, hearing emotion lace his words. Emotion he tried to disguise by making his voice hoarse.

"Yes," she whispered, reaching for him, her fingers tracing a light, invisible line from cheekbone to jaw. She saw the muscles tense as he clamped his jaw closed and stared over her head, taking several long even breaths.

Behind them the door opened, spilling a wedge of light into the gravel. Glenn stepped outside.

"You get a call, too?" Matt said, as his hands slid down Erica's arms and released her.

"Yeah. And we'd better move it," Glenn said. "Seems our arsonist has been busy."

Chapter Eighteen

There was very little traffic on the Bay Bridge and Matt drove fast, his reflexes in control while the rush of adrenalin cleared his mind of everything but the job that lay ahead. He slowed as he took the off ramp into the glittering heart of San Francisco. "What's the address, Glenn?"

"Russian Hill. An apartment house. I'll tell you where to turn."

He felt Erica stiffen but a quick glance revealed only a slight frown creasing her forehead. Maybe she was having second thoughts about leaving Gallagher standing in the parking lot. Matt's mind forged ahead. The seventh damn fire and still no leads.

The car crested the hill. "Turn here." Glenn pointed to a dead-end street running off Vallejo. As soon as the car turned the corner, Matt could smell smoke. He parked behind two police cars.

The door of the darkened high rise stood open, the acrid smell of smoke emanating from inside. Tenants in robes or overcoats, some barefoot, clustered around the fire chief or spoke with reporters.

Beside him Erica gasped, the sound hitting him like a fist in the gut. He turned to see her clutching at the dashboard as though she might faint. He pulled her to him, and she buried her ashen face against his chest, shuddering convulsively.

"Erica?" He gentled her with his hands, massaging her shoulders and her neck under the thick dark hair.

She pulled back, sucking in a long draft of air. She exhaled and struggled to get words out. "That's where...my mother...our house..." She took another deep breath. "The house was demolished. That apartment was built on the site."

He envisioned a six year old girl in her nightgown, crying on the lawn for a mother she'd never see again. She shouldn't be here, reliving that nightmare. He tightened the arm that still spanned her shoulders, but she moved away. "I'm all right now. It was just the shock."

He blew out a pent-up breath. It had been a shock to him as well. "Put it out of your mind. It's just one of those weird coincidences."

"I'm fine." Color seeped back to her face but her voice still trembled. She looked down at her elegant black pumps. "This is hardly the garb for investigating fires."

"I have some extra gear." He got out and went around to unlock the trunk. He'd called the fire site coincidental for Erica's sake, but there'd been too many coincidences. There was a connection. There had to be.

Glenn was with the fire chief and Kandowski, an SIS officer. Matt had found a pair of spare rubber boots and retrieved a wrinkled raincoat from among the Big Mac containers in the back seat and given them to Erica to wear. She walked beside him toward the small group, carrying his extra flashlight, his boots and coat looking incongruous with her silky turquoise dress.

The fire chief nodded. "Matt. Erica. Just telling Glenn this was a cellar fire; laundry room in the basement. Mainly smoke damage except for the laundry equipment and the power box."

"Incendiary?"

"Yeah. Gasoline. A tenant smelled smoke and called us before the thing got out of hand. However..."

Glenn's tone was somber. "There's a body."

Erica's face had paled again. Matt grabbed her hand with a steadying pressure. She drew back her shoulders and her chin came up in that stubborn gesture he'd admired the first time he saw her. But her hand clung to his as though she'd never let it go.

Kandowski said, "Yeah. Hodgekiss is here already."

"Erica? You want to stay here?" She had guts, but this might be more than she could handle.

The chin came up another notch. "No. This is my job. I'm going in."

"You don't have to."

"Yes, I do."

Given the determined angle of her chin, he knew it was a waste of time to argue. "Lead the way, Kandowski. Give us the details as we go."

Slipping quickly past the reporters, they moved through the lobby, where a uniformed policeman with an emergency light was riding herd on nervous tenants, and headed for the stairs leading to the basement.

Kandowski turned on his powerful flashlight and said, "The perp got in through a window."

"And I bet I know how," Glenn said. "It was jimmied, right?"

"Right," Kandowski said. As they neared the bottom of the stairs, two men appeared with a stretcher, the body covered with a white sheet. Hodgekiss, the ME, followed, reaching for the pipe sticking out of his pocket.

Matt heard Erica's footsteps hesitate but when he reached the bottom she was right behind him.

"Well, Matt!" Hodgekiss said, his cheerful grin conflicting with the darkness and the pervading smell of smoke and chemicals. "Got a new angle for you this time. He was shot."

"Shot!"

Hodgekiss shrugged. "Might be murder or suicide. The position of the gun was such that he could have pulled the trigger himself. Be tricky to figure out which. Anyway, we've ID'd him, so that's a start."

Noting Erica's white face, Matt wished she'd abdicated from the case when he'd told her to. "What's the name?"

"Dale Todd."

Erica's sharp gasp mirrored Matt's reaction. Damn it, there *was* a connection! He had no doubts now.

Erica moved toward the stretcher, turning her flashlight on. "If that's Dale Todd, I can confirm the identification."

Matt put a restraining hand on her arm. "Wait." To Hodgekiss he said, "What kind of shape is he in?"

Hodgekiss gave Erica a concerned look. "Fire didn't get to his face. You sure you want to do this now?"

"I need to know." She pulled back the sheet. Dale Todd's bald head and freckled face were illuminated in the glare of her flash. Her voice dull and flat, she said, "Yes, that's Dale."

Hodgekiss said, "He a close friend?" The gentleness in his voice belied his usual brisk cheer.

She rubbed her face and Matt saw tears in her eyes. "I've known him since I was little."

Matt reached for her. "Let me take you home."

"I'm all right! Just leave me alone."

Stung by her tone, Matt let his hand fall to his side. "When do we get the autopsy report, Harry?"

"Well, hell, boy, I'm up now." He looked at his watch. "Going on three. Shall we say about noon?"

"I couldn't ask for better." Hodgekiss knew as well as he did how important it was to find any clues that would stop the arsonist. And find them fast.

Hodgekiss followed the stretcher bearers up the stairs. The sweet aroma drifting down from his freshly lit pipe did nothing to drown the stink of gasoline.

In the laundry room, SIS men were working through the blackened chaos with hand held lights. Wet dripping foam covered everything and black water formed puddles on the concrete floor. Matt turned to Kandowski.

"Okay, give us the rest of it. Gasoline cans?"

"Yeah, two. They're burnt bad so we won't get any prints. A locker was busted open. I figure the perp got something outta there to help things along."

Matt grunted. "Where's the gun?"

Kandowski handed him a plastic bag.

Glenn said, "Hey, that's a silencer. If Todd committed suicide, would he bother with a silencer?"

"Doesn't make much sense," Matt agreed.

"None of it makes sense," said Erica, weariness threading her voice. "I can't believe Dale killed himself. I can't believe he'd set fires, either."

Kandowski handed another plastic bag to Glenn. "This here's the Detroit door opener the perp probably used to get in that window. With any luck, we might get some prints off that."

"There are times," Matt said, leaning against the doorjamb, "when I wish I'd gone in for something easy, like being an accountant."

"Accountants don't have pulpits," said Erica. Her face was drawn, her eyes huge. To Matt she sounded as if she hadn't slept for a year. "Is it okay to go in there?"

Her face was much too white, Matt thought, and her squared shoulders didn't disguise the fact that she was emotionally shell shocked.

"No, it isn't. Not for you." She opened her mouth as if to protest, but he ignored her. "Glenn, you can run this show. I'm taking Erica home."

"I'm all right," she protested.

"Yeah, I know. And you could probably handle this but you don't have to. There's a limit."

Outside, reporters angled microphones and floodlights toward him. He blinked against the glare and tried to shield Erica.

"Is this the work of a lone arsonist, Lieutenant?"

"What about the victim? Was he involved in the fires?"

"When the hell are you going to stop this looney?" The voice blared out, distinct from the rest. "Or you gonna let the whole city burn down first?"

Matt's hands clenched into fists. Two steps and he'd be close enough to deck Mr. Big-mouth. A satisfying thought; too bad he couldn't afford to translate it into action.

Erica's clear voice rang out. "The Insurance Crime Prevention Bureau is working closely with Lieutenant Nicols' Special Investigation Squad. I'm confident that our joint efforts will soon bring the investigation to a close." She actually flashed a smile. "I'll be happy to tell you more as soon as I know more myself." Matt blinked again as she moved forward and the reporters fell aside, clearing a path for her.

"Just like Moses, parting the bloody Red Sea," he murmured under his breath.

Chapter Nineteen

Erica saw the clock on the dash flip to 3:30 as Matt pulled into her driveway. He'd hardly said a word during the drive. Was he thinking about Dale's death? Did he wish he was with Glenn and the others? No, he'd have put her in a patrol car with a uniformed officer if he hadn't wanted to be with her.

She rested her head against the seat back, feeling keyed up, her nerve ends buzzing. She ought to be dead tired. Matt stared straight ahead. Was he waiting for her to move? She cleared her throat, dry and scratchy from the smoky basement. "I think I'll make some coffee." Matt stretched his right arm along the back of the seat. If she turned her face she could rest her cheek against his palm. But she didn't.

"Better make it decaf, or you'll never get to sleep."

She couldn't imagine being able to sleep, decaf or no. Not after seeing Dale's pale, freckled face so still on that stretcher.

Suddenly they both turned and spoke at the same time.

"Would you like to come in?"

"Maybe I should come in."

Erica managed a faint smile which Matt answered with one of his own. "Well, that settles that."

Inside, Erica pulled a bag of coffee beans from the freezer and plugged in her coffee grinder. Matt watched her from across the room. "Instant coffee would be quicker."

She pulled a face. "But it wouldn't taste as good. This will only take a minute."

"I know."

The sound of the electric grinder was shrill in the pre-dawn quiet. She went to the sink to fill the glass carafe, then started in surprise to find Matt was beside her, turning her into his arms.

"Screw the coffee," he said, voice husky.

She set the coffee pot down and moved against him, winding her arms around his waist, resting her cheek against his shirt front. She closed her eyes and took a deep shuddery breath. This was what she had missed all her life. This sense of sharing, of completeness, a wholeness that had nothing to do with physical desire and everything to do with bonding to another human being.

She had no idea how long they stood like that, their bodies pressed together, giving and taking, each absorbing the very essence of the other. If it was up to Erica, she'd never move again in her life.

His chin began sliding back and forth across the top of her head. The sensation was delicious. Then he started on her back, his hands soothing her spine from the base to the dip between her shoulders.

He gave a heavy sigh, his hands coming to a rest on her waist. She drew back enough to raise her eyes to his.

"It's been a night and a half," he said.

"It has."

"And I know the time isn't right. There's been way too much going on and it's late and..."

"And?" she prompted, feeling his hands tighten.

"And none of it means a damn to how much I want you."

Erica took a deep breath and let it out again. Her heart hammered against her ribs.

He went on, his voice a little rough. "And I know it's not fair to you. Taking advantage of the circumstances and your vulnerability."

Her eyes locked on his with steady intensity. Who was the most vulnerable right now? Her or Matt? "Why don't you let me be the judge of what's fair?"

He glanced at the ceiling as though looking for the right answer. For one terrible second, Erica thought he was going to leave. Then he scooped her into his arms and carried her across to the bedroom.

A wedge of light spilled through the open doorway and threw shadows across the white carpet and the queen-size brass bed, draped with a white cotton eyelet spread and piled with pillows.

He laid her down with a tenderness she hadn't known he possessed and stood back, as if to study her in the half-light. Did he see her, Erica? Or did he remember that other woman? The one who had died?

"What is it?" she murmured.

He touched a strand of her dark hair fanning across the pillow. "I don't deserve this. I don't deserve you."

She caught his hand and drew him down to her. "I was hoping that maybe, for a change, we deserved each other."

She watched the steady rise and fall of his chest, the emotions on his face as he leaned over her. Reaching up, she unfastened, one by one, the buttons fronting his shirt. Pushing aside the soft fabric, her hands stole across his middle, absorbing the warmth, the texture, the feel of his skin. He caught his breath as she explored the definition of masculine pectorals, the ropy sinew of shoulders and upper arms.

With one fluid movement he was on the bed, kneeling astride her, his hands tracing the curves of her body through the thin silk dress.

She drew her index finger along his jaw line. "Your beard grows fast." Her voice was hoarse, but not from smoke. She wanted to know absolutely everything about him, like Christmas morning when she unwrapped one parcel after another, not stopping until every gift had been revealed and exclaimed over.

"Do you want me to shave?" They both spoke barely above a whisper, as if afraid of shattering the fragile mood encompassing them in their own little world.

She shook her head, unable to speak. He'd discovered the mother-of-pearl buttons marching from shoulder to hem down one side of her dress. "I love the feel of this stuff," he said. "But I love the feel of you more."

Erica was glad she'd put on her seldom-worn black lace bra and bikini panties. The contrast of black lace against her pale skin made her feel sexy, a feeling bolstered by the look in Matt's eyes as he slowly peeled away her dress.

He shrugged out of his shirt and dropped it to the floor. She watched as he reached into his hip pocket and pulled out a couple of foil-wrapped packets, tossing them on her white wicker bedside table. She'd never seen a condom up close, though she certainly knew what they were. And, while part of her appreciated that he cared enough to protect her, another part wondered if he was always so well-prepared.

He stretched out beside her and seemed to read the mute questions in her eyes. His touch was gentle, unthreatening, as he raked the fingertips of his hand from her collar bone to her navel and back again. He blew a soft breath across her chest, rewarded by the instant puckering of her nipples, plainly visible through the sheer black lace.

He covered her hand with his. "Am I making you nervous?"

In their previous embraces he'd been aroused in seconds, hard, hot and demanding. She'd expected him to come at her fast and furious, the act over in minutes. Instead he seemed like a totally different person. Patient. Relaxed. More gentle than she'd have thought possible. She almost wished he'd rush her through, allowing no time for thought. That was the way her ex-husband had operated.

She gazed up at him, trying to keep the tremor of uncertainty from her voice. "I'm just not...I don't know what you want me to do."

"Well," he said, his lips a breath above hers, "we could start with this." Even the pressure of his kiss was a surprise. Gentle. Coaxing. Drawing an immediate response that sent hot blood coursing through her. She threaded her fingers through the hair on the back of his head, loving its heavy fullness, the way it teased the nerve endings on the tips of her fingers, the palm of her hand.

"Or this." He spoke against her lips, unclasping the front of her bra. She shivered as he reached to palm her breast, reshaping its soft weight in his hand.

"Or we could try this." The tip of his tongue touched the valley between her freed breasts before snaking a course down her ribs and belly to her navel. As his mouth explored the concave hollow stretching from hipbone to hipbone, his hands were busy stroking the soft skin of her inner thigh from stocking top to panties' edge.

Erica had never experienced anything like the riotous sensations his touch evoked. From the roots of her hair to the tips of her stocking-clad toes was a clash of hot and cold, goose bumps and perspiration. To her acute embarrassment she was actually squirming on the bed, unable to stop some part or other of her body from moving.

"That's it," Matt said in soothing tones, as his fingers trailed over the sheer swath of lace protecting the downy triangle of her femininity.

He stretched atop her, his male hardness outlined through his jeans and angled insistently toward that most vulnerable area of her body. He nuzzled the side of her neck, his breathing ragged.

"Erica. You make me crazy. Right from the first I wanted you so bad I was crazy with it."

She thrilled to his words. Abandoning conscious thought, she began touching him all over, her hands instinctively sliding into the back of his jeans and cupping his buttocks. At his groan, she redoubled her actions, her legs tangling with his. The sensation of stockings and skin against denim was wildly erotic.

"Don't," he groaned.

She froze. "What?"

"Don't stop," he whispered. He guided her hand to the clasp of his jeans. She had to struggle with the zipper, the jeans grown shockingly tight with him inside. Finally he

sprang free into her waiting hands. She swallowed her
nervousness. He was so big. So hard, yet so soft. Irresistible.
She formed a circle with her thumb and forefinger and
slowly slid it the length of his engorged shaft.

He allowed her sensory exploration for scant seconds,
then pulled away to tug off his jeans and her panties. When
she reached for the garters holding up her stockings he
stopped her with a touch.

"Leave them on," he whispered.

Erica hesitated, then gave a jerky nod. He fumbled on
the table for a condom and handed her the packet which she
promptly dropped. She flashed him a nervous smile.

"I'm sorry," he said. "I don't want to rush you. You just get
me going like..."

"Me too," she said, finding the foil square and raising it in
triumph. "Show me how."

"I don't need to show you a thing."

Erica let the melting effect of his kiss send her floating in
languid bliss. If only their lovemaking could be the same.

She couldn't help it. When Matt kneed her legs apart she
tensed. All of her. Closing her eyes she willed herself to relax.
When he didn't do anything further she opened her eyes,
afraid of what she might see in his expression. He'd propped
himself above her and was gazing at her face with concern.

"What is it?"

Erica gnawed her lower lip. It seemed so silly. Such a
small thing, really. "I, uh, I've never..."

"Never what?" he asked, smoothing her tangled hair
back from her face, his touch unbearably gentle.

She turned her head away. "Forget it."

"Whatever it is, you can tell me."

She opened her eyes wide. Why did she believe him? As if there should be no secrets between them. Ever. "I've never had a...you know..."

"An orgasm?"

She nodded, wishing she didn't sound like such a freak. She'd read about women who had multiples, five, ten, even twenty, while she herself would happily settle for one.

"In that case," he said, his words a throaty murmur, "allow me to be the first."

She swallowed. What if she couldn't? What if there was something wrong with her?

"The big secret is to relax. Totally."

"I'll try," she whispered, as he began stroking her in places she'd never been stroked before, the inside of her elbow, behind her knee, the soles of her feet. And while his fingers were busy, so was his mouth, moving from her breasts to her navel to the palm of her hand. His tongue, his lips, his fingers all combined to chart such a wondrous journey of eroticism that she hardly noticed when his touch climbed from the inside of her thigh to the place between her legs where the pressure had been steadily mounting.

As he separated the sensitive folds she realized that she was incredibly hot and slickly damp, a sensation that increased tenfold as his thumb slid past the swollen lips to a spot which felt as if every nerve ending centered in it. Her legs felt limp and she was certain she couldn't move them if she wanted to, but when his fingers brushed that sensitive nub her whole body jerked. His movements stilled and she almost groaned in frustration, aware of her entire being straining toward some unreachable distant point.

Switching tactics, he tongued her breasts, first one and then the other, suckling them greedily, and she felt her body react with a huge outpouring of heat, like a scalding wall of flames, threatening to incinerate the two of them. His movements escalated, as did the pressure of his fingers and mouth. She was unable to inhale deeply, managing only little panting gasps as her limbs strained, her entire body stretching for something just out of reach.

And then it came. A tidal wave of shattering sensation. She threaded her fingers through Matt's hair. Her legs stiffened. She cried out as her entire body convulsed against his.

The experience left her dazed. When Matt leaned over and brushed her lips with his she realized she was bathed in perspiration and still had her fingers twined tightly in his hair. She inhaled with a shuddering breath. She'd never be the same again. Releasing him, she smiled against his lips. "I was going to say thank you but that seems rather inadequate," she whispered.

He smoothed the damp strands of hair back from her face. "Happy to oblige."

"But what about you?" She struggled to a sitting position.

"My turn's coming. Shall we try for a record? See how many orgasms you can have before sunrise?"

"Could we?" She laughed with newfound delight. Suddenly, with Matt, anything seemed possible.

He groaned in pleasure as she eagerly caught on to the knack of unrolling the thin plastic, pausing to marvel at the pulsing heat she held in her hands.

"Erica!" His teeth were clenched and beads of sweat had popped onto his forehead.

"Oh, sorry," she murmured. "I just can't believe how it stretches." He gave a little groan, then a laugh, and she buried her face in his shoulder. "I can't believe I just said that."

"Nothing you say surprises me."

Erica held her breath as he raised himself over her, poised at the opening to the core of her womanhood, using her liquid heat as lubricant before he eased into her.

She raised her hips as leverage, urging him deeper, feeling the wondrous friction as their bodies became joined. She wasn't prepared for the rush of heat as he started to move, slowly at first, teeth gritted as if in pain.

"Is something wrong?"

"You're just so tight. I'm afraid I'll hurt you."

"You couldn't possibly." As she spoke she wrapped her legs around his waist, raising herself to him, increasing the momentum of their bodies.

As he matched her thrust for thrust, Erica felt again that swamping heat low in her belly, radiating outward with growing intensity, until she was gasping for breath, and when her release came, so did his, a shared explosion of sensation.

**

Matt sank down, propped on his elbows so as not to crush her with his full weight. Their wet bodies, joined from shoulder to ankle, throbbed with ebbing heat as if they were one body rather than two. His muscles felt like mush, but his blood was singing with a power he'd never known before.

He stared at her closed lids and parted lips, listened as her breathing slowed. What had she done to him? Rolling to lie beside her, he thought, for a second, of getting up to have a cigarette and regain his sense of separateness. To stand back and think about what had happened to him.

No. He wanted to stay close to her, mind and body, exploring this unfamiliar sense of oneness with her. He took her hand and held it against his lips until his own breathing and the beat of his heart was normal again.

But he shouldn't let his guard down like this. Better if he forced his mind back to the case. Reaching out, he tangled his fingers through her thick hair. Her eyes opened and her smile was almost his undoing.

"This is a rotten time to bring it up, Erica," he said, his eyes caressing her face as his hand stroked her hair. "You've just lost two people you loved. But I'm positive there's a connection to the fire that took your mother." He smoothed her eyebrows with the tips of his fingers. "You're the key. Will you undergo hypnosis; see if you can recall what happened that night?"

Her relaxed expression was replaced by a haunted look. "Matt, please don't ask that of me. What good can it do? That night was so long ago."

"It might accomplish nothing," he admitted, "but I know there's a link. Even one tiny detail might be enough to crack the case."

She stirred, his words turning the languid aftermath of love into restlessness. "I don't want to rake up the past again. I can't believe there's anything to remember."

"You won't do it? Even if it might solve the case?"

She slid off the bed and went to the window, pulling the curtain aside to gaze out. The pale dawn backlit her breasts and the smooth sweep of her hips and he yearned to taste her skin again, feel the length of her body against his. Desperate, he tried to shift his mind back to the case, but it was no use. Desire pounded in his veins, bringing every nerve to quivering anticipation.

Turning, Erica spoke. "All right, I'll do it." She came toward him, the sheen of her skin like music in the dim light.

He held his hand out. "I know it's asking a lot..."

"But you'd do anything if it meant maybe solving the case. So would I. Let's not talk about it anymore." She looked down at his body for a long moment. The caress of her eyes brought instantaneous reaction and he pulled her down beside him.

"Your wish is my command," he whispered. Sliding a hand under her head, he bent to taste the soft fullness of her lips. His other hand moved to the satin skin of her breasts and the hardening nipples that thrust against his palm.

He heard her quick intake of breath as she took him in her seeking fingers and found him as hot and hard and urgent as before. The sweetness of her stroking swept him, mindless, into the full flood of passion.

***

Later, he stood watching her sleep, dark lashes curling on her cheeks, tired lines smoothed away by the release of love. He ached to hold her, fall asleep beside her. Instead, he reached for his clothes. Better leave now. He needed to get away, needed space and time to get his emotions under control.

At the door he stopped for one last look. It seemed callous to slip away without a word, without acknowledging the incredible intensity of what had happened between them. So what was he going to do? Leave her a note like some half-baked teenager? Pointless. He'd never find words to describe the effect she had on him.

Outside in the fresh, damp air, birds were chattering in the trees as the first faint golden light from the sun warmed the eastern horizon. Matt lit a cigarette, inhaling the smoke deep into his lungs. It tasted great, even if he was a little light-headed and his tongue felt thick. He ought to go home and sleep, but his mind was wide awake. Besides, he should relieve Glenn; his partner hadn't had any sleep, either.

He looked up at Ronya's tattered mansion and remembered Dale had been her friend, too. Or her tool? But the idea didn't feel right. Damn it, he had to lay off the gut feelings. He didn't really know what Erica's aunt was capable of.

He butted his cigarette in a niche in the stone wall and straightened up to see Ronya, swathed neck to ankle in sweaters and skirts, wandering among the roses, followed by three cavorting tabby cats. He walked up the slope to meet her.

She didn't seem surprised to see him. "Hello, Lieutenant. Did you bring Erica home from the fire?"

Startled, he said, "How did *you* know about the fire?"

Her gaze was penetrating. "I wasn't there, if that's what you're thinking. They said on the news just now there was a fatality."

He decided to postpone the evil moment. "Erica says you're doing a series of paintings on fires."

"Oh, yes. Yes." She stared at the bright horizon. "I'm doing preliminary sketches and studies just now. That's why I was at the fires, you know. Erica said you have pictures of me." She said it as if the photos were a compliment to her.

"We always photograph crowds at a fire. Pyromaniacs usually can't resist watching what they've done."

"Poor Philip," she sighed. "Lieutenant, was that a bad fire this morning? Was it one of the tenants who died?"

He couldn't put it off any longer. "I wish I didn't have to tell you this, but the man who died this morning was Dale Todd."

Her body jerked as her hand flew to her mouth. "Oh, no! Not Dale!" She turned to look at a shrubbery version of a giraffe. When she turned back, tears were sliding down her cheeks. Her voice was an anguished whisper. "Lieutenant, when is this going to end? Suzanne, Philip, Dale. Why? *Why?* Which of us will be next?"

Matt followed her gaze to Erica's carriage house. Could Erica be in danger?

His thoughts raced. Not only was she investigating the fires, she was part of this ill-fated family. She might have incriminating knowledge without being aware of it. Yes, there was danger. The hypnosis seemed doubly urgent now. The arsonist *had* to be caught before he struck again.

Ronya's quavery voice broke in on his thoughts. "That apartment house is built on the spot where my sister Suzanne died. Does Erica realize that?"

He resisted the urge to put his arm around her slumped shoulders. "Yes, she does." Matt thought of Erica's body entwined with his, her joy in her new-found capacity for ecstasy. He was tempted again to go back to her bed and sleep beside her, but he couldn't do that. Not yet. "She'll need you to be with her when she wakes up."

Ronya's eyes seemed to look right inside him. "More than yourself, Lieutenant? I think not."

He couldn't keep the derision from his words. "An Irish cop from the wrong side of the tracks?"

"How a person sees himself is more important than how others see him." Her gaze was ingenuous, earnest.

He reached for a second cigarette. She was right. It was now that mattered, not the past, not their roots. Not what anyone else thought.

He sucked in smoke, exhaling it into the clear morning air. Funny how good it made him feel that Ronya approved of him being with Erica. Funny and scary. He hadn't bargained for all these emotions muddying his clear goal of playing a lone hand.

He didn't need the emotions. His life had space for only one need: to work. He'd needed Lynne and lost her, she'd needed him and he'd failed her; he'd done enough damage for one lifetime.

"I'll keep an eye on her." He paced away, then back. "Do you think Dale could have committed suicide?"

Her eyes opened wide. "Never! Dale was a survivor."

"What about setting fires?"

She looked dazed. "A man who cared for plants and animals like Dale did, setting fires?" She turned and waved a hand at her house. "In there, curled up in a little blanket-lined box that Dale made for her, is the kitten he rescued yesterday. I can't believe he set those fires."

He didn't want to believe it either.

"I'm going to name the kitten 'Toddy,'" Ronya said. "She looks like him, you know."

Matt threw his cigarette down and ground it under his heel. Why had Dale been in that apartment house?

And what made Ronya Germaine tick? At times she was quite sane and sensible. At others, she seemed to be in a different world. Had her lover's death soured her so much that she preferred fantasy to the real world?

She put her hand on his arm. "Lieutenant, watch over Erica." Her voice dropped to a whisper. "The Fates are closing in on us."

Matt's shiver was involuntary. His mother used to say a shiver like that meant somebody had walked over his grave. "I will. Don't worry." It occurred to him then that she might be able to help him with the twenty-two year old fire, the one that had killed Erica's mother.

"The night of Mrs. Rawlins' death, she and Erica cancelled plans to be away overnight. Perhaps something to do with Mr. Rawlins' business trip?"

"Suzanne's plans had nothing to do with Eric." Ronya sighed and rearranged the voluminous folds of her clothing. "Philip was taking her and Erica to Mandellini that evening but something happened to prevent it. I don't recall what, though knowing Philip, it was likely some theatrical crisis."

She reached down to pet one of the tabbies rubbing around her ankles. "Eric idolized her, you know. I think he felt so guilty about not being there to save her from the fire that he blocked out all memory of it."

"Memory of the fire?" asked Matt, incredulous.

"Oh, no, Lieutenant. Memory of the separation. He and Suzanne were separated at the time."

Chapter Twenty

Stuck in the Monday morning commuter traffic crossing the Golden Gate bridge, Matt thought about Eric Rawlins. How could a man 'forget' he'd been legally separated from his wife? But Rawlins had an ego the size of Texas; he'd never admit that any woman would think of leaving him, let alone do it.

It was already after eight when he walked into the SIS squad room, eyes gritty, stomach rumbling. He hadn't taken time to go home and shower or eat. There was just too damn much to do.

Mendoza, looking chipper with a fresh shave and a clean shirt, grinned. "Hey, the boss came to work straight from the party, fellas. Musta been some party, Matt, huh?"

"The Russian Hill fire was no party," he snapped. Now he wished he'd taken the time to change, at least. He'd be hearing about this for a long time.

"Musta been a fire he lit himself," somebody else said, setting off a ripple of snickers. "Davenport's been looking after the Russian Hill set."

Matt gritted his teeth and grabbed a coffee. The cop was wrong about one thing. He hadn't set the fire that consumed him and Erica before dawn this morning. Neither had she. The spark had been there, between them, from the beginning. A slow burn, until the flames had erupted a few hours ago. There'd be no stopping it now. Unless he stayed away from her.

As Matt sat down, Glenn walked in. "I got Todd's address. You coming to have a look-see or are you going to drink that poison?"

Matt left the coffee without a second thought. "Let's go!"

Dale Todd's rooming house was almost as old and shabby as the landlord who answered their knock. He handed over the key to Dale's room and said, "Help yourself," as soon as they'd flashed their IDs.

The room was big but without character, containing only a sagging double bed, a wardrobe, a chest of drawers, one worn armchair and stacks of newspapers and racing forms. There weren't even any pictures on the wall. All very dull and dreary. Except for one thing.

In the middle of the bed lay a folded sheet and printed on it in big letters were the words, "For the cops."

Matt flipped it open with his pen. The words were printed, too. "I set the fires in the warehouse, garage, boat shop, ladys store, theater, Fillmore. Mandell was an accidint. I can't live with it no more." The note was signed 'Dale Todd.'

Glenn, grinning, said, "Looks like the son of a bitch chickened out before we got him! Maybe I can go home and get some sleep after all."

Matt's elation on reading the note began to subside. "You think this confession is for real?"

Glenn said, "I'd sure like to think so, but let's get the fingerprints and writing checked before we open the champagne."

Matt nodded. He couldn't help thinking of Erica's conviction that Dale wouldn't have committed suicide or set fires. And Ronya agreed with her. "Let's take a quick look, then get the homicide boys in here to do a real search. Grab a couple of those racing forms for handwriting samples."

Five minutes of rifling through drawers produced nothing, not even a list of phone numbers. "Todd must have had a great memory," Matt said. His fingers found a small object in the back of the bedside table drawer. "Looks like a safety deposit box key."

There was no number on the key, no tag to indicate what it might open. Matt frowned, then pocketed it. "Let's talk to the landlord. Todd's got to have a car somewhere. The old guy might know where it is."

The landlord grumbled about being disturbed again but told them the car was parked around the back. Glenn said, "Let's leave it for the Homicide boys. They might as well do it the same time as the room."

As they drove back to the station, Matt said, "If Philip Mandell's death was an accident, like the note says, why was he being tailed?"

"Jealous husband, jealous girlfriend?"

Matt said, "Could have been Hans Zeigler."

"Anything's possible, I guess, but Zeigler doesn't seem to have any real motive for murder. I can't believe he'd want to take over the Peninsula Players so badly that he'd kill for it."

"Let's see what Homicide and the autopsy report give us. We might not have to look any further than Todd," Matt said. He felt nostalgic for Homicide. If he was still with them, he'd be helping the boys take Todd's room and car apart, trying to make sense out the things they found. Or should have found and didn't. SIS was a move up, but it hadn't given him much satisfaction.

Still, all he'd dealt with was the Gilbey case and these seven apparently senseless fires, so it wasn't surprising that he felt no sense of accomplishment. Time he quit brooding about Gilbey, anyway.

But what about Todd? The suicide note didn't feel right. It confessed to setting the fires, but gave no reason. If the note wasn't genuine, somebody had killed him. And if he was right about a link between Suzanne Rawlins' death and Philip Mandell's, the criminal almost had to be one of Erica's family.

Which meant that Erica, because she was investigating the fires and might come up with something incriminating, was definitely in danger. Too early to phone her, though. She needed to sleep.

At the station, Mendoza said, "Matt, I found the PI that was tailing Mandell. She's waiting in the second interview room."

The woman was middle-aged, her looks nondescript, but her smile was friendly. "Glenda Wilson," she said, rising to shake hands with him.

"Lieutenant Nicols. We're investigating the murder of Philip Mandell, director of Peninsula Players. I understand you were tailing him earlier this month."

"I'd never heard of Philip Mandell until your detective mentioned the name."

Matt felt his jaw sag. "What?"

"I'm sorry, Lieutenant, but I was never assigned to anyone of that name."

"Then who..."

She smiled. "The name 'Peninsula Players' told me which case I must have been working on and since that case is closed, I can tell you who. Though I'd appreciate if you kept the details to yourself."

"But we were told by two members of the Peninsula Players that Mandell was being followed."

"It may have looked like that, but it was Hans Zeigler I was tailing."

"Zeigler!" Matt felt as if someone had smacked him between the eyes. "Can you tell me who hired you?"

"Sure. A jealous wife."

Matt swore.

"It's all over with," Glenda Wilson said, smiling. "Her husband and Zeigler are now living in cozy domesticity in an apartment off Geary."

Back in the squad room, Matt bit down hard on a sugar cube as he said to Glenn, "Well, that didn't get us anywhere. And I may just charge that bastard with wasting police time."

Glenn rose and stretched. "I wouldn't bother. Zeigler probably thought he was telling the truth. He's too full of himself to imagine that anyone would dare interfere with his love life. Anyway, I'm heading home for some shut-eye." He grinned. "About time you went to bed, too. Or could that be *back* to bed?"

"Piss off, Davenport."

Glenn left and Matt considered his next move. At the top of his list was Eric Rawlins. He'd been Dale Todd's boss for a lot of years. He reached for the phone.

***

At noon Matt got two take-out cheeseburgers and a can of Coke, then phoned Erica. There was no answer at the carriage house, and her cell went to voice mail. Where could she have gone? Surely not to her office already. Frowning, he dialed ICPB.

"Sorry," said the receptionist. "Ms. Johnson hasn't checked in yet today. Can I take a message?"

Matt hung up. Where in hell was she?

He was scrabbling in his pockets for a sugar lump when Hodgekiss called. "I'm sending the autopsy report over by courier, Matt. Todd was shot once through the heart at close range."

"Close enough range for suicide?"

"It's possible."

"I hope the damn gun shows some prints," Matt said. "If it doesn't, either the fire burned them off or the killer wore gloves and we still won't know whether it was suicide or murder."

Matt chewed up yet another sugar cube, hoping the sugar hit would get his brain moving so he could eliminate some of the 'ifs.'

By three-thirty he'd roughed out a report on the Russian Hill fire and the lab had phoned to say that the gun found with Todd had killed him but they couldn't get any prints off it. Figured. Maybe the St. Christopher medal wasn't doing him any good at all.

Between sessions on the phone and studying the report, he called the carriage house, Ronya, and Erica's cell a dozen times. Why couldn't the damn woman check in? Had something happened to her?

At four, a team from Homicide walked in. "Here's a list of the stuff in Todd's room, for what it's worth."

"How about the car?"

"You're gonna love this, Matt. We found a big leather briefcase in the trunk. And guess what, it smells like gasoline."

"You mean an honest-to-God piece of evidence? I couldn't be so lucky."

The cop chortled and tossed a plastic bag on the desk. "Thought you might like to see what we found in his room. Under the bed, right where they'd be handy." He upended the bag and out tumbled bright purple, lacy peek-a-boo panties and bra, a length of silk rope and a pair of handcuffs.

Matt stared at this haul. From the little he'd seen of Todd, the man didn't look like a Romeo, especially not a kinky Romeo. He didn't look like a cross dresser, either. He reminded himself that looks, like money, didn't define the person. He put the things back in the bag and handed it to the Homicide cop.

As the cop left, Erica walked in.

"Where the *hell* have you been? I've been trying to reach you all day and nobody knew where you were."

***

Erica glanced from Matt to the interested faces of his fellow officers. "Doesn't look like you've been home lately yourself," she drawled. No one but Matt had to know he was responsible for the color in her cheeks and the spring in her step. Or that she couldn't move without recalling in scintillating detail the intimacy they'd shared a few hours before and the precious gift he'd given her.

Matt reddened at the barely suppressed guffaws from the other men and glanced away, but not before she saw the beginnings of a grin tugging at his lips.

"Score one for Erica," said one of the junior officers.

"You, uh, didn't think to text me?" she continued.

Open laughter now. "Score two," someone else called.

"I was busy," Matt muttered.

"So was I," Erica murmured, swooping close to him. "Shall we get together and compare notes?"

"Compare notes on what?" This from the back of the room.

Matt glowered at his task force and snapped, "We may have had a breakthrough in the case. That doesn't mean the paperwork disappears. Everybody got that?" The answering grumbles and murmurs confirmed that everybody did.

Erica's eyes were riveted on Matt, her lips forming the words soundlessly. *What breakthrough?*

"Let's get out of here!" In the hall he grabbed her hand and yanked her along behind him. She almost had to run to keep from being dragged. Outside, around the corner of the station house, he pushed her up against the wall and gave her a long bruising kiss.

Erica was breathing hard when he finally released her.

"God, I've been wanting to do that all day," he said. "Where were you?"

Erica caught his face between her hands. "Can we do it again, with a little advance warning?"

"Anything you want." This time she kissed him, her tongue swirling light teasing patterns inside his mouth, which she'd discovered earlier drove him out of his mind. She felt him harden against her immediately, felt her body respond with a sweet melting rush of heat. She clung to him, afraid her legs would betray her if she tried to stand unaided. They both fought for breath.

Stepping back, he tucked her arm through his. "We'd better quit this before we embarrass ourselves. Come on, I'll buy you a coffee," he said, with a gruffness that Erica knew was designed to disguise the effect she had on him.

She ran her tongue over her still throbbing lips. "Missed me, did you? Serves you right for running out this morning without waking me."

He stopped so abruptly she plowed right into him. "I kind of figured you might need your sleep."

She tilted her head and gave him a saucy look. "But not you, Superman?" She looked again. "I knew something was different." Her hand went to his jaw and stroked it. "You shaved this morning."

He resumed his pace. "Guilty as charged. But I'd like to talk to you about that poor excuse for a razor you keep in your bathroom."

"You used my razor?"

"Nicked myself good for my troubles, too," he said as he pushed open the door to the dingy neighborhood coffee shop and ushered her to a dark booth at the back. "Two espressos, Nicky," he called to the counterman.

Erica glanced around and gave him a cheeky grin. "Well," she said, "first McDonald's and now here. It just keeps getting better with you, Matt."

The way he shifted around on the seat, she knew he was uncomfortable. Because of his arousal? Or because he wanted to say something she wouldn't like? Reaching across the table, he captured her hand in both of his, turning it over to smooth the lifeline in her palm. Even this light touch sent blood pulsing through her veins.

Matt cleared his throat. Here it comes, Erica thought. He's going to say he wants me off the case. "Tell me about the breakthrough."

Nicky brought the espressos and Matt released her, settling back in his seat. Erica watched in disbelief as he dropped five sugar lumps into his cup. "You first."

Her coffee was black as mud. Why did she have the feeling she'd need its caffeine jolt? "Ronya told me about the talk you had with her this morning. I'd never heard of a separation, so I went and asked my father about it."

Matt blew on his coffee. "I assume he denied it?"

She couldn't help the sharpness of her tone. "How did you know?"

"Paid him a visit myself. He didn't mention you having been there, though."

"He wouldn't," Erica said. "After I left his office I got a message to call Justin Mandell." Matt sat up straight, poised on the edge of his seat.

"And?"

"We had lunch," Erica said, before taking a cautious sip of her own coffee.

"You planning on telling me what you both ate, or cut to the chase?"

"Justin heard about Dale on the news this morning and called me. It seems that his loyal loving wife, Cheryl, had been having an affair with Dale for quite some time."

She heard the hiss as Matt exhaled through his teeth. "That *is* interesting. But why tell you?"

"He guessed I'd be working with you on the investigation. He didn't want the police stumbling onto the fact and maybe making public disclosure."

"You mean like newspaper headlines screaming, *Mystery woman sought in arson investigation*," Matt drawled. "Complete with a police artist's sketch."

"Something like that," Erica said. "He's never confronted Cheryl. He just hoped it would run its course."

"And now it has, poor bastard."

Erica didn't know if he meant Dale or Justin.

"So if we talk to his wife he'd appreciate us being discreet, is that the upshot?"

"In a nutshell."

Matt sat back and crossed his arms. "I'm always impressed when good citizens come forward and cooperate."

"Don't be such a cynic," Erica said. "He's thinking about Auguste's delicate health, not the Mandell family name."

"I guess." Matt was staring off past her head. "Think Cheryl Mandell's capable of arson and murder?"

"I think she's capable of anything if she stands to gain from it. Now it's your turn. What breakthrough?"

"We searched Dale Todd's room this morning," Matt said. "Found a suicide note. In it he confessed to setting all the fires, including the one that killed Philip."

Erica sucked in her breath.

"I take it that surprises you."

Erica thought about the tiny orange kitten whose life Dale had saved. She glanced up at Matt, but doubted he'd be very impressed with the story. "Yes, it does."

"Why?"

Erica pursed her lips. "In some ways he fits the psychological profile of a criminal. He's a loner and not terribly well-educated. But in other ways he doesn't fit at all because..."

"He's got a record for breaking and entering," Matt cut in. "Spent ten months inside for that. He either went straight after he was released or never got caught. Until now. So what doesn't fit?"

"I've known him forever. I never felt he had a lot of pent-up anger or frustration or hostility, the way most arsonists do. Yes, he was a loner, but he'd had the same job and the same support network, my father and Ronya, for years. That provided more stability for him than many non-criminals can lay claim to."

"He could have been acting on someone else's orders."

"Like who?" She studied his face. Damn it, he looked good! It was hard to keep her mind on the case. Then it hit her what he was getting at. "My father? Give it up, Matt. There's nothing in it for him. He never does anything unless it benefits him personally."

Matt shrugged. "What about Cheryl?"

"Well, she's certainly got a lot of pent-up anger and hostility. Do you suppose...? No. It's entirely too far-fetched."

"What is?"

She leaned toward him and dropped her voice to a whisper. "Unless it was part of some weird sex ritual?"

Matt burst out laughing. "You mean like they watched the flames together and got it on at the same time?"

Erica flushed. "It was just a thought."

Matt sobered. "Don't worry, we'll check on Cheryl. She must have known Justin would inherit once Philip was dead and that gives her a major motive. Community property being what it is, she'd walk away with millions for her half of the vineyard."

Erica propped her chin on her hand. "Something doesn't ring true about the suicide note. It's too pat."

"That's what my gut's been screaming all day, too. But unless we come up with something new, Bailey's going to close the book on this one. I know how he thinks. We lost a lead today, too."

"What happened?"

"We found the PI who was supposed to be tailing Philip and guess what? It was Zeigler she was after." He frowned at Erica, who had started to giggle, then shook his head. "Anyway, the whole case stinks. And I still think it goes back twenty-two years."

Erica flinched. "How could it?"

"I don't know, but I have this hunch that just keeps gnawing at me and if I'm right, you're in danger. Promise me you'll be careful."

She leaned forward and caught his shirt, drawing him closer. "You could, uh, not let me out of your sight."

"A pleasant prospect, except I'd never sell Bailey on it. Especially if he decides Todd's death closes the case. But there's the idea of hypnosis. I still think it's worth a shot."

Erica released him and sat back, lips pressed in a thin line. "That's not fair. You caught me in a weak moment."

He clasped her wrist, his thumb stroking and teasing the soft flesh on the inner side. "You mean you'd have agreed to anything I said?"

Her eyes closed as she recalled their closeness. The heat of their embrace. The incinerating passion that flared between them, hotter than any arson blaze. Her lids lifted. She gazed into his eyes. "Anything."

Without releasing her he stood and dug into his pocket with his free hand, tossing a few bills onto the table.

She scrambled to her feet. "Where are we going?"

Matt snugged her against his side. "Some place you'll agree to anything I say."

"You mean an interrogation room?"

"No, I mean my place."

Chapter Twenty-One

"Why do you keep looking at me like that?" Matt leaned toward her, his voice a husky whisper in deference to the occasion.

Erica managed a careless shrug. "I wouldn't have pegged you as owning a suit, that's all." She'd been looking more at him than his suit, but he didn't have to know that. Probably wouldn't want to know it.

Somber music issued from the organ at the back of the tiny chapel. He frowned and looked down at himself. "Something wrong with my suit?"

"Not a thing." Indeed, the three-piece charcoal wool suit hugged his rangy frame and lent him an unexpected air of respectability.

"I bought it for all those baptisms. Seems my family views the bachelor uncle as the ideal godfather."

Erica turned toward him. "You come from a big family, don't you?" Their early morning session of love-making had included very little sharing of other intimacies. Matt seemed reluctant to discuss his past and she knew it had to do with that girl Francie had told her about. Yet more than once he'd said only the present mattered. Who was he trying to convince?

The music swelled and she missed his response. "What did you say?" she whispered, touching his arm and letting her fingers linger there.

He dipped his head closer. "There were eight of us."

"Eight?" Erica repeated, incredulous.

Matt tugged at his tie. "Yeah."

"Aren't you lucky!"

"Not in a house with only one bathroom."

She envied him the experience of growing up in a real family. He must have had a deep sense of belonging. "Were you the oldest?"

He shook his head. "Middle."

She heard footsteps and looked back to see her father and Ronya. Her aunt, bulky and rag-tag in layers of black, slid into the seat next to her. Her father saw her hand resting on Matt's arm, glared at her and went to sit directly behind them.

He knows about Matt and me, she thought. Or suspects. And I don't care. I want his approval, but it's no longer the most important thing in my life. The realization was like a weight being lifted from her shoulders.

Her father had to learn to accept her for who she was. That what she did for a living or who she spent time with was her choice.

Few chairs were occupied when the minister stood to say a few words about Dale Todd. Even Cheryl hadn't bothered to show up. Afterwards, the chapel emptied quickly. Erica thought of the way Dale had loved to tend plants and animals and felt a pang of sadness that so few people were affected by his passing.

"I wasn't aware that attending memorial services numbered among the duties of our hardworking law officials," her father said as the four of them walked out into the mellow fall day.

"It doesn't. I'm here because I wanted to come," Matt responded. Erica heard a funny note in his voice and shot him a long look. There was something odd about the way he looked at her father.

"Come along, Ronya," Rawlins said, his voice brusque with impatience. "I have a pressing appointment. Erica, can I drop you at home?"

"I'll see the ladies home, sir."

Erica's jaw dropped. Matt being deferential? She'd never have believed it if she hadn't seen it. And in the car, even after shedding tie and jacket and rolling up his sleeves, he was silent. Ronya, seemingly unaware of the undercurrents, prattled on about old times until they reached the house, where she heaved herself out of the car and gave them a cheery wave.

"Will she be okay alone?"

"She's tougher than she looks," Erica said. "And she hates being coddled."

Matt nodded. "You ride Western?" he asked.

She slanted him a cautious look. "Sure. Why?"

"Riding's the best way I know to blow the cobwebs out of my head. You wanna tag along?" He made it sound as if he didn't care one way or the other.

"You mean like a real date?" Erica teased.

Matt scowled. "Something like that."

"Sure. Just give me a minute to lose the basic black."

He waited in the car while she tossed on jeans and a flannel shirt and grabbed her hat, boots and gloves.

As Erica settled onto the seat, not crowding him, but not hunched against her door either, Matt flipped his half-smoked cigarette out the window. "I'm not your mother," she said. "I'm not going to yell at you for smoking."

He turned the key. "Yelling wasn't her thing. Just a sad, disappointed look on her face when we screwed up. The old man cornered the market on yelling, especially after he'd downed a few whiskies, and nobody paid him any attention anyway. But all Ma had to do was give us one look and she had us squirming."

"She must be an amazing lady. To raise eight kids without ever raising her voice."

"Yeah."

"Is your family still in the east?'

"Most of them."

"And do you all get together? Christmases and stuff?"

"Some do. I haven't been back in a while."

"How long?"

He shot her an impatient look. "What is this? Interrogation time?"

Matt's bluster didn't fool her for a minute. It was merely his protective shell. She'd had several glimpses of his vulnerable side and she was willing to bet the knowledge scared him. Turning toward him, she laid her arm across the back of the seat, fingers not quite brushing his shoulder.

"You know everything about me. I want to know about you."

Matt blew out an impatient breath. "Why do women do this? You sleep with a guy and suddenly you need to know the name of his kindergarten teacher."

Erica laughed. "I bet it was Sister Mary Somebody. And don't you know most women believe that talking is the glue that holds a relationship together?"

With a wary look, he said, "Is that what we have? A relationship?"

"Of sorts."

"How do you figure?"

"Simple. You invited me riding. For men, a relationship is held together by shared activities."

Matt snorted. "You should have been a shrink."

"I thought about it but, actually, I started out to be a lawyer. My father liked the idea of having a lawyer in the family."

"How's he feel about the detour?"

"It doesn't matter. It used to, but I'm learning to lead my own life, not the one he wants for me." She hesitated. "I'm sure you realize what made me choose arson investigation as a career. Subconsciously, I wanted to solve the mystery of my mother's death."

As if unable to help himself, Matt's free hand snaked out and gave her knee a light, reassuring squeeze.

Erica caught her breath. He cared how she felt. He had to care; there was no other explanation.

"Do you know a woman is more likely to be hurt by a man's silence than by his words?"

"Who imparted that bit of folk wisdom?"

"No one. I learned it living with my father."

"That your way of telling me I'd better keep talking?"

"Darn right," Erica said, her tone light. "It's accepted wisdom that women like to talk about their thoughts and feelings. Men, on the other hand, dismiss their feelings or keep them buried. Result? Basic communication breakdown between the sexes."

"If you're so smart, how come your marriage failed?" He gave her a quick look. "Sorry, I was making assumptions. Maybe you're a widow."

"No, you were right the first time. I married Trevor for all the wrong reasons." She shifted uneasily, feeling the ghost of the dead girl a tangible barrier between them. She wanted to know what had happened, the same as she wanted to know about everything in his life, but asking questions like that would only make him clam up.

The air smelled cleaner among Mill Valley's sloping green and brown hills. At the sight of a 'For Sale' sign, Matt braked to a sudden halt at the side of the road and, without a word of explanation, stared at the run-down barns and unkempt acres.

"Thinking of moving out here?" Erica asked eventually.

"I might."

"Pretty long commute to the station."

"There are other things in life besides police work."

"Owning a ranch, for example?"

"Not just any ranch." As he spoke he guided the car back onto the road.

"A special ranch?" Erica probed. "Show horses?"

"More than that. Some place where kids can get a taste of life away from the street." He glanced over at Erica. "What? You're looking at me like that again."

She smiled. "That's two surprises in one day, Lieutenant. I'm not sure how many more I can take."

Matt was silent as he navigated the winding driveway to the stables and parked beside a corral. She got out of the car, stretched her legs and soaked up the smells of stable, grass and crisp fall air. But it seemed no time before Matt was back, garbed in his familiar jeans and a soft denim shirt, and leading two horses.

***

"Tony saddled Ginger for you," Matt said. "Blackie's got a soft spot for her."

"I get the feeling Blackie's not the only one."

"Here." He dropped several sugar lumps into her palm. "Ginger's got a sweet tooth."

Erica grinned, a teasing twinkle in her eyes. "We both *know* she's not the only one."

Matt gave her a leg-up into the saddle. "When did you get so mouthy?"

She grinned. "Blame your bad influence."

He grunted and mounted Black Satin. His influence couldn't be all bad. Erica's eyes were sparkling as Ginger pranced beneath her.

Matt indicated a trail that led toward a wooded area. "Go ahead," he said. Erica clucked to Ginger and headed off down the trail, Blackie trotting to catch up.

Matt watched Erica closely, admiring the way she rode. Especially the way her pert butt bounced along in front of him. Sex with her was great. So why wasn't it enough? Why did he have the urge to plumb the depths of her mind as well as her body? Until now, possession of a woman's body had been enough.

Matt reached over and patted Blackie's neck. The creak of leather and smell of horse was heaven after the exhaust fumes and noise of the city. So Erica figured he should keep talking, did she? Maybe, if he wanted what she called a 'relationship.' But he didn't. He just wanted to ride and relax, let his mind go blank.

So why wouldn't it?

He knew why. The answer was trotting along right in front of him.

Cresting the hill, they looked down on rolling pastureland. "Let's go!" Matt nudged Black Satin to a trot, then a canter and finally, a full gallop. He heard Ginger's hoof beats close behind.

The horses were breathing hard and snorting as they slowed to walk up the next hill. Erica was smiling, pink-cheeked. "I'll have to introduce you to my mare someday."

"I'd like that." His words came spontaneously and he realized that he meant them, that he wanted to commit himself to doing things together. He rolled the word 'relationship' around in his mind, getting used to the sound of it.

"I'm thinking about having Missy bred again. Her colt, Merlin, looks like he's going to be a winner."

"Missy?" said Matt. "That's not a very classy name."

"And Blackie is?" Erica retorted. "I'll have you know her full name is Mistress Morgana. She lives up to the name, too. She can be a witch when she wants."

"Blackie is short for Black Satin."

"She looks like satin, too."

An hour later they stopped to let the horses rest. Seated on the ground, back against a tree trunk, Matt uncorked his canteen. Across from him Erica seemed as relaxed on the ground as in a saddle, knees bent, jeans tucked into the tops of well-worn riding boots. She was so damned easy to be with! And dynamite in bed. His loins stirred at the memory.

She'd discarded her hat and a slight breeze played with the ends of her hair. She'd got under his skin in a big way. Being with her seemed to deepen his need for her instead of sating it. He hadn't felt this way since Lynne died. He hadn't wanted to ever feel that way about a woman again.

He turned his head toward the grazing horses so he wouldn't have to see her expression when he told her. "By the way, I've set up an appointment for you with a hypnotherapist. Tomorrow at nine."

Chapter Twenty-Two

Matt hadn't been in Lee's office for months, not since he'd brought in a murder witness for hypnosis, back when he was in Homicide. The leather sling chair were still comfortable, the soft jazz from the wall speakers soothing, but neither calmed his thoughts. Lee had warned him that even if Erica was susceptible to hypnosis, regression to her childhood might not be possible.

He prayed, surprised at how easily the old habit came back to him, that Erica would remember something he could use. But more important, that she'd come through the ordeal unscathed.

The door to Lee's inner sanctum opened and the hypnotherapist said, "You can come in now, Lieutenant." He added, in a low voice, "She went into the trance very quickly. I think this is going to work."

Almost holding his breath, Matt went in, closed the door, and sat in the chair Lee indicated. Erica was lying back in a recliner, eyes closed and, unlike him, seemed completely relaxed. He took out his notebook and listened as Lee began taking Erica back through the years. As Lee had predicted, Erica responded well to suggestion and it didn't take long until she was back to the time of the fire that killed her mother.

As the years fell away in her mind, her voice changed. Matt thought how strange it was to hear a high-pitched juvenile voice from her lips. "Daddy's gone away. Mommy says he'll be away a long time. Her eyes are red. I think she was crying."

"Erica, are you sad that your Daddy's gone away?"

"I miss him." Her tone seemed to threaten tears.

"Is Mommy giving you special treats to make up for him being away?"

Sounding happier, Erica said, "She got me a puppy! His name is Cookie because he's so sweet and he's got big eyes and he likes to play. I had a sleep-over with Aunt Rony, too. I love her big house and all the animals. Uncle Philip is going to drive us to Mandellini and we get to stay there two whole sleeps!"

"Erica, this is the day Uncle Philip is going to drive you to Mandellini. Is Mommy packing some clothes for you? Are you going to take Cookie?"

Erica squirmed on the recliner and pouted. "She says we can't go. Uncle Philip's too busy. That's not fair after he promised." Her voice lightened. "But he's going to take us out for dinner."

"Where are you having dinner? Is it special?"

"Oh, it's beautiful! It's *huge*! There's thousands of people and candles and big sparkly chan...chandeliers! I want to come here for dinner every day but Uncle Philip says it would cost too much." She confided, "He's acting kind of silly now."

"Erica, what is he doing that's silly?"

"He kissed Mommy's hand, right in front of everybody. Daddy wouldn't do that. Mommy's face got all red."

"What did she say?"

Matt realized he was holding his breath.

Erica giggled. "She said, 'Philip, don't be silly! We're best friends. That's all we can be.' I like it when she calls him silly. Silly Philly."

"Erica, has Uncle Philip brought you home now?"

"Mommy's letting me stay up while he drinks some coffee. It's way past my bedtime. He says he's taking us to dinner tomorrow, too, and Mommy's promised to do my hair different."

"All right, Erica, Uncle Philip's gone home. Are you in bed now?"

"Mommy put Teddy and me in her bed but I can't sleep."

Matt's jaw was tense with anticipation.

"Erica, what's Mommy doing now?"

"She...she...oh, no! Please don't!" The small voice was shrill with distress.

"Erica, what's the matter?"

"Mommy! Auntie Cheryl! Please don't yell!"

"Can you hear what they're saying?"

"Auntie Cheryl's shouting at Mommy." Erica moaned. "She says Mommy had her chance with Uncle Philip a long time ago. I think she's mad 'cause he took us out for dinner. She could have come too." Erica's hands were clenching. "She says for Mommy to leave him alone. But Mommy wouldn't hurt him. She'd never hurt anybody."

"Erica, what is Mommy saying?"

"She says, 'You don't know.' And she's crying. Auntie Cheryl, don't make Mommy cry!"

"Please go on."

"Auntie Cheryl says she'll tell Daddy. Mommy says it doesn't matter, Daddy's never coming back." Tears rolled down her cheeks. "I don't understand! I don't want them to be mad at each other! And why isn't Daddy coming back? I want him to come home."

"Erica, just relax, everything will be all right. What's happening now?"

She sniffled. "Auntie Cheryl's leaving. She banged the door. I can hear her car. I don't want her to hurt Mommy. I hope she doesn't come back, ever." A pause. "Mommy's coming to bed. I'm pretending I'm asleep."

"Why are you pretending?"

"Cause I don't want Mommy to know I can't sleep. She'll be upset and she already feels bad. Mommy and Auntie Cheryl keep shouting in my head. Mommy's asleep, though. And Cookie's asleep, but she's in the basement, in the nice basket Mommy bought for her."

"Erica, why don't you go to sleep now? Then you can tell me what happens when you wake up."

Suddenly she screamed.

Matt jumped.

"Mommy! Mommy! There's smoke!" She moaned and twisted on the recliner. Matt bit his lower lip hard. "Mommy, I'm scared. I'm hanging on tight, don't let go, Mommy, is our house going to burn?"

"Erica, what is Mommy saying now?"

"She says I'm to stay put. The grass is wet. There's smoke and big flames coming out the windows. I'm scared, I'm so scared and I'm cold." She folded her arms across her chest. "I'm holding Teddy so he won't get cold."

Then she screamed again. "Cookie's in there! Mommy, please get Cookie! Cookie! I want my puppy!" Tears were rolling down Erica's face.

"Erica, has Mommy gone to get Cookie?"

Her sobs were heart-broken. "Why doesn't she come back? I'm scared by myself. I can hear sirens. They're coming close. Mommy! Mommmmy, don't leave me alone!"

"Is anyone else there?"

Still crying, she said, "The lady from next door. But I don't want her, I want my Mommy. Why doesn't Mommy come? Where's Cookie?"

"Erica, it's okay, the fire's all over. It's a year later and you're seven now and staying with Aunt Rony. What do you do there?"

Gradually the sobs subsided. "We play with the kittens and she lets me paint pictures with her."

While Lee guided Erica through her growing up years, college, and back to the present, Matt paced. His forehead was damp with sweat and he felt as if he'd been wrestling a giant demon.

The sound of their voices stopped and Matt halted, realizing that Lee was looking at him.

"Matt, before I bring her out of the hypnosis, I can suggest to her that she will remember nothing of what she's said or I can tell her she'll have total recall. What's your recommendation?"

Matt felt his guts knot. "You expect me to decide?"

Lee gave Matt a probing glance. "Who better?"

Matt tried to avoid Lee's gaze. "She told me once she wished she could remember. But I don't know. Maybe there's a good reason she blocked it."

"I'm prepared to follow your advice. Would I be wrong to surmise the lady's happiness is important to you?"

Was it that obvious?

Damned if he did, damned if he didn't, Matt thought. It was a hell of a situation to be in. "I don't know. Yes, I do. I think she'd want the truth. Go ahead, tell her to remember." He snuck one last look at Erica before he left the room.

"Coffee, Lieutenant?" Matt blinked at the smiling receptionist. Where had she come from? Automatically he reached for the steaming cup.

He hardly tasted the coffee. How would Erica feel knowing her mother had gone back to rescue her puppy? Had he made a mistake insisting she do this?

Too late now. He paced, longing for a cigarette. Abruptly he stopped in mid-step. The coffee soured in his stomach. He'd let Erica down. The same way he'd let Lynne down all those years ago. Half a lifetime had gone by and he was still screwing around in other people's lives, convinced he knew best.

He knew squat! Except for one thing. It was imperative he distance himself emotionally before he screwed up even worse. Erica was capable of figuring things out for herself. But, as far as her physical safety went, the onus was on him. And he could do that part. He'd been trained for it.

He took a breath. He felt better now. More in control. Emotional involvement had a way of throwing everything out of whack. Move back a pace, review the facts from a distance, that was the way to go.

The Auntie Cheryl she'd mentioned had to be Cheryl Mandell. And the fire had broken out soon after she'd left the house. Had Dale set it? Had Cheryl been Dale's mistress and manipulator back then as well? And, if Cheryl was guilty of setting that fire, was she guilty of manipulating Dale to set the last seven in San Francisco? Did she suspect that Erica had overheard her fight with Suzanne that night? If all that was true, Erica could be in more danger than he'd thought.

At the sound of Lee's door Matt turned, his thoughts a jumble. Erica and the ordeal she'd just been through, Cheryl's possible involvement, his own guilt over what he'd done. He took a half step forward and stopped.

***

Erica hesitated at the door, then moved into the waiting room. The last person she wanted to see right now was Matt. Her thoughts were a kaleidoscope of fragments and half-remembered images. She needed to be alone to sift through them.

Across the room Matt's eyes flashed questions, questions she couldn't answer, underscored by emotions she couldn't name. One thing was certain. This man knew everything about her. Every deep, intimate secret of her woman's body and her twenty-eight years on earth. Erica shivered. She felt wounded and raw and stripped utterly naked and it was all Matt's fault.

Because she loved him.

The revelation took her breath, stopped her short. She didn't want to love him. Love gave people incredible power. Loving Matt left her wide open to being hurt. She couldn't face being hurt. Not right now.

She watched as if from a great distance, saw him don his armor, his protective 'tough cop' mantle, before he crossed the room to her side. She felt as if her insides were splintering into a million pieces. It was too much. First reliving the night her mother died. And now facing Matt. She'd fallen in love with a man who ran like hell from the slightest hint of commitment. A man who didn't believe in love.

When he took her arm in a solicitous but impersonal way she realized he was regarding her as merely a witness in one of his cases. She shook him off. "If you don't mind, I need to be alone." She hardly recognized the strained tones of her own voice.

His searching gaze bored into her eyes. What more did he want? What more could she possibly give? "I'm not sure you should be alone right now."

She thrust back her shoulders and lifted her chin. "Don't worry. If I remember anything that might help the investigation you'll be the first to hear."

"That's not what I meant."

"What did you mean?" Erica winced. What was she trying to do? Pick a fight?

Her feelings of vulnerability were underscored by Matt's hesitation. He started to reach for her, then stopped. Opened his mouth to speak, then didn't. Her heart was beating a million miles a minute. What she really needed was for him to pull her into his arms, hold her tight, and tell her everything would be all right.

But he didn't even look at her. "I'll be at the station. Call me if you need anything."

Fat chance! "Sure." He didn't even notice the faint sarcasm. It seemed to Erica that he couldn't get away fast enough. Into his car and out of her life.

He was gone when she went out to the parking lot. Her hands shook as she tried to start the MG and she clenched them together in her lap, fighting for control. A moment later she managed to turn the key. Nothing. She tried again. Still nothing.

Retrieving the wrench Matt had given her, she opened the hood and faced something tangible and real to concentrate on instead of the vague 'what-ifs' of the past. Leaning over, she gave the rotor the barest nudge the way Matt had taught her, then returned to the driver's seat and turned the key.

"Don't you let me down too," she whispered.

The gods must have heard the desperation in her voice, for the motor turned over first try. Stomping hard on the clutch, she shifted into first, determined to show the world she wasn't some helpless female, dependent on a man to make things right. Determined to prove to herself that she wasn't depending on a man to return her love.

She drove like a robot, not fully conscious of her destination until she reached the burial park. How many years had she prayed for total recall of that long ago night? Now she knew why she'd blocked out the memory. Deep down, her six year old self believed it was her fault her mother died that night.

Moved by her pleas, Suzanne had run back inside to rescue Erica's beloved Cookie. How could she have blanked out the memory of Cookie all these years? But, of course, blocking her guilt had been what it was all about.

Guilt was the cause of so many hasty actions and wrong decisions. Probably her mother already felt guilty about the separation; she didn't want to deprive Erica of her new pet as well as her father. And for that final act, she'd paid with her life.

Erica had always wondered what sort of mother would abandon her child to rush back inside a burning building. What was so damn important she'd risk her life for it? Now, at last, she had the answer.

For her daughter's happiness! Her mother had risked her life for that. And lost.

A mature and caring mother, Suzanne had made her choice. She hadn't been forced to go back into that house for a puppy, but she'd made up her mind to do it. And, accepting that she was not responsible for a choice her mother had freely made, Erica felt something new in her life. Closure. Finally she could lay the past to rest and move forward into the future.

Beside the headstone that bore her mother's name, Erica folded her legs beneath her and sat staring at the grass blanketing her mother's remains. She mourned not only for her mother, but for Matt Nicols and a love that would never bear fruit.

"Everybody wears a mask," she said. The faint echo of her voice sounded loud and startling on the deserted hillside. "And makes his own choices." They'd all chosen. Her mother. Philip. Ronya.

Even Cheryl, remaining married to a man she didn't love, while his brother, Philip, mourned for Suzanne, a ghost these last twenty-two years.

Not for her!

It was obvious that Matt held himself accountable for choices made by others. Which meant he'd never let go of the past. She had to get beyond that. Make her choice. Get on with her life.

Sadness gave way to resentment. Matt Nicols had treated her like every other man in her life who wanted something from her.

She had to face it. He'd turned his back on love but freely taken the sex. Turned his back on her needs but taken her help and expertise. He'd used her to help him crack this case, to make himself look good.

Hearing a car approach, motor straining as it droned up the incline, her feelings of peace, solitude and closure evaporated as if she'd imagined them. Sunlight glinted off the interloper's windshield, rendering the driver unidentifiable. The car slowed to a crawl, then continued past.

So much for introspection. Time to look forward. So what if her father had shuffled her off to boarding school first chance he had? Or Trevor had married her for her looks? What really got her steamed was the way Matt had manipulated her, bending her to his will with sweet talk and sensual acts. Then walking away from her.

She tensed, hearing what sounded like someone moving behind her, feeling the hair stir on the back of her neck. Slowly she turned, her gaze skimming the surrounding area. All was serene. Except her heart, which galloped erratically.

Don't be stupid, she told herself, willing her heart rate back to normal. It was a sunny afternoon and no one was creeping around spying. Nonetheless, she stood and dusted off her backside, craning her head with instinctive wariness in every direction. The car that had interrupted her wallowing was parked a short distance away and she couldn't tell if the driver was inside or not. Probably just someone else come to pay their respects.

She needed more time alone. No, not alone. With a warm, listening presence who demanded nothing and knew how to give and receive love.

Chapter Twenty-Three

Glenn slouched into the SIS squad room and sat beside Matt's desk. "How'd it go?"

Matt shrugged. So what if he'd just seen his life flash before his eyes? It was over between him and Erica. Better this way. Better to end it before it really began. It was no good Erica coming to rely on him only to find she'd picked the wrong guy. "It seems Cheryl Mandell was at the house that night cat-fighting Suzanne Rawlins over Philip Mandell." He recapped the details Erica had revealed under hypnosis.

"I've got news, too," Glenn said. "Suzanne Rawlins filed for divorce a month earlier. Still, people split up all the time. It's no motive for arson."

"I think there's a good possibility Cheryl could have torched the house. Or made Dale do it for her, to keep Suzanne away from Philip."

Glenn polished his glasses. "Hell of a risk to take for a guy who wasn't interested in her. Unless she was sure she could change that."

"Then there's Justin." Matt leaned back. "Maybe he killed Dale out of jealousy and tried to cover it by lighting all those fires."

"Maybe," Glenn said. "He had good reason to be jealous of his brother, too, Philip being the favorite son and all. Maybe he knew Cheryl had been in love with Philip. He seems to have a better motive than anybody else, especially when you consider he'd get the vineyard if Philip died before the old man."

The door opened and the smell of Bud Bailey's cigar preceded him into the room. "What in hell is going on? I thought you guys were wrapping up the Todd case."

Matt took a deep breath. "It's possible Todd was just a hired torch."

"That's all you got?"

"Captain, right now I'm listening to my gut." Bailey'd been a street cop; he knew the value of gut instincts as well as any of them.

Bailey snorted. "Nicols, this case is gift-wrapped! The guy confesses, then commits suicide. What more do you want?"

He wanted to be sure it was Dale who was guilty, that the murderer didn't go free. More than that, he wanted to be sure Erica wasn't in any personal danger. He'd never forgive himself if anything happened to her. Time to try a different tack.

"Suppose the writing on the suicide note isn't the same as on those racing forms?"

"Can you prove it?"

"Not yet."

"Get me the proof." The Captain waved his cigar. "For now let's make the mayor happy. Not to mention the voting public." He left in a cloud of cigar smoke.

The door opened again and a courier came in and dropped an envelope on Matt's desk.

Matt signed for the package and ripped it open. "The report from Homicide," he said, scanning it. "Todd's our fire-setter, no doubt about it. His prints are all over that Detroit door opener. And two rectangular gas cans fit neatly into his briefcase, which shows recent staining from gasoline."

Glenn stood up and stretched. "Still got that safety deposit box key?"

"Yeah. I doubt if it can be traced, though."

"And in the meantime?"

"In the meantime," Matt said, reaching for the phone, "let's do like the good captain says."

Glenn skewered his partner with a long look. "Since when do you listen to the powers-that-be?"

"When I'm being discreet." Matt grinned at the look of disbelief on Glenn's face and swung around in his chair to ensure a measure of privacy in his conversation.

***

By the time Erica reached the stables, gray clouds and gusting winds signaled an approaching storm and she changed her mind about riding. She jumped as a few fallen leaves blew across the driveway in front of her.

She stroked Missy's sleek neck and inhaled her warm horsy scent while the mare crunched an apple. "Avoidance tactics never solve a thing, Missy. We both know the best way to deal with a problem is to face it head on, right?" Missy nuzzled at her for a second apple. Erica displayed her empty hands and the mare snorted.

Erica smoothed the horse's satiny nose. "When it comes to Matt Nicols and his gut feelings, I'll go one better. I've got a plan."

While Matt was off on a wild goose chase trying to link the recent fires to the old one, she'd get to the bottom of this case and hand it over to him. She'd even see to it that he got the credit, since his career was so almighty important to him.

She felt happier as she headed back to the city. She now knew she wasn't responsible for her mother's death. And she'd learned there was nothing wrong with her physically when it came to enjoying sex. Like it or not, Matt Nicols was directly responsible for these benefits.

A glance in the rear-view mirror made her stomach muscles clench. Her hands tightened on the wheel. The city was full of nondescript gray four-door sedans. It might not be a coincidence to see one at the cemetery, one at the stables and now, one behind her, but it was definitely peculiar. Why would anyone be tailing her? Just because she was investigating a series of fires, two of which had also produced corpses, didn't mean that she knew anything important.

She reviewed the main facts in the other ICPB cases she'd worked on recently. Nothing suspicious there, she decided, as the first fat drops of rain landed on the windshield. She'd proceed to the office as planned and get a whack of work done now that everyone else had gone home. The golden arches sprang into view, reminding her she was hungry.

Matt should see her now, she thought as she turned into the McDonald's drive-through lane. Apparently the driver of the gray car had suffered a Big Mac attack, too. But he was parking as if to go inside, so her overactive imagination had been leading her astray again, just as it had at the burial park.

The hot food smelled delicious and her stomach was rumbling by the time she reached the office. She nibbled a few fries in the elevator and took the first bite of her fish filet sandwich as she reached her desk. A blob of tartar sauce squirted out, splattering some papers. Now she knew why Matt's desk was such a pit, she thought, swiping at the spill with a napkin.

Erica exhaled angrily. That man invaded almost every thought that entered her mind. It had to stop!

Suddenly she tensed. Was that the outer office door opening? Had she remembered to lock it behind her? No crack of light showed beneath her door. If someone was out there they weren't advertising the fact. Erica reached for her flashlight. "Who's there?"

No answer.

"Anyone out there?"

She counted silently to ten, then flung open her office door, flicking on the powerful flash at the same time. Her racing heart slowed. She was alone.

The ringing of the phone pulled her back to reality. She hurried to her desk and grabbed it before the answering service could cut in.

"Erica." It was Cheryl's voice. The voice that had haunted her since the session with the hypnotherapist.

"Cheryl," she said. "How did you know I'd be here?"

"I need to talk to you right away."

She propped her hip against the desk. "So talk."

"Not on the phone. Can you come up to the house?"

Erica glanced out at the inky darkness. Rain spattered against the window pane. "Right now?"

"It's important. It's about the night your mother died."

Erica's heart zoomed into triple time. "What about that night?" Abruptly the connection was broken.

Had Cheryl hung up? Had the storm knocked down a line to Mandellini? Or had someone else severed the connection? Erica bundled into emergency rain gear and went down to the almost deserted parking garage. She caught herself listening for footsteps in the silence but there was nothing except the eerie hum of fluorescent lights.

Traffic was light and she'd crossed the Bay bridge and turned north before she noticed the steady beam of headlights, at a discreet distance, in her rear-view mirror. She slowed. So did he. She accelerated. So did he.

"Hold onto your hat, mister," she said aloud, her breath fogging the windshield. "You're about to be taken on the ride of your life."

***

He gripped the phone tightly in his fist. "What in hell do you mean you lost her?"

"Listen. It's as black as sin out here. And raining to boot. I think she did it on purpose."

"On purpose? Like she knew she was being followed?"

"Yeah. What do you want me to do now?"

"Tell me again exactly where you are. And where you last had her in sight."

***

Her headlights barely penetrated the darkness of the winding road up the hillside guarding Mandellini. It was lucky she knew the road so well. The house was dark, the bell rope sodden, and she hunched into her rain gear as wind gusted into the entrance. No answer. She tried the door, not surprised to find it open. Auguste had never believed in locking doors.

She stepped inside, flipping back the hood of her slicker. "Anyone home?" Her footsteps sounded loud on the tiled floor of the hallway. "Justin? Cheryl? Auguste?"

She heard a muffled clink and, rounding the corner, saw a faint glimmer of light coming from the dining room. "Who's there?"

"Who do you think?" Cheryl sat at the head of the polished cherry wood table. A lone candle shed an inadequate puddle of light and misshapen shadows lurked in the corners of the huge room. Cheryl poured herself a fresh drink from the bottle in front of her. "Nishe of you to come." Pouring a second drink, she gave the glass a push toward Erica.

Erica stripped off her slicker and sat down. "What happened to the electricity?"

Cheryl shrugged and took a healthy slug from her glass.

"Where's Justin?"

Cheryl shrugged again.

Erica's temper kindled. Had she driven for more than an hour in nerve-racking wind and rain for this? "You said you had something important to tell me."

"Thash right." Cheryl indicated Erica's untouched glass. "You're going to need that."

Erica sat back and crossed her arms. "No, thank you."

Cheryl shrugged yet again and refilled her own glass, slopping liquor on the table. Erica shoved the bottle out of Cheryl's reach. Leaning forward, she said, "I know you were at my mother's house the night of the fire. Did you set it?"

"No." Cheryl fumbled for her cigarettes. By the time she'd taken her first drag she seemed to have herself in hand. "I know who did, though."

Erica forced herself to act unimpressed. "Really?"

Cheryl inhaled again and managed to execute a wobbly smoke ring. Her speech was surprisingly clear now. "I had it in my mind that Philip would come back later that night, so I drove down the road a little way and parked my car to wait."

"And did he?"

"I don't know," Cheryl admitted. "I'd had a fair bit to drink and I guess I dozed off. The sirens woke me up. But I saw *him* driving away."

Erica leaned forward. "Saw *who* driving away?"

Cheryl appeared to be engrossed in aiming the ash from her cigarette at the ashtray. "Took me awhile to put two and two together. Started out as sort of a joke, you know. Kidding around. But I could tell by his reaction I'd hit the jackpot."

Erica had to restrain herself from reaching across the table and shaking the woman. "Damn you! Who was it?"

"Dale Todd."

Erica couldn't repress a shocked gasp.

Cheryl crushed her cigarette with one long orange fingernail. "And now he's dead, poor bastard. One thing, though. He never meant for your mama to die. He'd been told the house would be empty."

"Told by whom?"

"I don't know. I worked on him for years but he wouldn't say."

Erica deliberately made her voice skeptical. "Did he tell you the rest of it? The reason?"

Cheryl slanted her a belligerent look. "Not exactly. But he paid me to keep quiet all these years."

"You were blackmailing Dale?"

"You'd be surprised what I do. Bet you didn't know it was me that went through your car that day you were here with the cop."

"You? What were you hoping to find?"

"I knew Dale was involved somehow. I wanted to know if your cop knew that. Figured there might be a notebook in the car. Something, anyway."

"Is that why he took his own life? Because you knew he'd set that fire?"

There was malevolence in Cheryl's eyes. "Dale wasn't the type to kill himself. Even though he felt guilty as hell over Suzanne's death."

"What about Philip?"

"I don't know anything about Philip."

"You wanted him."

"Says who?"

"Don't play dumb with me. I was there. I heard you."

"You were just a kid."

"Does Justin know he's second choice?" Listening to her own words Erica felt little prickles of warning creep up her spine. Instinctively she glanced over her shoulder. "Cheryl, where's Justin?"

Cheryl took another swallow of liquor. "Don't know and don't care. Only married him to piss Philip off. Even with Suzanne gone he wouldn't give me the time of day."

Erica leaned across the table and clamped her hand over Cheryl's. "Justin knows about you and Dale."

The older woman blinked. "Not likely!"

"He knows, Cheryl. He told me himself."

Cheryl's eyes narrowed. "Why would he tell you?"

"Because of the investigation into Dale's death." Erica straightened. "Oh, God! You don't suppose Justin had something to do with...?"

The lights flickered and went on. Cheryl's heavy eye makeup was smudged into black rings around her eyes.

"Don't suppose Justin what?"

"Had anything to do with Dale's or Philip's death," Erica said, horrified at the thought. Justin had always seemed so calm and somehow...good. Could it be the facade of a killer?

Cheryl waved her hand, obviously dismissing the idea. "Nah! Justin doesn't care about anything except his precious vines."

Abruptly Erica stood up. No matter what Cheryl thought, Justin did care for her. And jealousy was a powerful motive. "Where's Auguste?"

"Bed, I guess."

Cheryl's shrugs were getting on her nerves. "Didn't you check on him when the power went out?"

The disdainful look she got from Cheryl made Erica hurry down the hall to the wing occupied by the padrone of the Mandell family. Even with the lights on she felt jumpy. Outside a loose shutter banged against the house.

From the doorway of Auguste's bedroom she could see, in the dim glow of a night light, his still, frail form beneath the covers. As she approached, horror clutched at her throat. The old man's eyes stared toward the ceiling, wide and sightless. The room was shrouded in the ominous quiet of death.

She heard a car race up the driveway as Cheryl came into the room. Erica swung on her, fists clenched. "What have you done?"

Cheryl didn't answer. Erica heard a door being flung open and the heavy tread of masculine feet coming down the hall. Her eyes moved from Cheryl's face to the doorway.

Matt burst into the room, gun drawn.

Chapter Twenty-Four

Erica stood near the entrance to Mandellini, watching the cars snake up the hill toward her. In strong contrast to the storm four nights ago, the sun was blinding, the breeze a faint caress on her shoulders.

Clayton moved closer and touched her elbow. "What time is the service?"

"In a few moments." It felt sad to be wearing basic black again. First Philip, then Dale, now Auguste. At least the old man had died from natural causes, not the foul play she had suspected in that emotion-charged moment when Matt stormed Mandellini like a medieval crusader.

Her father's car glided past. Erica's lips tightened as she saw the brash blonde occupying the passenger seat. "Who invited her?"

"Ms. Cameron, you mean?" Clayton asked.

"Auguste is barely cold, and she's up here angling for a real estate listing."

Clayton didn't appear to hear the note of disgust in her voice or even her actual words. "I didn't know they were planning to sell."

"My guess is she's here to persuade them that it's a good idea."

Clayton gave her elbow a reassuring squeeze. "At least the lieutenant isn't here, invading our privacy with his pointless questions."

Justin came out of the house and signaled to the mourners. As Erica and Clayton followed the others to the terraced hillside where the service was to be held and Auguste's cremated remains sprinkled, her mind returned to the last time she'd seen Matt, putting away his gun as she stood beside Auguste's lifeless body.

She'd turned on him, primed to do battle, her grief and fear making her want to hit out at whoever was handy. "What the hell are you doing here?" She rarely used such words, but Matt's presence pushed her to heightened levels of emotion. After he confirmed that Auguste was indeed dead, and Cheryl had returned to her solitary drinking, he'd had the nerve to say, "I was worried about you."

"How did you know where I was?"

His hazel eyes had met hers unflinchingly. "You managed to lose the guy I assigned to keep an eye on you. I made an educated guess."

"How dare you! I'm quite capable of looking after myself!"

"I didn't know what we were up against." He lowered his voice. "I still don't." He inclined his head in the direction Cheryl had taken. "Did she tell you anything of importance?"

Erica sucked in her breath. "Auguste is dead. But nothing takes precedence over the all-important investigation, does it, Lieutenant?"

His jaw muscles clenched and he waved a hand in the direction of Auguste's body. "There's nothing I can do for him. But I don't want the next corpse I stumble over to be yours."

"There won't be any more corpses," she said, her voice fading as exhaustion caught up with her.

"How do you know?"

"Cheryl saw Dale leaving the scene of the fire the night my mother died. He told her the house was supposed to be empty. No one was supposed to get hurt. She says he never got over it and I believe her. So there's your arsonist, Lieutenant. Nice and neat the way you like it. You've no further need of me. And with luck we won't see each other again."

They were empty words, of course. As long as she remained with ICPB she was bound to run into him.

The early afternoon sun beamed down on the mourners gathered around the minister. Taking a deep breath of the fresh fall air, Erica joined her aunt and put an arm around shoulders that had become noticeably stooped in the past two weeks. She made brief eye contact with her father, conscious that he appeared undisturbed by the recent trio of deaths. No surprise there.

She focused next on Cheryl, whose sober face and dark glasses concealed the jubilation she must feel over Auguste's death. Confronted by what was surely the end of an era, Erica's throat tightened. Justin had no heirs. Would the vineyard be swallowed up by some huge commercial vintner? Or, one day, would the very spot where Auguste's ashes were now being scattered become the site of a garish modern subdivision?

Watching the breeze catch and toss Auguste's ashes, Erica was struck by the irony. Ashes had shaped her destiny from childhood, beginning with the ashes of her home and the fire's tragic theft of her mother. And her chosen work, where she sifted through ashes, like an archeologist sifting through dirt looking for clues to lost centuries of civilization. Ultimately, ashes had brought Matt Nicols into her life, changing a part of her forever.

She couldn't concentrate on the minister's words, much as she wanted to glean comfort from them. Her eyes wandered to Dolores, here with her relatives, men and women who had tended the vines for generations. How much longer would they be able to call Mandellini their home?

Background movement caught her eye and, as her mind registered the identity of the latecomer, her heart lurched. The aching sadness made a mockery of the message she recited to herself a dozen times a day: she no longer cared two figs about Matt Nicols.

For a change, he was conventionally dressed in a white shirt, dark jacket and tie. His eyes were masked by sunglasses, but she could feel his gaze trained on her over the heads of the crowd separating them. Although she knew it was ridiculous and fought against it, every particle of her body trembled.

At last, the minister ended the service and invited everyone into the house for food and a sip of Auguste's finest.

"Aren't you coming?" Clayton had started forward, Ronya leaning heavily on his arm.

"In a minute."

The hillside emptied until it was just the two of them, face to face.

It was ridiculous to hope Matt had come because he missed her, because he wanted a life with her. She knew it was ridiculous, kept hammering that fact into her brain. Yet she couldn't stop the rush of heat through her body, or the way her soul reached for him. Watching him, feeling a terrible let-down, she knew that he wasn't here because of her. And that she'd never love another man the way she loved him.

In one way he'd given her the future. He'd freed her from the nagging torment of not knowing what happened the night her mother died. A torment that had clouded everything she thought and did and felt in her search for self-identity. In that respect she was finally free and she owed it all to him.

On the other hand he'd stolen the future. If she couldn't spend it with him, she didn't have a future at all. How could she face the empty years the way Ronya had, pining away for a love not meant to be?

She watched him remove his sunglasses. Watched the loving way the sun gilded his hair, the way his hazel eyes looked into hers. "I wasn't expecting to see you here today." She was proud of herself. She sounded quite civil, given the previous words they had exchanged.

"Something came up," Matt said.

"Something to do with the investigation, no doubt."

"Yeah. We found Todd's safe-deposit box."

"Well, well. I bet it was full of fascinating stuff."

Matt shook his head. "Just cassette tapes."

"Cassette tapes of what?"

"Of someone giving him instructions. Time and place. Coinciding with..."

"Let me guess. Seven recent fires in the city."

He nodded.

She tilted her head and crossed her arms over her chest. "Are you here to make an arrest?"

"Not yet. We need to do some voice analyses."

"So this isn't a social call."

His eyes never left hers as he shook his head.

She waved her hand in a grand gesture. "Don't let me stop you. After all, a funeral is the perfect place to suggest the prime suspects don't leave town."

"Don't do this, Erica."

"You've got that wrong, Matt. All wrong. The doing is entirely yours." Head high, back straight, she turned and walked toward the house.

***

Matt watched until she disappeared through the massive carved door, the pain inside him intensifying a hundredfold. She might just as well have knifed him as look at him as though she hated him. Putting her through the hypnosis hadn't been a mistake; it had been a total disaster.

He'd known, ever since racing after her four nights ago, that he loved her. His fear that her life was in danger had forced him to face it, made him admit how tight a hold she had on his heart. He'd spent the last four days fighting it, trying to erase her from his mind. Without any success.

But he'd get over her. He'd have to. Because there was no hope that he could love her the way she needed and deserved to be loved. It would only end by his failing her the way he'd failed Lynne. If he'd loved Lynne enough she'd have had the strength to say no to her father and the abortion; she'd still be alive.

Matt abruptly turned his back on the house, feeling as if a giant hand was squeezing his heart. Erica was still in danger, and would be until the murderer was caught. There was only one thing he could do for her: find the killer and release her from the shadows dogging her every step.

Until then he had to endure the tension that vibrated at a screaming pitch between them. He couldn't walk away from it until she was safe. And he couldn't risk letting her close to him. He had no choice.

"Choices," he repeated aloud, the word bitter in his mouth. People faced them every day of their lives. The right choice meant rewards and happiness. The wrong choice resulted in disaster. Like Lynne. She'd made her choice. Opted to appease her parents rather than do what her heart told her was right. And she'd paid the highest price there was. Paid with her life.

So how long are you going to beat yourself up about other people's choices?

The thought stunned him with its clarity. Is that what he was doing? Beating himself up for other people's choices and decisions?

The crusader side of him always wanted to make sure everyone made the right choices—and then felt guilty if they screwed up. He stared at the terraces where Auguste's ashes lay and shook his head. Life was too damn short to carry a load of guilt that didn't belong to him.

He turned back to face the house. For twenty years he'd chosen to dedicate himself to police work. It was a choice that could be changed. He could stop acting out his subconscious wish to punish Lynne's father for 'murdering' her, and think about the other things he wanted to do. If he wasn't responsible for Lynne's death, then perhaps, after all, he deserved to have his dreams come true.

His lips twisted in a wry smile. Not all of those dreams would come true, now. Certainly not the most important one.

But there were other causes for a crusader, other 'pulpits' to preach from. The gang he'd run with as a kid flashed into his mind, as it often had lately. He'd like to do something for wild kids, help them stay clear of crime and jails.

In the meantime, Mandellini stared back at him, forbidding, impassive, refusing to release the secret behind eight fires and three deaths. What he had to do right now was walk down there and breach that door, force the secret into the open, strip it bare and render it harmless.

He hadn't seen Erica since Wednesday night, hadn't told her the suicide note had been faked. The handwriting was not Dale Todd's. There hadn't even been any fingerprints on the paper. Why would a man choosing to die wear gloves to write a note? No, Dale Todd had been murdered.

Murdered by the same person responsible for the fires. The Captain, to give the devil his due, had praised him for sticking to his guns. Bailey had even gone along with Matt's crazy scheme.

Inside the house, Matt was acutely aware of heads turning in his direction and sudden lulls in the conversation. Out of the corner of his eye he saw Erica standing with Ronya, Gallagher hovering protectively. Resolute, setting his lips in a firm line, he turned his head away and approached Justin Mandell.

"I'm sorry about your father."

Justin was haggard but serene. "Thank you. I'll miss him a great deal but I accepted long ago that his time was coming." He eyed Matt thoughtfully. "I suspect your presence here signifies more than respect for my father. Am I right?"

Matt cleared his throat. "I need to make an announcement. I'm sorry to intrude, but I can't let this opportunity go by."

"Does it concern Dale Todd?" Justin waved his hand at the people thronging the big room. "Everyone who knew him has been talking about him, speculating about what really happened. There's been nothing in the papers except that his death appeared to be suicide and the police suspect he was involved in all those recent fires."

"Yes, it's about Todd. We've deliberately withheld all details from the press because of the way the investigation is developing."

"You've piqued my curiosity, Lieutenant. To be honest, I've wondered ever since Todd's death whether he deliberately killed my brother. And why."

Matt was curious about Justin Mandell, too. Had he killed both his brother and Todd because he couldn't stand Cheryl's indifference and infidelity any longer?

"With any luck we'll soon have the answers." Matt scanned the crowd.

To his left was Cheryl Mandell, heavy makeup failing to disguise her strained expression. She could have killed Philip in order to inherit Mandellini, then Dale in order to cover her tracks.

Beyond her, chatting with Gallagher, face impassive, was Eric Rawlins. Had he killed Philip because of jealousy over Suzanne?

Matt's glance slid over Francie, her arm through Eric's, and on to Ronya Germaine, who looked tired and lost. She peered around the room as though not quite sure where she was. Was her vagueness just an act?

Matt picked up an empty wine bottle and tapped it with a knife for attention. Heads swiveled and conversations died as people turned to face him.

"Ladies and gentlemen," Matt said, "I apologize for the interruption but I have an announcement about the death of Dale Todd, a man known to many of you here."

He paused. Every face was intent on his, some showing indignation, others avid curiosity.

"It's not yet clear whether Dale Todd's death was murder or suicide."

He heard a few startled gasps and murmurs.

"If any of you have information about Todd that might be relevant, please contact the Special Investigation Squad of the San Francisco police." He paused again.

"Several cassette tapes belonging to Todd have been found in a safety deposit box he rented. They contain recordings of telephone conversations he had."

More shocked murmurs. People glanced at one another, some shifting as though uncomfortable.

"The other speaker on the tapes isn't identified, so we'll be asking some of you, during the next few days, to do voice tapes for comparison with the evidence tapes."

He scanned the room again. Ronya looked as though she hadn't heard a word he'd said. Rawlins seemed shocked. Cheryl's face was white, Justin's impassive.

"Thank you for your attention."

Matt nodded to Justin and strode from the room. The conversation rose to almost a roar of excitement behind him.

Outside the front door, he paused. Would his ploy to spook the murderer into revealing himself work? Nothing he could do now but wait.

Chapter Twenty-Five

Erica glanced at the wine glass she clutched, surprised the stem hadn't snapped in two.

"I knew it was too much to hope for," Clayton said, his voice heavy with disgust.

Erica forced her attention toward him. "What?"

"That the Lieutenant would be capable of showing a little decorum. Of showing respect for the family on this of all days."

Erica turned on him. "I'd guess he believes the end justifies the means. Much like yourself."

"You're certainly quick to defend the man."

"No quicker than you to accuse him."

Clayton flushed. "This is a really charming side of you that I'm seeing lately, Erica."

She put the wine glass down, already regretting her hasty words. "Sorry."

He subjected her to one last disapproving glance. "Believe me, so am I." He straightened his tie, made sure his jacket hung just right, and moved toward her father.

Cheryl's voice, already a little slurred, sounded from behind her left shoulder. "Looks like you pissed the boyfriend off but good."

Erica turned. Her animosity toward Cheryl faded as she recognized her for what she was; a frustrated and bitter middle-aged woman. "What's it to you?"

Cheryl shrugged. "Not a damn thing. I suppose you knew about those tapes beforehand?"

Erica studied the older woman. It was obvious that Cheryl was still drinking heavily. Was she worried? Or just curious? "I'm not exactly the Lieutenant's confidante these days."

Cheryl rocked on her four inch heels. "Who all do you think he'll be getting voice samples from?"

"Your guess is as good as mine," she said before heading toward the other side of the room. She could do without Cheryl's company, especially today. Halfway there, Justin pulled her into a deserted corner.

Justin, usually so calm, seemed agitated. His forehead was shiny with perspiration and his tongue darted nervously between his lips. "What did Cheryl want?"

Erica felt a flash of sympathy. It couldn't be easy to lose a brother and a father in quick succession. And while Justin looked like he needed a hug, he'd never been demonstrative. It was Philip who'd been given to extravagant displays of affection. She still expected to look up and see him across the room; he'd been so much a part of this family. And hers. "She was asking if I knew about the tapes."

"What did you tell her?"

"I'm as surprised at their existence as everyone else."

Justin's eyes narrowed as he studied the room's occupants. "The Lieutenant suspects someone here?"

"It looks that way."

"But if Todd was the arsonist..."

"It appears he was taking orders from someone else." Was Justin sweating because he knew who had hired Dale? Or because he didn't know and was afraid it might be Cheryl?

Justin finished his wine in one swallow. "It's bad business, Erica. Bad all the way around. Ms. Cameron says I ought to sell the place, start life afresh."

"You can't do that!"

He flashed her a startled look.

"Mandellini is your life. It's much more than just a home. How can you even think about selling?"

He stared at her for a moment, then his face relaxed. "You're right, of course. I'd be lost anywhere else." He shook his head. "With Philip's death, and now my father, I guess it isn't surprising that I haven't been thinking very clearly." He gave her an awkward pat on the shoulder and walked away.

Erica's gaze moved to the Cameron woman, who was holding Clayton captive with one hand and clinging to Erica's father's arm with the other. Matt's paramour! Had he already gone back to her?

Feeling leaden, she detoured to the buffet where Ronya was nibbling on a sandwich and looking much more alert and cheerful than she had half an hour before. "Your lieutenant certainly knows how to liven up a dull gathering."

"He's not my lieutenant," Erica responded at once.

"Nonsense," her aunt said, an affectionate twinkle in her eye. "Well, I'm glad they found out Dale didn't commit suicide. Not for one moment did I believe he was capable of taking his own life."

Erica gave her a searching glance. For all her weird affectations her aunt was usually a good judge of character. "You sound convinced."

"I am. He told me how he survived even though his mother abandoned him at birth. He survived prison, though he hated it. Yes, I know about his time in prison, but at heart he was a good man."

Erica swallowed. Her throat felt constricted. "Supposing he did start the fire that killed my mother?"

"I don't believe it. He worshiped Suzanne."

But Cheryl had seen him there that night.

"Then Philip died," Erica continued. "Being the cause of two accidental deaths might have sent him over the edge. You can't be sure."

Ronya shook her head. "I'll never believe it."

A scene from the hypnosis session flashed into Erica's mind. "Did Philip love Suzanne?"

"Oh, yes. He was devoted to her. Always." Ronya took a step backwards, alerting Erica to the presence of a third party behind her.

"Excuse us for a moment, Ronya," Rawlins said in a voice that brooked no argument. Taking Erica's arm he steered her forcefully out the french doors to the brick terrace overlooking the driveway.

"I'm afraid your aunt is making less sense every minute, dear. I really do think she should have special care."

"Out of sight, out of mind, don't you mean?" Erica said, her voice flat. "What are you afraid of? She's already told Lieutenant Nicols that you and my mother had separated before the fire."

Her father's eyes blazed with anger. "Your aunt is mistaken. Suzanne and I were very much in love. As for the Lieutenant, I've already been in contact with the Mayor. He tends to agree that the wrong man is heading the Special Investigation Squad."

"You'd do that, wouldn't you? Alter the course of a man's career with no qualms. No second thoughts."

She watched her father's face as he tried to control his anger. It was rare for his control to slip even this far. Suddenly, as though pulling on a mask, he had it back.

"Waste of time." Releasing her, he dusted his hands. "Life is too short for second thoughts. One does what one has to, that's all. No room for emotional pandering." He indicated the open doors. "Shall we be social?"

"Let's!" Erica brushed past him, her hands shaking. Once inside she spent a moment composing herself, determined to exercise the same iron-clad control as her father.

She turned, her gaze sweeping the crowded room. Voices rose and fell and she caught snatches of conversations.

"...poor Justin...the last of a line..."

"...heavy tax burden...not really sure..."

"No one could produce a Chardonnay like Auguste."

"...think you might consider selling? The market is down right now but I..."

Francie Cameron had wasted no time moving in on Cheryl, who was looking at the realtor with glazed eyes.

She caught the sound of a familiar masculine voice off to one side. And the name Dale Todd. "I tell you, Ronya, the man was unbalanced. Despite what the police might say, I'm convinced he took his own life."

Her aunt murmured a response.

"After all, no sane person would start a fire using sleeping bags, would he? There must be so many more appropriate ways to do it. That alone shows his delicate mental health."

Sleeping bags? There was nothing inappropriate or odd about using sleeping bags to start a fire. He was going to outrageous lengths to convince Ronya that Dale had been unbalanced.

Erica pushed closer. Her aunt's back was toward her. Facing Ronya, his sleek head bent as he spoke to her in low urgent tones, stood her father.

Erica's heart began to pound. Her palms broke into a sweat as she stared at him and realized the real implications of what he was saying. Just then he looked up. Their eyes met. Blindly she turned and pushed through the crowd toward the door.

"Erica. Where are you going?"

She didn't answer, weaving and dodging until she made her way outside. Supporting herself with one hand against the brick wall, she sucked in huge gulps of fresh air. There were footsteps behind her. She prayed she was mistaken about what she'd heard him say.

"Erica, are you all right? You looked pale."

She faced him. "You tell me. Am I all right?"

"What? I don't..."

"Sleeping bags," she said, forcing herself to say the words clearly. "I heard you tell Ronya how Dale started that last fire with sleeping bags."

His face went taut with impatience. "What of it?"

"That particular detail was never made public."

He brushed her comment aside. "I read the police report, naturally. Being the building's architect I was entitled to know how the structure had fared."

Erica shook her head and stepped back. "I also read the police report. There was no mention of sleeping bags."

"Someone told me, then. What difference does it make?"

She kept her eyes riveted on his face. "Only the professionals who were there that night saw what was left of the sleeping bags. After the material was removed and analyzed, it was decided to keep that particular piece of evidence hushed up."

He bristled. "I don't know what it is you're trying to say, young lady..."

"Don't you?" Erica said. She felt cold steel pierce her racing heart. This was her father. A stranger.

"I think you're overwrought."

"Dale did whatever you told him. Did that include setting fires?"

"Now see here, Erica!"

But what she was seeing was a monster. She turned and raced down the steps, one goal uppermost in her thoughts. Matt. She had to find Matt.

"Erica, wait. I can explain."

At the last step, she was pulled up short, almost tripping. He had hold of her dress. She wrenched from his grasp and ran toward her car. Luckily she'd left the keys in the ignition.

His voice followed. "Listen, Erica. Let me explain."

Erica jumped into the MG and turned the key. The starter motor turned over but the engine didn't catch. No! Not *now*! She tried again. Still nothing. Her father's hand was reaching for the passenger door. She released the emergency brake and depressed the clutch. The car started to roll, slowly at first, then picked up speed.

He wrenched open the door. Erica popped the clutch. The car lurched but the motor didn't catch. Her father dove inside, slamming the door after him. She steered down the driveway as the rolling vehicle gathered speed. Without taking her eyes from the road Erica popped the clutch again. This time it worked. The motor roared to life.

"You have to listen to me, Erica. I can explain."

"Save it for the police," she said, her voice grim, her grip on the wheel tightening as they hurtled down the gravel driveway toward the first switchback.

"It was an accident, a terrible accident. I needed the insurance money," he panted. "But the house was supposed to be empty. Believe me; I was sure no one was in there. Or I would never..."

"You killed my mother!"

"I loved her. I worshiped the ground she walked on."

"She threw you out!"

"You're not listening to me." Reaching across, her father grabbed the wheel.

"What are you doing?" The car see-sawed wildly, rear wheels spinning on gravel as Erica brought it back under control. Fresh fear assaulted her. This stranger, her father, was capable of anything. Capable of killing.

"I'm making you listen," he said, his words distinct as if he was speaking to a child. "You have to understand. I needed the money to win Suzanne back. Without money I was nothing. She treated me as if I was nothing." As he spoke he fastened his seat belt with unhurried movements. They could have been taking a country drive.

"So you had Dale set fire to the house. And made a bundle building an apartment block on the site." She tried to laugh but it became a sob. "And your little girl grew up to be an arson investigator. Ironic, isn't it? Investigating fires engineered by my own father. No wonder you didn't approve of my career."

She risked a quick glance at him. "Was Philip's death accidental? Or did you intend him to die?"

Her father's lips grew taut. "He had a debt to pay."

Tense with concentration, she guided the car into the switchback. His voice was now a monotone. She needed to keep him talking. "What debt?"

"You were there when he turned Suzanne against me. You remember. He filled her head with his foolish, useless dreams. We were happy until he forced his way into our lives."

She sucked in her breath. "Why wait all this time? Why not eliminate him years ago?"

"Killing him wasn't enough. It was his fault Suzanne died. I wanted him to suffer. To waste a lifetime chasing his stupid dreams. Without her." He gave a humorless laugh. "He actually thought he was going to make something out of that old theater. But I knew, weeks before, that the time for his final punishment had come."

"So you set those other fires to cover up the fact that Philip's death was deliberate, not accidental."

"I thought that was clever. Wouldn't you agree?"

Erica's jaw clenched. It was hard to concentrate on the road, on the gravel flying from the MG's wheels. Her father actually sounded proud of himself. "You fooled everyone.

Francie told you Philip was going to look at the theater, didn't she?"

"It was perfect. I knew then that was the place to carry out my plans for his destruction. Him and his pipe dreams. Up in smoke. An eye for an eye."

"Rather coincidental that Philip's visit to the theater was exactly five days after the previous fire."

"Oh, no, that wasn't coincidence. It was meant to be. I knew as soon as she told me that fate had taken a hand, that I was doing the right thing. And it was so easy. When Philip let me into the theater and took me up to the office to show me the building plans, I knocked him out."

"Was he alive when Dale set the fire?"

"I have no idea." The question seemed to bore him.

Erica shuddered as she skidded the MG around another curve. It was her father who was unbalanced, not Dale.

"But I don't understand why you got rid of Dale."

"Dale always held your mother's death against me. He was afraid of going back to jail, but after Philip, he began to act erratic, get things wrong. Take Fillmore Street. He did that on his own. When he didn't adhere to my schedule, I knew his usefulness had come to an end. Besides, I'd discovered he was spending time with Cheryl. Sooner or later he was bound to shoot off his mouth. I couldn't allow him to do that."

"Of course not." Her heart was racing, her damp palms sliding against the steering wheel.

"It was fitting that he should die on the same spot as your mother. My memorial to her."

Her foot pressed the accelerator pedal to the floor. She had to hurry. She had to reach Matt.

"I knew you'd understand. Once I had a chance to explain."

The car flew around the next corner on what felt like two wheels. The sound of spraying gravel pounded in her ears but couldn't drown out the terrible things her father had just told her. That he was responsible for her mother's death and had convinced himself Philip was to blame. That he had murdered two men apparently without a twinge of conscience.

"Watch out!" The expressionless tones vanished, replaced by genuine fear as she spun into the next switchback. "Erica! Slow down."

"What's the matter?" she ground out. "Are you afraid I might kill you like you killed them? Dale. Philip. My mother?"

"I explained that. It was a mistake, Erica, a terrible tragic mistake."

She stomped on the gas as the car cleared the switchback. The driveway still seemed to stretch ahead forever. She glanced quickly at the stranger who had fathered her. He stared at the road, his lips drawn back, his hands clutching at the dashboard. She deliberately nudged the car closer to the edge of the road. It was a straight drop down more than a hundred feet.

"What are you doing?" he shrilled.

"What do you think?" She accelerated, swerving the car to the far side of the road in preparation for the next switchback.

"You'll kill us both!"

Abruptly the rear end fishtailed. The steering wheel jerked out of her grasp. Eyes wide, mouth open, her father lunged for it, wrestled with it. The MG lurched and swayed, hovered on the edge of the road, then half rolled, half plunged through the sparse underbrush into thin air.

Chapter Twenty-Six

Behind the house, Matt scratched Dolly's neck, fed her sugar lumps, and speculated. Tomorrow he'd take the charade a step further and start taping voices—for comparison to tapes that didn't even exist. Would the killer panic and reveal himself? It seemed the only hope.

He wished Glenn would hurry up and come back for him. He was less than keen to hang around and watch Gallagher fawning over Erica.

The slam of a car door caught his attention and he headed for the front of the house.

The cough of an engine sputtering to life hastened his footsteps. That wasn't Glenn's car, that was Erica's MG. Why would she be leaving so soon?

As he reached the parking area he glimpsed the roof of the MG careening around the first curve of the driveway. She was going way too fast! He ran across to the brow of the hill.

Below him, the MG accelerated along a straight stretch and swung into the next curve, rear wheels spitting gravel. There was someone in the passenger seat. Eric Rawlins.

He sprinted down the driveway. Something was desperately wrong. Why was Erica driving like a crazy fool? Was she trying to get away from Rawlins?

He quit the driveway and skidded straight down the steep slope, slipping and sliding in his leather shoes. He hit the switchback at a run and was halfway to the next when the sickening sound of skidding rock and gravel brought him panting to a halt.

The MG teetered at the edge of a sharp curve. His heart stopped. Silence thundered in his head as the car careened to one side, as though in slow motion, then disappeared over the edge of the bank.

The world condensed to one word, one thought.

Erica.

Running, rolling, falling, he reached the edge.

Fifty feet below the car lay on its side in a gully.

He stood frozen in sick horror for a second before his training kicked in and took over. He swung down toward a narrow ledge, thudding to a painful halt on his knees. As he grabbed the branch of a tree and struggled to stand up, he glimpsed a movement to his left.

Erica!

Her dress was torn, and there was blood running down one arm but she was on her feet.

"Erica!" He scrambled toward her, heedless of pain, of his own bloody scratches, of everything but exploding joy that she was alive, that she'd been thrown clear.

As he took her in his arms, he knew everything had changed. No more holding back. No more treading the safe path. She melted against him and he found that he was the one who was shaking. Then she tried to pull away. His arms tightened around her. He'd never let her go.

She clawed at him, struggling, her physical strength surprising. "Let me go!"

"Never!"

The instant he spoke he heard the ominous crack of an explosion, then the roar of flames.

"My father!" she screamed.

Rawlins. In the car.

He released her and slid down the bank. If he could just reach the car before the flames spread...

Hopeless.

He skidded to a halt, shielding his face from the heat, the stench of burning gasoline acrid in his nostrils. The MG was engulfed in flames.

Not even an act of God could save Rawlins now.

Erica stumbled down after him, her face white, eyes huge and glazed with shock. He met her halfway and scooped her into his arms. She laid her face on his chest, her body shuddering against his.

There were urgent voices on the road above, pounding footsteps, a car motor. Someone had heard the explosion, seen the flames and smoke. Help was close at hand.

He peeled off his jacket and draped it around her shoulders, possessively cradling her against him. Inside, he was at war with himself. He wanted to protect her, to have her tell him what happened in her own way and her own time. But there wasn't enough time to allow either of them that luxury.

"What happened?" He winced at the professional, uninvolved sound of his words. This was Erica, for God's sake. The woman he loved.

Her words were halting, punctuated by sobs, but he understood.

"Dear Lord!" He held her by the shoulders, at arm's length. "What was he trying to do? Kill you both?"

She rubbed her eyes with one dirt-stained hand. "At the end he was trying to get the car under control, trying to save us both." She drew a deep, shuddery breath. "He thought his explanation would make everything all right. But I had to find you."

He looked down at her. And knew what he wanted to say couldn't wait. "You've got me, Erica. All of me. For as long as you want."

She blinked up at him. "What are you saying?"

"A future together. You and me. Marriage, if that's what you want."

She stared at him for so long he thought she hadn't heard. A shout came from the road above, and he knew with a sinking feeling that it would be hours, maybe days before they were alone again.

"Matt!" Glenn was climbing down the slope toward them.

"Here," he said, releasing Erica, even though it was the last thing he wanted to do.

***

Erica burrowed into the comforting folds of Matt's jacket and rubbed her nose against the collar. It smelled like him, made her feel safe. Almost as if he still held her wrapped protectively in his arms, still looked at her in a way no man had ever looked at her before.

She couldn't control her shaking body and her head was buzzing with a confusing clash of thoughts; Matt and marriage, her father's death, the facts she'd learned from her father's own lips, the horrible things he'd done...

She felt a light touch on her arm and looked up into Justin's concerned and kindly face.

"Erica? Are you all right?"

All she could do was look at him. Her muscles refused to obey the order to nod her head. Was she all right? Would she ever be all right again?

Erica didn't realize how close the sirens were until they stopped, until the noise and confusion of a rescue operation surrounded her. Firefighters came charging past and she felt as if she'd come full circle to the flames of twenty-two years ago. Except now the sun was shining. Back then the stars had been bright in a black sky, the midnight dew on the grass cold and wet beneath her bare feet.

She hugged Matt's coat closer, clinging to a precarious sense of reality. It was the sun shining in the sky, not stars. It was Matt's jacket on her body, not a cotton nightie. One thing remained the same, though. She felt alone, surrounded by people yet very alone. Only one man could erase that loneliness.

As if from a great distance Erica heard Matt tell Justin to see that an ambulance attendant checked her over. Dazed, she allowed Justin to lead her to the road. Allowed someone to remove Matt's jacket and examine her forearm. Felt no pain as they cleaned and dressed the gash. She blinked and looked away as one attendant shone a light in her eyes. Shock? Ridiculous. This wasn't shock. This felt like paralysis.

"Erica, darling." Ronya clasped her hand in one soft, plump paw. "There's nothing you can do here. Let me take you home."

Erica shook her head, stubborn, determined to stay. Matt was issuing orders. Taking charge. She loved that about him. Loved everything about him. Loved knowing he would have rescued her father if there had been any chance at all. Black smoke hung above the burned-out carcase of her car. Two firefighters struggled up the bank with a covered stretcher and she turned away. Justin and Ronya, one on either side of her, moved to shield her from the sight.

"Did you know? Did you have any idea?"

"Know what, dear?"

"He had Philip killed, you know. Jealous of something that happened twenty-two years ago."

Why were Ronya and Justin looking at her strangely? They patted her and made soothing murmurs, as if she was a child, and seemed relieved when Matt joined them.

Matt. Her anchor. Her bulwark in the sea of life. He made everything seem sane, even when it was anything but. Even now, when she was drained and numb, he made her feel that everything would somehow turn right side up.

"I suppose," she said, forcing her voice into a semblance of normalcy, "this means quite a tangle of paperwork for you to unsnarl."

Matt's gaze traveled from Ronya to Justin before he spoke. Almost as if the three of them were using some kind of sign language she couldn't understand.

"I don't think so," he said finally. "We can prove Dale Todd was the arsonist. Overcome by guilt, Todd committed suicide. Case closed. Nice and neat."

"But what about...?"

"What about what?"

Was that a challenge in his eyes? Her heart began to gallop, the numbness easing away. Could it be that he didn't intend to implicate her father in the fires?

What would that accomplish?

But she wasn't sure if she'd heard him say the case was closed, or just imagined the words. She'd find out later; there were other things she wanted to know. "What about your ranch?" she asked, vaguely aware that Rony and Justin had been discreet enough to step out of earshot.

"What ranch is that?"

"The one we were talking about the other day. For troubled teens."

"Oh, that." He lowered his eyes to the ground between them. "It would probably never work."

"Why not?" It was her turn to challenge him. "Why not?" she repeated, trying to make her lips form the words the right way, willing him to look at her.

Slowly he met her gaze. "Burned-out cop? Poor risk. Besides, people tend to be suspicious of a single adult male who opens his home to troubled youngsters."

"And if the adult male was married? With a family?" He didn't answer. She watched him swallow thickly, saw his internal war with the past.

"Did you mean what you said earlier?"

"What did I say?"

"That you're mine if I want you?" She could swear that his face had paled.

"I kind of hoped you'd put that down to the emotionalism of the moment."

"Is that all it was?"

Matt shifted his weight from foot to foot, stared off over her head, finally leveled his gaze at her. "No."

Erica released a pent-up breath. The emptiness in her heart began to fill and she found her lips could smile after all. "Didn't I tell you once before, I'm used to getting what I want?"

"Better be sure you know what you're getting."

She took a step toward him. "There's not a doubt in my mind." Another step. "More than I've ever wanted anything in my entire life, I want you."

Matt exhaled, opened his arms, welcomed her into them. Feeling his heart racing next to hers, she knew that if he could manage to let go of the past, so could she.

Starting now. Together, they could start over. And set their sights on any damn thing they wanted. Together. It had such a feeling of completeness.

A soft breeze rustled through the trees and played tag with the ashes of her ruined car. Ashes didn't have to signal an ending, Erica thought. Not always. Not without leaving room for the beginning of something new.

Epilogue

Matt nailed a board on the paddock fence he was rebuilding, then straightened up, dropped his hammer and stripped to the waist. The sun was warm in the sheltered valley.

In the next paddock Black Satin and Mistress Morgana cropped spring grass while the yearling, Merlin, danced skittish circles around them. He and Erica had almost finished dickering for another brood mare, so there might be three foals come fall.

Another movement caught his eye. Erica was walking down the lane toward him, followed by Toddy, the orange kitten Dale had rescued. Toddy was a healthy half-grown cat now, thanks to Ronya's care, and seemed to think he was in charge of the whole ranch, though Erica was obviously at the top of his list.

Matt's chest tightened with love and pride as he watched her walk toward him. His woman. His wife. The mother of his child. He took a sugar lump from his pocket and crunched into it.

She smiled as she approached, then ran her fingers softly through his damp chest hair. He held her tight against him for a moment before they turned to watch the sleek horses.

"I brought your lunch," she said. "And there were two phone calls. The second group of teenagers is arriving tomorrow."

"How many?"

"Two boys and a girl."

"Good."

But would it work this time? He couldn't stop thinking about the boy who'd sneaked out the first day and gone back to the city. "I still want to know what I did wrong that Bruce took off."

Erica stroked him lightly on the upper arm. "Matt, it was his choice. You can't force people to do what's best for them."

"Yeah." Sometimes he still had a hard time remembering that he wasn't responsible for other people's choices.

"Glenn called, too. He and Penny are bringing their kids out after lunch. He said he'd give you a hand with the fence while we take the kids riding."

He turned a fierce look on her. "You be careful!"

She grinned. "You're worse than Rony with your fussing. I'm fine, the baby's fine. The doctor says exercise is good for me."

"Damn doctors don't know everything," he growled. "Promise me you'll take it easy. You've still got five months to go."

It would be good to see Glenn. Hashing things out with Glenn was the one part of police work that he missed. Not that he'd had much time to miss it – this ranch took every moment. He eyed the boards he'd just nailed up. Wouldn't hurt the next batch of kids to paint them, learn about maintaining a working ranch.

"You invite them for dinner?"

"Of course. If the weather holds we can barbecue outside."

"Great!" He linked her arm through his. "In that case I'll make a Caesar salad. Be nice to baptize our new dining room, though."

Erica had done wonders making the old house into a home. Hollis Hearne's painting, 'Moon Dance', which she'd refused to let him sell, hung above the huge fieldstone fireplace and the two, the new and the old, looked fine together. In his den the antique roll top desk from Philip's apartment complemented a brilliant abstract of Ronya's that hung above it.

"When does Rony's show open?" he asked.

"Next week. I'll have to get out of my jeans and wear something smashing while I still have the chance."

"You'd look gorgeous in an old sack."

"That's about all that fits me these days."

He smoothed her hair. No one would even know she was pregnant, except for that special glow in her eyes. It told the whole world her secret. "Rony's worked hard to get this show together."

Erica nodded, a fleeting sadness in her expression. "I think it helped her to cope with losing Philip, then Dale and Auguste."

She almost never mentioned her father. He knew her grief had been eased by their happiness together but she'd never completely forget; how could she? And the baby she carried would never know its grandfather. His folks would more than make up for that, though. His entire family was driving him nuts these days, now that he finally had what they considered a normal life.

At first he'd worried that Erica might miss her work but she insisted arson investigation had served its purpose and she had no regrets about closing the book on that part of her life.

"You haven't forgotten that Justin and Cheryl are throwing a celebration dinner after the opening, have you?"

"At Mandellini?"

"No. Cheryl managed to convince Justin to splurge on the Carnelian Room."

Matt groaned. "I'll have to wear a suit. Damn."

"Just think how good it will feel to take it off afterwards." A teasing gleam appeared in her eyes. "Think how much fun it would be letting me take it off for you."

Heat spread through him. "I'll hold you to that. I even promise not to complain about wearing the damn thing. Want to practice? I'll go put it on right now and you can take it off for me."

"We don't need to waste time with that," she murmured, her hands moving on his back, shoulders to buttocks, and sending shivers of delight to every part of his body. "You're half undressed already."

Lowering his voice, he said, "So let's see you finish the job." Desire poured through him as her knuckles grazed his belly while she unfastened his jeans. He reached out to undo the buttons on her shirt, then stopped and took a closer look. "Who said you could wear my shirt?"

"Any objections?"

"Damn right. Take it off. Now."

His breath caught as she tossed the shirt on the grass and opened her arms to him.

###

Dear Reader:

I think every book a writer works on eventually becomes that author's *Book of the Heart*.

This one was particularly special to me, so if you enjoyed it please take a few moments to leave a short, honest review wherever you purchase your books.

ABOUT THE AUTHOR:

Kathleen Lawless' earliest memories are of wanting to be a writer. To create stories that would touch the lives of others who love to read the way she does.

"I'm working on my 30th novel and it's amazing to see the changes in traditional publishing, including ebooks and the opportunities writers have to interact with their readers." She enjoys pushing the boundaries of traditional romance, erotic romance, romantic suspense, women's fiction and stories for young adults.

She also knows firsthand about happy endings. "Can you believe I wrote A HARD MAN TO LOVE with a hero named Steele, years before I met my own hero named Steel? His proposal to me on a remote island in the Caribbean was more romantic than anything I could have written about."

Sign up for Kathleen's newsletter to receive updates, give-aways and special fan-priced offers.
www.kathleenlawless.com[1]

Website: www.kathleenlawless.com[2]

Twitter: https://twitter.com/kathleenlawless

---

1.   http://www.kathleenlawless.com

2.   http://www.kathleenlawless.com

Facebook: https://www.facebook.com/
kathleenlawlessnovels/

Instagram: https://www.instagram.com/
kathleenlawless/

Blog: http://www.gemsintheattic.blogspot.ca

More Books by Kathleen Lawless

Deliver Me

Raised on small Arkansas farm, Maddie Winslow craves excitement, but an escaped convict seeking shelter in her barn is more adventure than she bargained for. Determined to help the brooding stranger clear his name, Maddie impulsively joins Judson Burke on a dangerous journey to his Texas home and finds herself the victim of relentless passion. When the prison wagon transporting Judson crashed, he fled, praying for a chance to prove he is innocent of his wife's murder. Betrayed by his past desires, all Jud wants now is his freedom—until his beautiful traveling companion convinces him that love is the only thing worth fighting for.

Callie's Honor

After the death of her brutal husband, Callie Lambert looks forward to peaceful years of hard work on her isolated Oregon ranch, doing things her way. All too soon a handsome stranger shows up, a man who slowly chips away at her strong facade and turns her dreams of solitude upside down. A drifter with a mission, Rafe Miller seeks only revenge for his brother's murder, and then he will move on. But something about Callie's proud, defiant green eyes makes him care more than he wants to, or should. Despite their wariness, neither can resist reaching out toward the promise of sharing a precious, golden love.

Anora's Pride

Anora King doesn't say she's married when she moves to a new town, but her new neighbors leap to that conclusion.

For Anora, struggling to raise money for her brother's operation, the deceit has its advantages, until the new marshal comes to town. Jesse Quantrill is shocked to find himself lusting after a married woman, but Anora doesn't act married and her mixture of innocence and feisty determination is irresistible. If the two fall in love it will be the town's biggest scandal but, no matter how hard they try to stay apart, lawbreakers, riots and ructions drive them into each other's arms.

Grace's Folly

Dr. Grace Abbot has deceived her father, who believes she stayed out East to become a proper doctor's wife. Now he wants her home, but if he learns she's the doctor, she may lose the inheritance to fund her passion, a women's clinic.

When a wounded stranger shows up at her Kansas City infirmary—with almost the same last name as the drifter she married to get her dowry money—Grace hits upon a wild scheme. This darkly handsome Mr. Abbott can pose as her doctor husband for the visit back home in California. She can view him as dispassionately as she would anyone. Can't she?

Pinkerton detective Dexter Abbott has found his client's willful daughter, and she's given him the perfect excuse to stick to her side while he returns her to her father. But his real problem begins when he doesn't tell her what his actual job is—and when being so close to her inspires longings Dex never expected in himself.

Untamed

When Paris Sommer finds the secret diary of her great-great-grandmother, who ran an infamous bordello in the old West, her secret fantasies are ignited. Putting her librarian career to good use, she goes to Forked Creek, Nevada, to stay at the brothel and do some research. There Paris discovers a forbidden pleasure of her own: Mitchell Brand, a dead-sexy cowboy who knows just how to treat a woman—and make her beg for more. Brand's hard-lovin' ways welcome Paris into a world of passion she's never known...until a mysterious treasure map hidden in the diary leads them to a place where peril and seduction collide.

Taboo

"Darling," wrote Fallon's best friend.

"You've been cooped up alone in the middle of nowhere far too long. I'm arriving to relieve your tedium. And bringing a very big surprise."

The surprise is Montague Bridgeman—and, courtesy of Fallon Gilchrist's dear friend, he's hers to do with whatever she pleases for one week. An inexperienced widow, Fallon is shocked at the idea of a private plaything. Shy and repressed, she decides to use him as her model and start painting again; he is a rather spectacular specimen of a man. Bridge, however, is hell-bent on awakening the reclusive Fallon to the sensual world, and she soon quivers under the force of his desire—and her own. Yet even more intense than these heady pleasures of the flesh is the haunted look in Bridge's eyes—a look that suggests he's much more than a lover-for-hire, and that seven days and seven nights might not be enough—for either of them.

Unmasked

No man had the slightest idea of her restless yearnings, her innermost desires.

Aurora Tremblay is a beautiful, headstrong woman with a powerful obsession: Grayson Thorne. Sensationally wealthy and handsome, he holds the key to Aurora's dream. But Grayson has his own agenda for this self-styled Grand Adventuress, who unknowingly invades a most private sort of party at his remote estate. Soon Aurora finds herself a pawn in a seductive, role-playing game in which cloaked strangers beg for her forbidden touch and temptation is everywhere—until the fiery passion between Aurora and Grayson brings them dangerously close to taking the ultimate risk—falling in love.

A Hard Man to Love

Montana Blackstone has big plans for the deluxe spa resort she's building at Black Creek Ranch. They don't include letting her know-it-all new foreman take the reins, even if tall, broad-shouldered Steele Hardt looks mighty capable of showing her how blissful it can be to surrender control—in and out of the bedroom. As the sizzling chemistry between them erupts in one mind-blowing encounter after another, Montana finds that Steele has a knack for knocking down her defenses and seeing through to the vulnerable core she's trying so hard to hide.

Once a pro poker player, now a renowned business troubleshooter, Steele came to Black Creek to give investors a covert report on the spa's potential—not to give its gorgeous owner such very personal attention. And once she learns the truth about why he's there, Steele stands to lose Montana forever. Convincing her that the heat between them is more than a diversion means taking the biggest gamble of his life. But Steele has never been known to take the easy way out and he's not about to start now.

Wicked Night Games

What's your fantasy tonight?

Welcome aboard the Fantasy Cruise Line, where luxurious private cabins use virtual reality to create any fantasy you've ever dreamed of—and a few you've never imagined.

Cassidy Ferrill's fantasy is to get revenge on her teen crush, Sloan Hardt, who broke her heart when he rejected her long ago. She wants to seduce the man, then leave while he's panting for more. When she discovers they'll both be guests on a Fantasy wedding cruise, Cassidy knows she's found the perfect opportunity. If she can just keep from losing her heart all over again.

Sloan doesn't immediately recognize the curvy auburn-haired beauty as his long-ago "pity date" to the prom, but he certainly recognizes what he's feeling: pure, unadulterated lust. The fantasy-themed cabins are a perfect opportunity for some truly wicked night games with this new, grown-up Cassidy. But while Sloan has always been a love-'em-and-leave-'em kind of guy, this fling somehow seems different. Why does he find himself fantasizing about a life with Cassidy after the cruise is over?

XXX Marks the Spot

Springing for an impromptu getaway with her two best girlfriends isn't entirely a selfless act on Kennedy James's part. Sure, she wants to help Lisa get over her cheating ex-husband, and Justine to quit obsessing about the ticking of her biological clock. But Kennedy has her own raging libido in mind when she books their trip to a southeast coast golf resort. What could be more fun than a week in a beach paradise surrounded by wealthy, eligible, and smokingly sexy men? What about an X-rated scavenger hunt? Kennedy's cooked up a checklist to die for: Your date's boxers...Sex in a limo...Skinny-dipping with him...A shooter he slurps from your belly button...and more wickedly erotic adventures sure to blissfully obliterate their heartaches back home in Seattle. The first one among their try-anything trio to complete the list is the winner—but in sexcapades this uninhibited, you just might bag a prize even bigger and more irresistible than you ever dreamed—with a lover who knows just the right spot for unleashing sensations not even these daring huntresses have experienced.

Fabulous at Fifty

SEX IN THE CITY GROWS UP!

Can newly-single Rachel Fontaine take her best friend's advice and never turn down a sexy romp?

Such brazen behavior goes against her character.

Or does it?

Is sex-with-the-ex a mistake?

What about sex with the hot new TV host?

Do younger men really like older women?

When did fifty become the new thirty?

Hold on for the fun as Rachel reinvents herself and discovers life after fifty is fabulous.

Final Heat

Tessa is secretly hunting a killer.

Hunter's mission is to stop the flow of arms to war-torn countries.

Pretending to like each other is the hard part.

The clues unfold in what should have been an easy race to win. Until it isn't.

And it turns out the stakes are higher than either of them knew.

Once their covers are blown, winning the race takes second place.

Afterburn

Arson never makes sense!

Except to the arsonist

When people die arson becomes murder.

Accidental or intentional? That's the puzzle for Lt. Matt Nichols, head of San Francisco PD arson squad, given a rash of fires in the city and no connection between the victims.

His career depends on solving this case despite the added pressure of hotshot specialist arson investigator, Erica Johnson dogging his every step. And his uncontrollable urge to kiss her.

Erica only wants to do her job, frustrated when Lt. Nichols refuses to cooperate. Doubly frustrated by the sexual sparks fly between them, generating a different type of heat.

When their investigation uncovers a link to the fire that took her mother's life when she was a baby, Erica becomes the arsonist's next target. And Matt races against time to save the woman he loves.

Intimate Strangers (a novella)

I can't tear my eyes from my yummy neighbor.

My camera finger itches to take his picture, while my body itches for other intimacies.

He would be the perfect subject for my upcoming erotic photography show.

He agrees to my proposal with only one string.

Our photo shoot turns into a disaster. Especially when I find myself between him and the camera.

Our sensual interlude nearly melts the film.

Do I destroy those pictures? Or use them to launch my career?

Also by Kathleen Lawless

Fabulous at Fifty
Afterburn
Anora's Pride
Callie's Honor

Printed in the USA
CPSIA information can be obtained
at www.ICGtesting.com
JSHW021952111023
50060JS00003B/5